Praise for *The Winter Vault*

'*The Winter Vault* shares from the first sentence to the last the inimitable DNA of her debut. And what a tenacious genetic signature it is . . . Read this book like poetry, or rather hear it like music, but stay if you can with Michaels' gorgeous melancholia . . . From inundated Nubia to pulverised Warsaw by way of the middle earth of Canada, she guides us to the top of some extraordinary peaks of feeling and perception. However rarefied the atmosphere, the vistas are spectacular'
Boyd Tonkin, *Independent*

'We regularly hear that progress entails loss. Anne Michaels has spent the last decade or so honing this generality into a particular of penetrating point and poetic reflection. Piercing the mental callus we grow around any dinned-in truth, her new novel, *The Winter Vault,* abducts the imagination and breaks the heart'
LA Times

'A tender meditation on loss and authenticity. Moving between Egypt, Canada and Poland, the novel's protagonists are rapt with the task of salvaging lives, buildings and memories'
Financial Times Summer Reads

'Written with intelligence and lyricism'
Mail on Sunday

'A graceful, melancholy new novel . . . [written] with the humane intelligence and lush language one might expect from the author of *Fugitive Pieces* . . . Michaels is a great poet of loss, and the challenges of memory in the face of it . . . Michaels produces passages of lyrical beauty, and eloquently expresses her horror at human violence inflicted on the land and its inhabitants'
Guardian

'Her dramas are internal, exquisitely expressed with the wisdom and precision of her other incarnation as a poet. *The Winter Vault* is a novel about memory and the part it plays in love; about how "inescapable sorrow" is the price love must pay. What can be preserved, or recreated, and what is lost forever in the search for a home is as uncertain for individuals as for communities'

Amanda Craig, *Daily Telegraph*

'A miracle of layering or patterning. At one point, Avery, who wants to be an architect not an engineer, dreams of making buildings that are "frank and spare, without irony; capable simply of both sorrow and solace". His creator has written a remarkable book with exactly those qualities . . . Full of arresting incidental detail and imagery'

New Statesman

'*The Winter Vault* is beautifully written, deeply considered, and ambitious in its historical, geographical and moral scope . . . Displacement, dispossession, obliteration of collective memory: these are Michaels' themes . . . It takes someone of rare integrity, courage and moral stamina to produce a book of this kind, a book that is serious and often dares to be beautiful. Anne Michaels is that person'

Literary Review

'Anne Michaels writes about tragic circumstances with an energy and attention that brings them fully to life. All characters in *The Winter Vault* are consumed by negotiations with a vanished past . . . Michaels writes with moving, melancholy richness about grief, to which there is no answer, only an echo'

Helen Dunmore, *Waterstones Books Quarterly*

'A lyrical exploration of love, grief and memory'   *Easy Living*

'A study of the way loss can dismantle love, and how hope and memory can repair the damage'   *Marie Claire*

'A love story that poses some thought provoking existential questions. Do we belong to the place we were born or the place we are buried? There are many poignant poetic passages and elegant ruminations on love, death, and marriage'   *Tatler*

'Michaels' graceful handling of language and her themes of displacement, memory, faith and the violence wrought on landscape make this a powerful novel'   *Metro*

'Michaels makes prose that feels wrought, every word serving a moral seriousness so intense as to broach a kind of sublimity. Like its predecessor, *The Winter Vault* reads [with] breathtaking power . . . Art, nature, science, history, music, food, architecture, language, culture, faith and philosophy intertwine densely, receiving glorious due in what's now recognizably Michaels' tone, a near-preternatural alloy of calm and passion. A reviewer despairs of selecting quotes. To highlight brilliant passages (each a prismatic emblem of the whole) is to stripe nearly every page with color'   *San Francisco Chronicle*

'This is a book that proposes great themes: a critique of progress, an exploration of the nature of human suffering, an interrogation of the relationship between past and present. And yet, for all of that, it remains at bottom a deeply affecting love story . . . Beautifully written'   *Globe and Mail*

'Every page quietly sparkles with metaphors that are often startlingly beautiful'   *Seattle Times*

'Every bit as ambitious, original and startling as its predecessor . . . *The Winter Vault* is sumptuous writing. Not sumptuous in the fleeting way a feast – consumed, then forgotten – is sumptuous, or finery, which fades and is likewise forgotten. Michaels' writing is sumptuous the way the morning sun on a garden is sumptuous, luminously, timelessly'   *Ottowa Citizen*

'A master of deft, pithy images . . . there is truth as well as beauty in this dark world'   *Spectator*

A NOTE ON THE AUTHOR

ANNE MICHAELS' three collections of poetry are *The Weight of Oranges* (1986), which won the Commonwealth Prize for the Americas, *Miner's Pond* (1991), which received the Canadian Authors Association Award and was shortlisted for the Governor General's Award and the Trillium Award, and *Skin Divers* (1999). *Fugitive Pieces*, her first novel, won both the Guardian Fiction Award and the Orange Prize in 1997. It has been published in twenty-nine languages and has also been made into a major motion picture. *The Winter Vault* was shortlisted for the Giller Prize 2009.

Anne Michaels lives in Toronto.

The Winter Vault

Anne Michaels

BLOOMSBURY

LONDON · BERLIN · NEW YORK

First published in Great Britain 2009
This paperback edition published 2010

Copyright © by Anne Michaels 2009
Published by arrangement with
McClelland & Stewart Ltd, Toronto, Canada

The extracts from the poems 'Annunciation' and 'Two Poems' on pages 119–120 are
taken from *The Selected Poems of Rosario Castellanos*, published by Graywolf Press.
Copyright © 1988 by the Estate of Rosairo Castellanos. Translation copyright
© 1988 by Magda Bogin. Used by permission of Magda Bogin.

The lyrics on page 253 are from 'Stoney End'. Words and music by Laura Nyro.
Copyright © 1966, 1968 (Renewed 1994, 1996) EMI Blackwood Music Inc.
All Rights Reserved. International Copyright Secured. Used by Permission.

The moral right of the author has been asserted

Bloomsbury Publishing, London, Berlin and New York

36 Soho Square, London W1D 3QY

A CIP catalogue record for this book is available from the British Library

ISBN 978 1 4088 0108 6
Export ISBN 978 1 4088 0604 3

10 9 8 7 6 5 4 3 2 1

Typeset in Perpetua
Printed in Great Britain by Clays Ltd, St Ives plc

Mixed Sources
Product group from well-managed
forests and other controlled sources
www.fsc.org Cert no. SGS-COC-2061
FSC © 1996 Forest Stewardship Council

www.bloomsbury.com/annemichaels

for R and E

Perhaps we painted on our own skin, with ochre and charcoal, long before we painted on stone. In any case, forty thousand years ago, we left painted handprints on the cave walls of Lascaux, Ardennes, Chauvet.

The black pigment used to paint the animals at Lascaux was made of manganese dioxide and ground quartz; and almost half the mixture was calcium phosphate. Calcium phosphate is produced by heating bone four hundred degrees Celsius, then grinding it.

We made our paints from the bones of the animals we painted.

No image forgets this origin.

The future casts its shadow on the past. In this way, first gestures contain everything; they are a kind of map. The first days of military occupation; the conception of a child; seeds and soil.

Grief is desire in its purest distillation. With the first grave – the first time a name was sown in the earth – the invention of memory.

No word forgets this origin.

I

———

Riverbed

Generators floodlit the temple. A scene of ghastly devastation. Bodies lay exposed, limbs strewn at hideous angles. Each king was decapitated, each privileged neck sliced by diamond-edged handsaws, their proud torsos dismembered by chainsaws, line-drilling, and wire-cutting. The wide stone foreheads were reinforced by steel bars and a mortar of epoxy resin. Avery watched men vanish in the fold of a regal ear, lose a shoe in a royal nostril, fall asleep in the shade of an imperial pout.

The labourers worked for eight hours, dividing the day into three shifts. At night, Avery sat on the deck of the houseboat and re-calculated the increasing tension in the remaining rock, re-evaluated the wisdom of each cut, the zones of weakness and new stress forces as, tonne by tonne, the temple disappeared.

Even in his bed on the river, he saw the severed heads, the limbless minions, stacked and neatly numbered in the floodlights, awaiting transport. One thousand and forty-two sandstone blocks, the smallest weighing twenty tonnes. The miraculous stone ceiling, where birds flew among the stars, lay dismantled, out in the open, below real stars, the real blackness beyond the floodlights so intense it seemed to be coming apart, like wet paper. The workers had first attacked the surrounding rock, a hundred thousand cubic metres carefully plotted, labelled, and removed by pneumatics. And soon, the building of artificial hills.

To free himself from the noise of machinery, Avery listened for the river flowing past their bed, his head against the hull. He imagined, clinging to the dark wind, the steady breath of glass-blowers in the city five hundred kilometres north, the calls of water-sellers and soft-drink vendors, the shrieking of kingfishers through the surf of ancient palms, each sound evaporating into the desert air where it was never quite erased.

The Nile had already been strangled at Sadd el Aali, and its magnificent flow had been rerouted before that, to increase the output of Delta cotton, to boost the productivity of the unimaginably distant Lancashire mills.

Avery knew that a river that has been barraged is not the same river. Not the same shore, nor even the same water.

And although the angle of sunrise into the Great Temple would be the same and the same sun would enter the sanctuary at dawn, Avery knew that once the last temple stone had been cut and hoisted sixty metres higher, each block replaced, each seam filled with sand so there was not a grain of space between the blocks to reveal where they'd been sliced, each kingly visage slotted into place, that the perfection of the illusion – the perfection itself – would be the betrayal.

If one could be fooled into believing he stood in the original site, by then subsumed by the waters of the dam, then everything about the temple would have become a deceit.

And when at last – after four and a half years of overwork, of illness caused by extremities of heat and cold, or by the constant dread of miscalculation – when he stood at last with the Ministers of Culture, the fifty ambassadors, his fellow engineers, and seventeen hundred labourers to gape at their achievement, he feared he might break down, not with triumph or exhaustion, but with shame.

Only his wife understood: that somehow holiness was escaping under their drills, was being pumped away in the continuous draining of groundwater, would soon be crushed under the huge cement domes; that by the time Abu Simbel was finally re-erected, it would no longer be a temple.

The river moved, slow and alive, through the sand, a blue vein along a pallid forearm, flowing from wrist to elbow. Avery's desk was on deck; when he worked late, Jean woke and came to him. He stood up, and she didn't let go, hanging from her own embrace.

– Calculate me, she said.

At dusk, the light was a fine powder, a gold dust settling on the surface of the Nile. As Avery took out his paints from the wooden box, thick cakes of solid watercolour, his wife lay down on the still-warm deck. Ceremoniously, he parted her cotton shirt from her shoulders, each time witnessing her body's colour deepening: sandstone, terra cotta, ochre. A glimpse of the secret white stripes under straps, the pale ovals like dampness under stones, untouched by the sun. The secret paleness he would later touch in the dark. Then Jean peeled her sleeves from her arms and turned on her side, her back to him, in the velvet light. The light of darkness, more evening than day.

Avery leaned overboard, dipped his teacup into the river, then set the circle of water next to him. He chose a colour and let it seep into the soft hair of the brush, infused with river water. Gently he released its fullness across Jean's strong back. Sometimes he painted the scene before them, the riverbank, the ruinous work that never stopped, the growing pile of stone physiognomy. Sometimes he painted from memory, the Chiltern Hills, until he could smell his mother's lavender soap in the fading heat. He painted, beginning from childhood, until he was again man-grown. Then, almost the moment he finished, he dipped the cup again into the river and with clear water drew his wet brush through the fields, through the trees, until the scene dissolved, awash on her skin. Some of the paint remained in her pores, until she bathed, the Egyptian river receiving the last earth of Buckinghamshire in its erasing embrace. Of course, Jean never saw his landscapes and, blind, was free to imagine any scene she wished. He would come to think of his wife's languor during that dusk hour – each dusk those months of 1964 – as a kind of wedding gift to him; and in turn, she felt herself open under the brush, as if he were tracing a current under her skin. In this dusk hour, each gave to the other a secret landscape. In each, a new privacy opened. Every evening that first year of their marriage Avery contemplated Buckinghamshire, his mother's smell, the distance of time from the wet beech forest to this desert, stress points, fissures and elasticity, the pressure map of the soon-to-be-constructed concrete domes, and the heavy mortal beauty of his wife, whose body he was only beginning to know. He thought about the Pharaoh Ramses, whose body above his knees had recently vanished and now lay scattered in the sand, stored in a separate area from the limbs of his wife and daughters. It would be many months before they would be reunited, a family that had not been separated for more than thirty-two hundred years.

He thought that only love teaches a man his death, that it is in the solitude of love that we learn to drown.

When Avery lay next to his wife, waiting for sleep, listening to the river, it was as if the whole long Nile was their bed. Each night he floated down from Alexandria, through the delta of date palms, past isolated *dahabiyah*, with their loose sails, beached on the banks. Each night before sleep, to dispel the day's equations and graphs, he made this journey in his mind. Sometimes, if Jean was awake, he spoke the journey aloud until he felt her drift into that state of near sleep when one still believes one is awake, hearing nothing. But Avery would continue to whisper to her nonetheless, elaborating the journey with a hundred details, in gratitude for the weight of her thigh across his. The river, he felt, heard every word, wove every sigh into itself, until it was filled with dreaming, swelled with the last breath of kings, with the hard breathing of labourers from three thousand years ago to that very moment. He spoke to the river, and he listened to the river, his hand on his wife in the place their child would some day open her, where his mouth had already so often spoken her, as if he could take the child's name into his mouth from her body. Rebecca, Cleopatra, Sarah, and all the desert women who knew the value of water.

While he painted her back, Jean remembered the first time – in the cinema in Morrisburg – that they'd sat together in the dark. Avery had touched her nowhere but her wrist, where the small veins gather. She felt the pressure move along her arm, his fingertips still touching only an inch of her, and she decided. Later, in the bright foyer she was exposed, in invisible disarray; he had crawled a slow fuse under her clothes. And she knew for the first time that someone can wire your skin in a single evening, and that love arrives not by accumulating to a moment, like a drop of water focused on the tip of a branch – it is not the moment of bringing your whole life to another – but rather, it is everything you leave behind. At that moment.

Even that night, the night he touched one inch of her in the dark, how simply Avery seemed to accept the facts – that they were on the edge of lifelong happiness and, therefore, inescapable sorrow. It was as if, long ago, a part of him had broken off inside, and now finally, he recognized the dangerous fragment that had been floating in his system, causing him intermittent pain over the years. As if he could now say of that ache: "Ah. It was you."

Avery was often lost, thinking through the mathematics by which a temple defines its space, attempting to enclose no less than sacredness. Constructing a plane where heaven meets earth. Jean argued that this meeting best takes place out in the open, and that the true plane where the divine vertical pierces this world is simply in the upright posture of a man. But for Avery, the body was one thing and the shaping of space – the human calculation of space to receive spirits – quite another.

– But we shape our inner space too, argued Jean. We are making up our minds and changing our minds all the time. And if we believe, I think it's because we choose to.

– Of course, said Avery, but the body is given to us. We arrive . . . prefabricated. A temple was the first power station. Think of the formulas invented, the physical achievement of thousands of men moving a mountain, hewing and hauling stone tonne by tonne, often hundreds of kilometres, to a site of precise coordinates – all in an attempt to capture spirits.

To define space, Avery continued, and then he stopped. No. Not to give shape to space, but to give shape to . . . emptiness.

At this, Jean grew fond and took her husband's hand. From the deck of the houseboat, they watched as workers disappeared into the newly fitted steel culvert that ran from Ramses' feet into the inner rooms of the Great Temple. The culvert burrowed its way through five thousand truckloads of sand, which had been transported from the desert to protect the facades and to provide lateral support for the cliffside. A century before, it had taken the discoverer of

Abu Simbel, Giovanni Belzoni, many days to dig his way down through drifted dunes to the temple; now Avery and his men had reburied it.

—You're like a man seen from a distance, said Jean, a man who we think has stopped to tie his shoelaces but who is really kneeling in prayer.

— Our shoelaces have to come undone, said Avery, before we ever think to kneel.

North of Bujumbura in Burundi, a small stream — Kasumo — bubbles out of the ground. This spring joins others — the Mukasenyi, the Ruvironza, the Ruvubu — into the Kagera, which in turn flows into Lake Victoria. This upper branch of the Kagera is one source of the Nile. Another source is the Rwindi River, which carries glacial runoff from the great Ruwenzori Range — the Mountains of the Moon. From the rainforest below, the snow peaks were thought to be salt, captured moonlight, mist. No one imagined snow in the equatorial rainforest, a place so verdant it sweats out a spell of giganticism.

Earthworms a metre long churn the soil, white heather sways ten metres above a woman's head. Flowers more than three metres tall sweeten the sun, their scent merging with the fragrance of cloves off the sea from Zanzibar. Grass grows tall as a man, moss thick as the trunk of a tree. Bamboo clatters into the sky like an image on accelerated film — a pace of fifty centimetres a day.

This is the habitat of the mountain gorilla, an animal that with one arm can snap the head off a human but who fears water and will not cross the river.

The equatorial snow – this frozen moonlight, this salt, this mist – melts and gushes with the force of gravity over sixty-four thousand kilometres of jungle, swamp, and desert; it swells the Nile and stains its burning banks bright green. Snow that comes to flow through a landscape so hot that it wrings a man's dreams from his head, the mirage shimmering in the air; so hot that a man cannot gain a moment's respite from his own shadow or his own sweat; so hot that the sand dreams of becoming glass; so hot that men die of it. A landscape so arid that its annual rainfall barely fills four teaspoons.

The desert abandons anyone who lies down. From the moment a body is covered in sand, the wind, like memory, begins to exhume it. And so the Bedouin and other desert tribes dig deeper graves for their women, a discretion.

Perhaps this is another reason for the immensity of the desert tombs, the sheer weight and mass of rock hauled and piled – ingeniously piled, yet piled all the same – at the gravesites of the kings.

In the desert we remain still and the earth moves beneath us.

Each night the temperature fell to freezing and the labourers began their day around the fire. By early morning one paid a price for even the slightest exertion. No one was seen to sweat because any moisture evaporated instantly. Men dipped their heads into whatever shade could be found, squeezed into the shadows of wooden crates and trucks. They gazed with desire across the Nile at the umbra of dom and date palms, acacias, tamarisk, and sycamore. Their faces sought the north wind.

Each morning from the houseboat, Jean watched Avery disappear into the throng of men. All around him, faces the colour of wet earth; Avery, pale as the sand. Soon she would climb to the plateau where a garden had been started, irrigated by the same pipes that provided water for the camp's swimming pool, and begin her lessons on desert fruits from the wife of one of the Cairo engineers, a gracious source of information – from recipes to plant medicines and cosmetics – who wore an elegant white shirt-dress to the garden, with white sandals, her hair elaborately sculpted and pinned under a white straw hat. She directed Jean, who was happy to sink her knees and hands into the work.

All day the temple rock absorbed the sunlight; any gap between the blocks trapped the heat like a clay oven. Then, each evening, the stone slowly cooled. Visitors came to experience Abu Simbel at dawn. But Jean knew that the true miracle of the temple was only revealed at dusk when, for one brief twilit hour, the great colossi came to life, stone lips and limbs cooling exactly to the temperature of skin.

One day, three hundred thousand years ago, one of our hominid ancestors in Berekhat Ram leaned down to pick up a tuff of volcanic rock whose shape, by chance, resembled a woman. Then another stone was used to deepen the naturally formed line between "head" and "neck" and between "arm" and "torso." This is the earliest example of stone made flesh.

In paleolithic Britain, a hunter chipped a handaxe out of flint, taking care not to damage a perfect fossil shell of a bivalve mollusc embedded in the stone. From the hunter fashioning the first tools (the first awareness that matter can be split to make a sharp edge) to the splitting of the atom – a minuscule amount of time in evolutionary terms, about two and a half million years. But perhaps time enough to consider the importance of preserving the beautiful mollusc in the stone.

The history of nations, Avery knew, was not only a history of land but a history of water. Flowing with the Nile over the border of Egypt into the Sudan, Nubia was a country without boundaries, currency, or government, yet an ancient country nonetheless. To the west and to the east, the Sahara. To the south, from the town of Wadi Halfa, the desolate desert of Atmur. For centuries, armies travelled by river for Nubia's gold, its incense and ebony. They came and built their fortresses and tombs, their mosques and churches on the lush thighs of the Nile. When stone is scarce, it is the clearest sign of conquest, just as a tree is a sign of water. The first Christians lived in the Pharaohs' ruins and built their churches in the Pharaohs' temples. Then, in the eighth century, Islam travelled upriver to Nubia, and mosques appeared where the churches had been. Yet conquest was never easy, even by river. The infamous Second, Third, and Fourth Cataracts — and cataracts within cataracts — the Kagbar, Dal, Tangur, Semna, and Batn el Hajar, "the belly of stones" — discouraged trespassers. From Dara to Aswan, caravans of a hundred camels crossed the sand, creaking and jangling with heavy sacks of rubber from the forests of Bahr el Ghazal, with ivory, ostrich feathers, and wild game. They passed through the dry valleys and hills, stopping at last at the oasis of Salima before reaching the Nile south of Wadi Halfa, then following the west bank of the river north into Egypt. Some believe the Nubians are originally from Somaliland, or that they crossed the Red Sea from Asia, by way of the port of Kosseir. Over the centuries, Arabic and Turkish occupiers married Nubian women, and tribes of twenty-eight different lineages lived together in scattered villages along the Nile.

Since the band of naturally fertile, silt-rich soil along the riverbank was only a few metres wide, for thousands of years Nubians have worked their *eskalays*. The *eskalay*, Avery had told Jean, holding his lamp close to an illustration in his journal that lay open beside him on their bed on the river, is the great machine of the desert. Its motor is a yoke of bulls. Countless generations of cattle have plodded tight circles in the sand to draw the river, waterbowl by waterbowl, into fields of chickpea and barley.

Farming land was so limited that shares were passed down,

single *feddans* divided and subdivided through generations so many times that, when compensation was to be allocated because of the dam, exasperated clerks found themselves dealing with shares as small as half a square metre. The divisions were so minute and the deeds of ownership so complicated – every single official landowner having died many centuries before – that any hope of straightforward compensation was abandoned. Instead, the Nubian way had to be respected – co-ownership in a communal economy.

In Nubia, families distribute the fruit of the palm among themselves, with shared responsibility for the care of the tree. Cows are the property of a collective of four, each owning a leg, and these shares can be sold and traded. An animal can be rented. The one who feeds and shelters the cow has a right to its milk and calves. Each owner has to provide food and shelter when the animal works his *eskalay*. Division but not divisiveness, for that would literally kill the enterprise.

Before the building of the High Dam at Aswan in the 1960s, a small dam was constructed, and its height was raised twice – ten, then twenty years later, the villages of lower Nubia, the fertile islands, and the date forests were drowned. Each time, the villagers moved to higher ground to rebuild. And so began the labour migration of Nubian men to Cairo, Khartoum, London. The women, with their long, loosely woven black *gargaras* trailing the sand, erasing their footprints, took over the harvesting and marketing of the crops. They pollinated the date palms, cared for their family's property, and tended the livestock. Men returned from the city to be married, to attend funerals, to claim their share of the harvest. And some returned in 1964 to join their families when, with hundreds of thousands of tonnes of cement and steel, and millions of rivets, a lake was built in the desert. Nubia in its entirety – one hundred and twenty thousand villagers, their homes, land, and meticulously tended ancient groves, and many hundreds of archaeological sites – vanished. Even a river can drown; vanished too, under the waters of Lake Nasser, was the Nubians' river, their Nile, which had flowed through every ritual of their daily life, had guided their philosophical thought, and had blessed the birth of every Nubian child for more than five thousand years.

In the weeks before the forced emigration, men who returned from labour exile walked through their villages to homes they had not seen in twenty, forty, fifty years. A woman, suddenly young and then just as suddenly old again, looked at the face of a husband barely seen since she was a girl, and children, now middle-aged, looked upon fathers for the first time. For more than three hundred kilometres, the river absorbed such cries and silences, the shock not of death but of life, as men, living ghosts, returned to look upon their birthplace for the last time.

———

The workers at Abu Simbel fell into small colonies: the Italian stonecutters – the *marmisti* – who could smell faults in the stone at twenty paces; the Egyptian and European engineers;

the cooks and technicians; the Egyptian and Nubian labourers; and all the spouses and children. Avery walked through the site and saw a hundred problems and a hundred singular solutions. He saw the clever adaptations made by workers who could not wait three months for replacement parts to arrive from Europe. It gave him a deep pleasure, his father's pleasure, to notice the wire and spring borrowed from another machine, transplanted with the fraternity of an organ donor.

When Avery first saw the Bucyrus machines squatting in the desert at Abu Simbel – the pumps, refrigerators, and generators – it was almost an ache he felt, for these were the machines his father had loved best. William Escher had put great stock in Ruston-Bucyrus reliability – in their famous excavators and in their machines for compressing, ventilating, pumping, winching, heating, freezing, illuminating . . . He'd had a boy's love of heavy machinery and favoured Bucyrus above all because of their machines born of the Second World War: midget submarines, flameproof locomotives, mine sweepers, landing craft, patrol boats, the Mathilda 400 and Cavalier 220 tanks, the 600 Bren Gun Carriers, and the tunnelling machine commissioned by Winston Churchill and constructed to his personal specifications, a box with a six-foot steel plough in front and a conveyor system in back, designed to dig trenches at the rate of three miles an hour.

–When my father worked for Sir Halcrow and Co., Avery told Jean, the company was building the great Scottish dams. And during the war they were consulted for the "bouncing bomb" missions, and tunnelled under London for the post office, and extended Whitehall for Churchill. My father was sent to North Wales to assess the Manod slate quarry to ensure it was sound enough to shelter paintings from the National Gallery. That's where he'd learned the sizes of Welsh slate: wide and narrow ladies, duchesses and small duchesses, empresses, marchionesses, and broad countesses. He loved the names of things: joists, trusses, sole plates, studs, footing, bearers, lintels, and spars.

– They could be plant names, said Jean. The flowering lintel, the spar nettle, the black-eyed joist . . .

– My father's first job, when he was fifteen, said Avery, was at Lamson Pneumatic Tubes. Ever since I can remember, we shared an affection for pneumatic tubes: ingenious, practical, inexplicably humorous. We loved the idea of an elegant, handwritten note, perhaps a love letter, stuffed into a cylinder and then shot through a tube of compressed air at thirty-five miles an hour or sucked up by a vacuum at the other end like liquid through a straw. My father believed this was the most unjustly neglected technology of the century, and we were continually thinking up new uses for pneumatic tube systems – it was a game he started with me in his letters during the war and we never stopped playing it. He drew maps of London criss-crossed with hundreds of miles of underground pneumatics – little trains of capsule-cars for public transportation; groceries delivered direct from shops to private residences, swooshed right into the kitchen icebox; flowers shot directly from the florist into the vase on one's piano; delivery of medicines to hospitals and convalescent homes; pneumatic school buses, pneumatic amusement rides, pneumatically operated brass bands . . .

My father was a splendid draughtsman, Avery continued. I have never known anyone who could draw machinery as he did. He pushed aside his plate at the supper table and I'd watch him sketch inner workings with fine clear lines. Suddenly the paper came alive and each part took its place in a moving, working mechanism.

It was over a draughtsman's drawing that my parents met. My mother was sitting across from him on a train. He had a drawing tablet open across his bony knees and she praised his work. Avery sat up in their bed below deck, very straight, and jostled against Jean as if they were in a railway compartment. '. . . Thank you,' said my father, 'though I must tell you, it's not the human circulatory system, it's a high-pressure vacuum engine. Though perhaps,' he added politely, 'it seems like a heart when viewed upside down.' He turned the drawing around and looked. 'Yes, I see,' he said. 'And now so do I,' said my mother. 'It's beautiful,' she added. 'Yes,' said my father, 'a well-designed engine is a thing of exceptional beauty.' My mother reports that he then examined her more closely, searched her face. 'Well, yes,' said my mother, 'but what I mean is the drawing itself, the pressures and flow of the pencil.' 'Ah,' said my father, blushing. 'Thank you.'

— Wait! said Jean, to whom one of the great, unexpected pleasures of her marriage was this free speech before sleep. Did your father really blush?

— Oh, yes, said Avery. My father was a mechanism for blushing.

The palm tree, Jean discovered, bears two fruits — not only dates, but also shade. Everywhere in Nubia they are tended, but in Argin and Dibeira, in Ashkeit and Degheim, the date palms grow so thick along the banks of the river that the Nile disappears. The shade there is green and the wind makes a fan of the entire tree. Even the south wind gathers there to cool itself among the leaves of the crown.

The Bartamouda palm gives the sweetest fruit, pouches bursting with brown liqueur, plump flesh with a tiny stone, which the tongue finds like a woman's jewel as the sweetness fills one's mouth. Gondeila dates, by far the largest but less sweet, just right for syrup. The Barakawi, barely sweet at all and therefore somehow more satisfying to eat by the handful. And the Gaw, thin flesh barely covering its bulbous stone, perfectly adequate for vinegar and *araki* gin.

More than half the palm trees in the Wadi Halfa district were Gaw, immense *buras*, ancient groves growing around a single mother, reproducing for generations. At pollination time, the Nubians climbed, the graceful trunk between their legs, and cut the male flower in the bud. Then the buds were ground to powder and small amounts were wrapped in a twist of paper. As each female flower opened, the climber would again ascend, his cap brimming with paper twists of pollen that would be broken over the open flowers. Any flowers left unpollinated grew a tiny date, a little fish, *sis*, and were fed to the animals.

When Jean and Avery first arrived in Egypt, the dates were still green, but soon the fruit drooped in heavy yellow-and-crimson clusters. By August the crop had grown dark and wrinkled with ripeness and then grew darker still. When at last the fruit was shrivelling on the branch, it was quickly har-vested, its sweetness reaching its deepest concentration. Men climbed, swung their scythes, and the bunches fell to the ground, where women and children gathered the fruit in sacks and baskets. Bunch after bunch rained down, sackful after sackful was carried back to the village and spread out to dry.

Shares in date trees were sold, mortgaged, given as wedding gifts and dowries. Not only the fruit but the core of fallen trunks, *golgol*, was eaten. The fruit was sold at market, used for jam and spirits, for cakes, as a special porridge for women in labour. The leaves were woven into rope for the waterwheel, the *sagiya*, for rugs and baskets; they were used as sponges for bathing, as fodder and fuel. Stems were fashioned into brooms. The branches were used for roofs and lintels, for furniture and crates, for coffins and grave markers. And when the train bearing the last inhabitants of Nubia left Wadi Halfa just before the inundation, its engine was decorated with the leaves and branches of the date palms that would soon drown. One could almost have believed a forest had risen from the ground and was making its way across the desert if it weren't for the wailing of the train whistle, a sound unmistakably human.

How much of this earth is flesh?

This is not meant metaphorically. How many humans have been "committed to earth"? From when do we begin to count the dead – from the emergence of *Homo erectus*, or *Homo habilis*, or *Homo sapiens*? From the earliest graves we are certain of, the elaborate grave in Sangir or the resting place of Mungo Man in New South Wales, interred forty thousand years ago? An answer requires anthropologists, paleopathologists, paleontologists, biologists, epidemiologists, geographers . . . How many were the early populations and when exactly began the generations? Shall we begin to estimate from before the last ice age – though there is very little human record – or shall we begin to estimate with Cro-Magnon man, a period from which we have inherited a wealth of archaeological evidence but of course no statistical data. Or, for the sake of statistical "certainty" alone, shall we begin to count the dead from about two centuries ago, when the first census records were kept?

Posed as a question, the problem is too elusive; perhaps it must remain a statement: how much of this earth is flesh.

For many days the great Pharaoh Ramses' men had journeyed upstream, past the foaming gorge of the Second Cataract where every sailor gives thanks for his passage. Then, in the peace where so few before them had travelled, their sail cutting the sky like the blade of a sundial, suddenly they saw the high cliffs of Abu Simbel that caused them to turn to shore. There they waited until dawn, when, following the angle of sunlight up the steep rock with a line of white paint, they marked the place of incision, the place they would open the stone to make way for the sun.

These men built two temples, the immense temple of Ramses and a smaller temple honouring Nefertari, his wife. They conceived the temple's epic proportions, its painted sanctuaries and hallways of statuary, and the four colossi of the facade, each Ramses weighing more than twelve hundred tonnes and, sitting, hands on his knees, more than twenty metres high. They carved the temple's inner chamber sixty metres into the cliff. In mid-October and in mid-February, they steered the sun to pierce this deepest chamber, illuminating the faces of the gods.

Like Ramses' engineers more than thirty centuries before, President Nasser's engineers drew a white line on the banks of the Nile to mark where his monument, the Aswan High Dam, would be built. Egyptian advisers strongly opposed the project, in favour of canals to link African lakes and a reservoir at Wadi Rajan – already a natural basin. But Nasser would not be dissuaded. In October 1958, after Britain declined to support the dam, in retaliation after the Suez conflict, Nasser signed an agreement with the Soviet Union to provide plans, labour, and machinery.

From the moment the Soviets brought their excavators to the desert at Aswan, the land itself rebelled. The sharp desert granite ripped the Soviet tires to strips, the drillheads and teeth of their diggers were ground down and blunted, the gears of their trucks could not endure the steep slopes, and within a single day in the river, the cotton-lined Soviet tires rotted to scraps. Even the great Ulanshev earth-moving machine – the pride of the Soviet engineers – which could hold six tonnes in its scoop and fill a twenty-five-tonne truck in two minutes, broke down continually, and each time they had to wait for parts to arrive from the Soviet Union; until, at last, defeated by the river that had so long been their ally, the Egyptians ordered Bucyrus machinery and Dunlop tires from Britain.

Every afternoon, a twenty-tonne pimento of dynamite was stuffed into each of twelve boreholes and exploded at 3 p.m. The shudder reverberated for thousands of kilometres. And every dusk, the instant the deplorable sun sank behind the hill, an army of men – eighteen thousand Soviet and thirty-four thousand Egyptian labourers – were loosed upon the site to recommence the cutting of the diversion channel. The banks of the river overflowed with shouting men, pounding machinery, shrieking drills, and excavators tearing into the ground. Only the Nile was mute.

At the ceremony to mark the first diversion of the Nile, Nasser had stood at the edge of the span, the captain of the ship, and beside him Khrushchev, the admiral. At the pressing of a button, the inundation began. Labourers clung to the sheer, man-made cliff, ants climbing aboard an ocean liner, slipping and falling into the river.

The dam would make a gash so deep and long that the land would never recover. The water would pool, a blood blister of a lake. The wound would become infected – bilharzia, malaria – and in the new towns, modern loneliness and decay of every sort. Sooner than anyone would expect, the fish would begin dying of thirst.

Hundreds of thousands of years before Nasser had ordered the building of the High Dam, or before Ramses had commanded his likeness to be sculpted at Abu Simbel, these cliffs on the Nile, in the heart of Nubia, had been considered sacred. On the stone summit high above the river, another likeness had been carved: a single prehistoric human footprint. Lake Nasser would melt away this holy ground.

———

In the evenings, those first months in Egypt, Avery and Jean often sat together in the hills above the camp, looking out upon what was as yet, to Jean, a scene of indecipherable activity. She felt that if the desert were plunged into darkness, all human presence would also instantly disappear, as if the incessant motion of the camp was activated by the generators themselves, the men in their service and not the other way around.

There had been many schemes proposed for rescuing the temples at Abu Simbel from the rising waters of the Aswan High Dam. It was understood, especially in the reality of post-war demolishment, that Abu Simbel must be saved.

The French had suggested building another dam, of rock and sand, to protect the temples from the reservoir that would form around them, but such a structure would require constant pumping and there would always be a danger of seepage. The Italians recommended the temples be extracted from the cliff and lifted in their entirety on gargantuan jacks capable of hoisting three hundred thousand tonnes. The Americans had advised floating the temples on two rafts, to higher ground. The British and the Poles thought it best to leave the temples where they were and construct a vast underwater viewing room around them, made of concrete and fitted with elevators.

At last, with no time left to prevaricate, the dismantling of Abu Simbel, block by block, and its re-erection sixty metres higher, had been chosen as the "solution of despair." It was believed that every block in three would crumble.

An international campaign was launched. Across the globe, children burgled their piggy banks and schools collected bags of loose change to save Abu Simbel and the other monuments of Nubia. When envelopes were torn open at the desks of UNESCO, coins from every country jangled to the floor. A woman in Bordeaux abstained from dinner for a year in the hope that her grandchildren might someday see the rescued temples, a man sold his stamp collection, students donated their earnings from paper routes, dog-washing, and snow-shovelling. Universities organized expeditions and sent hundreds of archaeologists, engineers, and photographers into the desert.

When Jean and Avery arrived at Abu Simbel in March 1964 for the vibrograph testing, which would determine more discriminately the fragility of the stone and the methods of cutting, the first task was already underway: the building of the immense cofferdam and its elaborate drainage system — 380,000 cubic metres of rock and sand, and a wall of 2,800 metric tonnes of steel sheeting – to keep Ramses' feet dry. Diversion tunnels and deep clefts lowered the water table, so the river would not probe its way into the soft sandstone of the temples. The cofferdam was conceived and constructed quickly, just in time. In November, Avery watched the water tempting the lip of the barrier. It was easy to imagine the colossi melting, toe by toe, the water slowly dissolving each muscular calf and thigh, and the Pharaoh's impassive courage as the Nile, his Nile, took him to her.

There was no town then, and in the rush to build the cofferdam, the workers lived in tents and houseboats, thousands of men in a vulnerable, makeshift camp. Although the Nubians had inhabited this desert with grace and ingenuity for many thousands of years, the foreigners at Abu Simbel lived with scraps of European equipment and their conditions could be described as primitive. But when the cofferdam was finished, the settlement quickly grew; housing for three thousand, offices, mosque, police station, two shops, tennis court, swimming pool. A contractors' colony, a governors' colony, a labourers' village. Two harbours were built for river barges heaped with supplies, and an airstrip for the delivery of mail and engineers. Machinery and food were brought by boat on the long journey up the Nile from Aswan or by jeep or camel caravan across the desert. Gravel and sand pits appeared, and ten kilometres of road, exclusively for the transport of the temple stones, the only paved surface for thousands of kilometres.

The camp was a living thing, born of extremes – river and desert, human time and geologic time. It contained such a babble of tongues that there was no attempt to provide a school for the forty-six children, since few of them spoke the same language.

Each cut, each of the thousands necessary to extract the temple from the cliff, was to be determined in advance and plotted on an ongoing master plan, a fluid web of forces continually shifting as the cliff disappeared. The sculpted faces were to be left whole when possible and no frieze separated at a place of particular fragility. Vibrations made by the cutting equipment and by the trucks were carefully accounted for. The sanctuary ceilings, which had, for generations, held themselves together according to the basic principle of the arch, would slowly be sliced and stored, taking the arch effect with them. And as the stress of the horizontal pressure increased, steel scaffolding with stanchions would be essential to assume the load. Avery worked with Daub Arbab, an engineer from Cairo who set off from his houseboat each day in an impeccably ironed, pale blue, short-sleeved shirt and whose hands – with shining nails and tapered fingers – seemed similarly finely tailored. Avery was at ease with Daub, and was impressed both by Daub's elegant shirts and by the enthusiasm with which he soiled them. Daub was always the first to get his hands dirty, always eager to kneel, to climb, to carry, to crawl into passages to read the gauges. Together each day, to remain ahead of the changing consequences, they monitored the strengthening tests and the stress-relieving cuts in the rock above; any omission or miscalculation of an altered force, disastrous.

Avery watched as the men sliced into the stone. Closer and closer, down to a distance of 0.8 millimetres from the hair on Ramses' head. The workers clenched their teeth against the motion of their own breath. While scaffolding supported the chambers, the walls of the temples were cut into twenty-tonne blocks. Gargantuan columns, like stone trees, were filleted by desert lumberjacks into rings weighing thirty tonnes.

Because lifting equipment was forbidden to touch the sculpted facade, holes were drilled in the top of the temple blocks and lifting bolts were sealed inside. Steel rods were inserted and epoxy (modified to withstand the high temperatures) held together fractures in the coarse-grained yellow sandstone. Cranes slowly lifted the blocks onto the sand beds of loading trucks and they were taken to the plateau above. In the storage area, the blocks were given steel anchor bars and their surfaces were waterproofed with resin. Meanwhile, the new site was readied. The foundation was excavated, frameworks were built for the facades, which would be placed in position and mounted in concrete. And then the concrete domes would be constructed, one on top of each temple, to bear the weight of the cliff to be built above them.

The most delicate work, inside the chambers themselves, was left to the *marmisti*, whose intimacy with stone was unrivalled. They alone were entrusted to cut into the painted ceiling; it was essential that the blocks fit into place within six millimetres, the maximum allowance for inaccuracy. The Italian stoneworkers possessed a daredevil nonchalance, pure *scavezzacollo*, an instinct so honed that the possibility of error was precisely calculated then disregarded. With handkerchiefs tied around their heads to keep any possibility of sweat from their eyes, they stroked the stone surface, reading like a lover every crevice with their fingers, then bit into the stone with the teeth of the saw.

Giovanni Belzoni contemplated the tip of Ramses' head: a few sculpted centimetres exposed from under the weight of the drifted sand. He saw that to clear a passage would be like trying to "dig a hole in water."

Giovanni Battista Belzoni was born in Padua in 1778, the son of a barber. Because he grew to more than six feet, six inches tall and was able to carry twenty-two men on his back, he had, in his youth, joined the circus as "The Patagonian Samson." But he was also an hydraulic engineer, an amateur archaeologist, and an unrepentant traveller; he and his wife, Sarah, wandered through twenty years of marriage in search of treasure in the desert.

At three o'clock in the afternoon of July 16, 1817, Belzoni climbed the dune at Abu Simbel, took off his shirt, and began to dig with his bare hands. Before dawn, by lantern light, until nine in the morning, when the sun was already murderous, then resting for six hours and continuing again into the night. For sixteen days, Belzoni dug. The cold of the night urged him on. The persistent chill of sand, wind, and darkness; ambition, failure, forsakeness.

Then, at last, at the edge of the lantern light, his hand fell into space and a small gap, barely big enough for a man to crawl through, opened up under the cornice of the temple.

For a moment Belzoni remained perfectly still, almost believing his hand was no longer attached to him. Then, something in the night changed, the desert changed, he could feel it, he could hear it: the ancient air inside the temple moaning from its new small mouth. Belzoni knew he should wait until the morning light, but he could not. Slowly he removed his hand from the hole (like the boy at the dyke) and felt an intense power released, as if a great furnace of sacredness had been opened and the heat of belief was pouring out. An intensity utterly unfamiliar, frightening. Later he remembered what the explorer Johann Burckhardt had said to him – "We have so long forgotten how to be intimate with immensity." He felt as if the black heat had burned right through him, a wound where now the chill desert wind was rushing – and indeed, when he recovered himself a little, he realized that the air coming from inside the temple was insufferably hot, hotter than a steambath, so hot that later the sweat would run down his arm and through his fingers onto his notebook and Belzoni would have to stop drawing. But now he knew he would have to wait for morning. When he pulled out his upper body, the night wind doused him; instantly, shockingly, the heat froze on his skin.

He squatted in the sand and looked out toward the river that was becoming almost visible, the sun beginning to crack open on the rim of the hills. It was dawn, August 1, 1817.

Soon the sun would enter the great painted hall of Abu Simbel for the first time in more than a thousand years.

From the small hole behind him, the immense roar of silence.

———

One day, a blind man appeared in the desert. His dark skin was smooth over his bones, and however old one guessed him to be, he was most certainly older. He wore European trousers and singlet but spoke no European language, only a whispered Arabic, as if he were afraid to be woken by his own voice.

At the blind man's request, the labourers carefully guided him up the contours of Ramses' powerful calves to the king's thick knees, each the size of a boulder. The old man would not be carried and took his time memorizing the way. After several ascents and descents, he knew his route perfectly, and they let him climb unaided to sit on Ramses' knee. So steady and interested was his blind gaze, a stranger might assume the old man was looking for something in the river, or keeping watch. It made all the imported engineers nervous to see a blind man at that height, but, after the first day, the labourers took no notice.

The blind man fascinated the stonecutters. The *marmisti* watched his fingers follow the clues in the rock with professional appreciation. They saw that he never faltered, that he moved with intense slowness and precision. If he moved, he was sure. When Jean first saw him in Ramses' lap, she gasped. How still he sat, how sculpted his face; he looked like a living Horus, the god with the head of a bird. One night she saw him, his singlet shining white, and he was singing. The machinery was loud; he could not be heard, his mouth open in silence. But Jean could tell the blind man was singing because he had closed his eyes.

———

Each river has its own distinct recipe for water, its own chemical intimacies. Silt, animal waste, paint from the hulls of boats, soil carried on skin and clothes and feathers, human spit, human hair . . . Looking out at the river, which at first had astonished Avery with its smallness – the great Nile seemed to him as slender as a woman's arm, incontestably female – Avery was pained to imagine the force with which it would soon be bound, its submission. Each year, for thousands of years, swollen with the waters from Ethiopia, the Nile offered her intense fertility to the desert. But now this ancient cycle would abruptly end. And end, too, the centuries-old celebrations of that inundation, inseparable from gods and civilization and rebirth, an abundance that gave meaning to the very rotation of the earth.

Instead there would be a massive reservoir reshaping the land – a lake "as large as England" – so large that the estimated rate of evaporation would prove a serious misjudgment. Enough water would disappear into the air to have made fertile for farming more than two million acres. The precious, nutrient-saturated silt that had given the soil of the floodplain such richness would be lost entirely, pinioned, useless behind the dam. Instead, international corporations would introduce chemical fertilizers, and the cost of these fertilizers – lacking all the trace elements of the silt – would soon escalate to billions of dollars every year. Without the sediment from the floods, farmland downriver would soon erode. The rice fields of the northern Delta would be parched by salt water. Throughout the Mediterranean basin, fish populations — dependent on silicates and phosphates from the annual flooding — would decrease, then die out completely. The exploding insect population would result in an exploding scorpion population. The new ecology would attract destructive micro-organisms that would thrive in the new moist environment, and introduce new pests — the cotton-leaf worm and the great moth and the cornstalk-borer — that would devastate the very crops the dam was meant to make possible. Insects would spread infectious — and excruciating — diseases in plague proportions, such as bilharzia, an illness caused by a parasite laying its eggs in almost any organ of the human body — including liver, lungs, and brain.

The silt, like the river water, also had its own unique intimacies, a chemical wisdom that had been refining itself for millennia. To Jean, the Nile silt was like flesh, it held not only a history but a heredity. Like a species, it would never again be known on this earth.

At the new site of the temple, without the ecology of the original shore, there would also be consequences — a kind of revenge. The desert and the river had always safeguarded the temples, but now their divine protection would come to an end. At the new height, there would be severe erosion by sandstorms, and lawns would have to be planted to replace the sand, the lawns in turn attracting a biblical plague of frogs, which in turn would attract a plague of snakes, which in turn would not attract the tourists . . .

More than five hundred official guests would attend the inauguration of the re-erected temples. There would be passionate speeches. "No civilized government can fail to give first priority to the welfare of its people . . . The High Dam had to be built, no matter what the effects might be . . ." "This is not the moment to go back over the actions and reactions to which the International Campaign has given rise . . ."

Simulation is the perfect disguise. The replica, which is meant to commemorate, achieves the opposite effect: it allows the original to be forgotten. Out of the crowd, the heckling of a journalist: "It looks exactly the same! What have you boys done with the forty million bucks?"

No word would be uttered of the Nubians who had been forced to leave their ancient homes and their river, nor of the twenty-seven towns and villages that had vanished under the new lake: Abri, Kosh Dakki, Ukma, Semna, Saras Shoboka, Gemaii, Wadi Halfa, Ashkeit, Dabarosa, Qatta, Kalobsha, Dabud, Faras . . .

. . . Farran's Point, thought Avery, Aultsville, Maple Grove, Dickinson's Landing, half of Morrisburg, Wales, Milles Roches, Moulinette, Woodlands, Sheek Island . . .

———

At the edge of the St. Lawrence River, near Aultsville, Canada, Avery awaited the arrival of the Bucyrus Erie 45 – The

Gentleman – an immense dragline that had been floated to the future site of the St. Lawrence dam from a Kentucky coal mine. All around him was a display that would satisfy even the most ardent machine-worshipper: nine dredges, eighty-five scrapers, one hundred and forty shovels and draglines, fifteen hundred tractors and trucks.

This was the moment his father had loved best, surveying the gathering of the mechanical infantry; making ready not to capture the hill but to eliminate it, or manufacture it, as circumstances demanded. William Escher knew this was not a simple battle of brute force between technology and nature but a test of will, two intelligences pitted against each other, requiring both probity and shrewdness.

Avery contemplated the St. Lawrence clay at his feet. He understood almost instantly that it would harden to rock in winter and in summer grip even the largest wheels immobile. Though it was compliant at the moment, this early afternoon in March 1957, he guessed correctly that the building of the seaway could easily become one of the most treacherous excavations on the continent. Avery had been hired on his own merits and under his father's supervision. But William Escher had died before even the first tree was felled. Since leaving school, Avery had always worked with his father. Now he found himself looking out upon the last moments of a landscape – always their shared ceremony – without his father's hand on his shoulder.

Along these leafy shores of the St. Lawrence, towns and hamlets had sprung up, founded by United Empire Loyalists, settlers made up of former soldiers in the battalion of the "Royal Yorkers." Then came the German, the Dutch, the Scottish settlers. Then a tourist by the name of Charles Dickens, travelling by steamboat and stagecoach who described the river that "boiled and bubbled" near Dickinson's Landing and the astonishing sight of the log drive. "A most gigantic raft, some thirty or forty wooden houses on it, and at least as many log-masts, so that it looked like a nautical street . . ."

Before this came the hunters of the sea, the Basque, Breton, and English whalers. And, in 1534, Jacques Cartier, the hunter who captured the biggest prize, an entire continent, by quickly recognizing that, by bark canoe, one could follow the river and pierce the land to its heart.

The great trade barons grumbled, unable to depart their Atlantic ports and conquer the Great Lakes with their large ships, groaning with goods to sell. Two irksome details stood in the way: the second largest falls in the world – Niagara – and the Long Sault Rapids.

The sound of the Long Sault was deafening. It ate words out of the air and anything caught up in its force. For three miles, a heavy mist hung over the river and even those at a distance were soaked with spray. The white water rampaged through a narrow gorge, a gradual thirty-foot descent.

In the mid-1800s, canals were cut to bypass the rapids but were too shallow for the great freighters. It was the way of things; Avery could not name a significant instance where this was not true, that early canals proved to be the first cut of a future dam, no matter how many generations lay between them. Building the seaway, with a dam to span the Canadian and American banks of the river, had been discussed many times, over many decades, until, in 1954, the St. Lawrence Seaway and Power Project was born. Hydroelectricity would be created for both countries; a lake, a hundred miles long, would pool between them.

To achieve these ends, the wild Long Sault would be drained to its riverbed. For a year, while the channels were widened, archaeologists would roam the ships' graveyard where, for centuries, the force of the water had welded cannonballs, masts, and iron plate into the rock of "the cellar" on impact. Nothing short of an explosion would pry them loose.

For some time, Avery sat on the shore of the river, in sight of the heavy machines, and thought about the wildness of that water, the elation of that force. It was familiar to him now, this feeling at the beginning, which he conscientiously registered as containing an element of self-pity; the first signs of a slow, coagulating grief.

In the flooding of the shoreline, Aultsville, Farran's Point, Milles Roches, Maple Grove, Wales, Moulinette, Dickinson's Landing, Santa Cruz, and Woodlands would become "lost." This was a term for which Avery had once felt contempt but now appreciated, for the sting of its unintentional truth; thousands would become homeless as though through some act of negligence. The former inhabitants would be conglomerated and relocated, distributed between two newly built towns — Town #1 and Town #2, eventually to be named Long Sault and Ingleside. Because the town of Iroquois was to be rebuilt a mile farther from shore and retain its name, officially it was not considered "lost," though it would lose everything but its name. To be flooded, too, were Croil's, Barnhart, and Sheek islands. Construction would soon begin on the northern edge of the town of Morrisburg to make up for the half of itself that would disappear. The First Nations, descendants of Siberian hunters who'd crossed the land bridge from Asia twenty thousand years before and who'd made these shores their home since the melting of the great glacier, were dispossessed of shore and islands, and heavy metals from the new seaway industries would poison their fish supply and their cattle on Cornwall Island. Spawning grounds would be destroyed. Salmon would struggle upstream, alive with purpose, to find their way blocked by concrete.

The Hydro-Electric Power Commission of Ontario had offered to move houses from the villages to Town #1 or Town #2. These were lifted from their foundations by the gargantuan Hartshorne House Mover. The house mover could lift a one-hundred-and-fifty-tonne building like a piece of cake on its giant steel fork and drop not a crumb. Two men, one standing on the other's shoulders, could fit in the diameter of one tire, and the machine could travel six miles an hour with a full load. The inventor and manufacturer of the Hartshorne House Mover, William J. Hartshorne himself, presided over the seaway operations; Avery had watched while two steel arms embraced the house, a frame was fastened under it and hydraulically lifted. Five hundred and thirty-one homes were being moved this way, two per day.

"Leave your dishes in the cupboard," boasted Mr. Hartshorne. "Nothing inside will shift an inch!" Even the spoon he had balanced theatrically on the rim of a bowl was still wavering there when they set the first house down and opened the door. The same night, the housewife who owned the spoon in question was so unnerved at being in her own kitchen, many miles away from where she'd eaten her breakfast that very morning, that she dropped and shattered the teapot she'd been so worried about — her mother's Wedgwood, in her family for four generations — as she carried it the short distance from counter to table.

In 1921, the chairman of the hydro-electric commission, Sir Adam Beck, had referred to the future drowning of the villages along the St. Lawrence and the evacuation of their inhabitants as the "sentimental factor." Now the paper mill had been taken over by the commission for its headquarters, and its regional offices had ensconced themselves in the stocking factory at Morrisburg. Not far from where Avery stood, public telescopes would be erected, overlooking the construction site, and bus tours would be organized for the millions of visitors. An historian would be employed to "collect and preserve historical data" from the places to be destroyed. The number of welfare recipients in the counties would increase 100 per cent. Already, Avery knew, there was a rumour one could earn ten dollars an hour moving graves.

Every Saturday, when Jean was a child, her father, John Shaw, a French teacher in an English private school in Montreal, took the train – the *Moccasin* – to tutor the children of the wealthy granary owner at Aultsville. When Jean came downstairs on Sunday mornings, a paper bag of sweet buns would be waiting for her on the kitchen table, the mysterious words *Markell's Bakery* in their flowing script, satin dark with butter. After her mother died, a silent Jean accompanied her father. They held hands on the train, all the way, and Jean's father learned to slip the book from his pocket and turn the pages with one hand while Jean slept against his shoulder. After his wife's death, John Shaw took to reading the books she'd loved, the books on her side of the bed. He memorized the lines she'd underlined, the verses of John Masefield she'd declaimed when Jean was a laughing baby in her arms, marching across the kitchen linoleum:

'Dirty British coaster with a salt-caked smokestack,
Butting through the Channel in the mad March days,
With a cargo of Tyne coal,
Road rail, pig lead,
Firewood, ironware, and cheap tin trays.'

Or the Edna St. Vincent Millay, when Jean was up in the night and her mother carried her across her chest wrapped in a blanket:

'O world, I cannot hold thee close enough . . .
Long have I known a glory in it all,
But never knew I this:
Here such a passion is
As stretcheth me apart — Lord, I do fear
Thou'st made the world too beautiful this year;
My soul is all but out of me . . .'

The villages along the St. Lawrence were enlivened by both the railway and the river. This created a vigour that Jean could not quite explain, though she recognized it somehow; two stories meeting in the middle. The nine-year-old Jean now knew what it was to starve of love and, in her hunger, was affected by what she saw: the old woman by the river who kept taking out and fingering the same few pages from her handbag, making sure she hadn't lost them, her handbag snapping shut with the same sound as Jean's mother's gold compact; the little boy who kept reaching for the tassel on his mother's coat as it swung from his reach with her every step. Once, in the general store she saw a woman give some potatoes to Frank Jarvis, the grocer, to weigh on his scale; then the woman passed over her baby to be weighed. She saw Jean watching. "Yes." She smiled. "Jarvis and Shaver sell babies. By the pound."

Jean began to yearn for these excursions with her father, and in the summer they disembarked at other stops after his morning's work; sometimes at Farran's Point, where John Shaw liked to visit the saw mill or the grist mill, the carding mill or the marble works. The foreman at the marble works was a former New Yorker and a master stoneworker. While John Shaw examined the cornices and archways lying about the grounds, Jean hunted out small animals, with their intricate stone fur, hiding in the long grass and peering out from behind the shrubbery. They admired the flower gardens at Lock 22, tended by the lock-keepers. They watched as the liquid heat rose above the limestone quarry and they held their noses at the stink of the paper mill at Milles Roches. Wherever the train stopped – Aultsville, Farran's Point, Moulinette – they saw a small crowd waiting on the platform for cargo to be unloaded: great spools of wire fencing, auto parts, livestock. They soon learned to listen for the thud of the mailbags before the train pulled away and to look out for the bulging dirty lumps of sailcloth that had been flung out onto the platform. They saw the train-men walking the track and filling the switch lamps with oil. They saw students returning from their week at college in Cornwall, and shoppers from the villages who'd spent the day in Montreal, awkward paper parcels in their arms or piled at their feet while they waited for someone to meet them at the station. Jean began to understand that there might be mystery for some travellers in both directions, though sadness always descended for her as the train approached the city, and by the time they reached home on Hampton Avenue, Jean, motherless, was emptied of any desire to look about her.

On private anniversaries, or when the seasons change, bringing memories, boats are rowed resolutely to seemingly meaningless coordinates on the St. Lawrence Seaway, where, abruptly, the rowers pull up their oars and spin to a stop. Sometimes, they leave flowers floating in the place, drifting in silence.

In the October shallows, one can stand once again in the middle of the Aultsville dairy. One can promenade ankle-deep through the avenue of trees on the main street, now water-logged stumps. In the first years, even gardens continued to rise out of the shallows, like pilgrims who had not yet heard the news of the disaster.

When the seaway was built, even the dead were dispossessed, exhumed to churchyards north of the river. However, not all the villagers were willing to accept the hydro-electric company's invitation to tamper with their ancestors and so instead six thousand headstones were moved and the nameless graves remained.

For many years after, the residents of Stormont, Glengarry, and Dundas counties were afraid to swim; the river now belonged to the dead and many feared the bodies would escape and float to the surface. Others simply could not bring themselves to enter the water where so many and so much had vanished, as if they, too, might never return.

———

Jean and her father disembarked at Dickinson's Landing. As soon as they'd left the train station they'd felt it, the whispered hysteria, the aimlessness. From the road they could see that all the houses had been plundered, gouged out from the inside, walls partly torn away. On the lawns, ganglia of wires hung from coarse brains of cement. Inside and outside merged, a fibrous pulpy mash – like seeds scooped from a pumpkin – of wood and plaster. Familiar patterns of broadloom and wallpaper were exposed to the open air. Lighting and plumbing fixtures, floorboards, ornate Victorian fireplaces, all with a palpable intimacy, were splayed on the grass, to be carted away in trucks. Amid the debris, fires were set.

It was a cold autumn day, the possibility of snow. The leaves against the dark sky glowed with the heavy colours of ripe fruit. Jean and her father joined the haphazard procession through the town to Georgiana – Granny – Foyle's front yard. Only the men who moved authoritatively back and forth across the lawn, and stood on the wide, wraparound porch, spoke with normal voices. No one would quite remember what it looked like, there was so much to comprehend; some said it started gradually and took a long time to catch, others said the wall of fire rose instantly, giving off a heat that drove all the observers back to the road. There was an enormous crowd; Georgiana Foyle was perhaps the only one from the county not watching her house as it burned.

Afterwards, Jean and her father walked to the river. Even there, where the air was refreshed by the water, they smelled the smoke.

The St. Lawrence flowed as always. But already it was impossible to look at the river in the same way.

They stood, staring out at the islands. It began to snow. Or at least it seemed to be snowing, but soon they realized that what was in the air was ash.

The white scraps glowed against the black sky. It fell faster than John Shaw could brush it from his coat. He pressed his fingers to his eyes. Jean put her hand in her father's coat pocket and with her other hand pushed her knitted hat low over her head. Jean, eighteen years old, knew that his emotion was not only on behalf of Georgiana Foyle. Her house is in the air, said John Shaw. Still they did not move, but continued to stand at the water's edge.

The crests of windwater and the shades of blue and black were so alive with the intensity of cold that Jean could almost not bear the beauty of it, and somehow she could not separate this sight from her father's sadness, nor from the feel of his hand.

Later, walking back to the train station, it truly began to snow, a heavy wet snowfall that came to nothing when it reached the ground.

Georgiana Foyle, who until that very moment had prided herself on a lifetime of good manners, banged on the side of Avery's Falcon with the flat of her hand. She began talking before he lowered his window.

— But they can move your husband's body, said Avery. The company will pay the expenses.

She looked at him with astonishment. The thought seemed to silence her. Then she said:

— If you move his body then you'll have to move the hill. You'll have to move the fields around him. You'll have to move the view from the top of the hill and the trees he planted, one for each of our six children. You'll have to move the sun because it sets among those trees. And move his mother and his father and his younger sister – she was the most admired girl in the county, but all the men died in the first war, so she never married and was laid to rest next to her mother. They're all company for one another and those graves are old, so you'll have to move the earth with them to make sure nothing of anyone is left behind. Can you promise me that? Do you know what it means to miss a man for twenty years? You think about death the way a young man thinks about death. You'd have to move my promise to him that I'd keep coming to his grave to describe that very place as I used to when we were first married and he hurt his back and had to stay in bed for three months – every night I described the view from the hill above the farm and it was a bit of sweetness – for forty years – between us. Can you move that promise? Can you move what was consecrated? Can you move that exact empty place in the earth I was to lie next to him for eternity? It's the loneliness of eternity I'm talking about! Can you move all those things?

Georgiana Foyle looked at Avery with disgust and despair. Her skin, like paper that had been crumpled and smoothed out again, was awash with tears in the mesh of lines, her

ANNE MICHAELS

whole face shone wet. She was so sinewy and slight, her heavy cotton dress seemed to hover without touching her skin.

Avery longed to reach out his hand, but he was afraid; he had no right to comfort her.

The old woman leaned against the car and wept unashamedly into her arms, her long, thin bones now standing out against her sleeves.

———

After the houses and farms of Stormont, Glengarry, and Dundas counties had been plundered for building supplies, and the remains eradicated by fire and bulldozers, the politicians gathered just west of Cornwall, at the town of Maple Grove, to push their golden shovel into the ground. Five years of construction and destruction lay ahead. Three major dams would be built, and cofferdams to allow the work to proceed, diverting first one-half of the river and then the other, leaving each half in turn drained for construction. To see the riverbed exposed this way, the intimate riverbed – private, vulnerable, tangled with vegetation, mosses, water life – shrivelling in the sun, sickened Jean, and she could not make out what she must do: to look or to look away.

It was unnerving, apocalyptic, to be walking on the exposed riverbed, as if the ghost of the river was swirling around Avery's legs. He kept looking down and looking back, feeling

48

that, at any moment, the St. Lawrence might suddenly begin flowing again, a powerful current that would throw him off his feet. But instead there was the new silence. Rocks lay emptied of purpose; it was as if time itself had ceased to flow.

Far ahead, on the bank, he saw something move. He discerned the shape of a woman. He watched her walking and bending, walking and bending, like a bird leaning down its head, here and there, for food. She was wearing blue shorts and a printed cotton short-sleeved shirt. A canvas bag was slung across her back. He watched her carefully wrap things in newspaper, write something, then cram them into the sack. She must have felt his eyes, for suddenly she stopped and turned and stared at him. Then, obviously having made a decision, she continued walking, away from where he stood.

In that second, as Avery saw her walking away, an inexplicable sadness came to him and a painful craving to follow. He climbed the bank and when he was quite close, he saw that she was collecting plants.

— Please don't let me disturb you, said Avery. I'm just curious what you're doing.

She looked up at him, surprised at his English accent.

— Have you come all the way from England to gawk at our dried-up river?

— I'm working on the dam, said Avery.

Hearing this, she pushed another fold of newspaper into her sack and began to move away.

— If you don't mind my asking, what are you collecting?

She kept walking. He saw the fine sun-bleached hair on her arms and on the back of her thighs.

— Everything that's still growing here, she said with a shrug. Everything that will soon be gone.

— But why pick these? They're only common plants, said Avery. Tansy and loosestrife, they grow all over.

— You know a little botany, just a little. This isn't loosestrife, it's fireweed.

She stopped. He saw her determined, sunburned face.

— I'm keeping a record, she said bitterly. I'm going to transplant these particular plants, this particular generation. Though of course they'll never grow and reproduce themselves exactly as they would have, if they'd been left alone.

— Ah, said Avery. I understand.

She started to bend and then stood, unable to continue with him watching her.

— My father was an engineer, said Avery. I went wherever he was working and the first thing I always learned in a new place were the trees and the flowers . . . It must have been very beautiful here . . .

She looked at him.

— The wrong thing to say . . .

— No. It was very beautiful here . . . a month ago.

She looked at the ground.

— I used to come here, she said, with my father.

She hesitated, then stepped down into the riverbed and leaned the full length of her back against a boulder. He followed and sat down, a few feet "upstream."

— A month ago we wouldn't have been sitting here, said Avery.

— No, said Jean.

Jean would never forget what Avery spoke of, their first afternoon in the abandoned river: of the Hebrides, where sea and sky are driven wild by the scent of land; of the Chiltern Hills, with its stone forests of wet beeches; and of his father, William Escher, who, in the months before he died, had arranged for this work on the seaway for Avery, as his assistant. Now he was working with another engineer, a friend of his father. Jean felt Avery's loneliness for him, even in this briefest recounting. She saw how nervously Avery wound and rewound the strap of his binoculars through the straps of his rucksack. Now it was her turn to feel an unaccountable depth of loss, fearing that at any moment he would stop talking and walk away from her.

— There's a cinema in Morrisburg, Avery said at last. Would you meet me there some time?

Jean looked into Avery's face. She had never been to the cinema with any man but her father. Then she looked away, downriver, feeling the poverty of her experience in the endless length of exposed clay.

— All right, said Jean.

They had emerged from the cinema into a long summer evening, not quite dark.

—You can drive me home, Jean said.

—Yes, of course, said Avery, feeling a sharp stab of dejection that she wished to leave so soon. Where do you live?

—About four hours from here . . .

It was past midnight by the time they reached Toronto. Clarendon Avenue was treelined, empty. The leaves of the maples gathered in the warm wind. Jean pushed open the wrought-iron door of an old stone apartment building, pendulous glass lanterns glowing in the entranceway.

— Step outside, said Jean, holding the door open for Avery to enter.

Inside, the foyer ceiling glowed with stars.

— This is where my mother and father lived when they were first married, said Jean. The painter J. E. H. MacDonald designed everything – the symbols of the zodiac, the patterns on the beams – and his apprentice, a young man named Carl Schaefer, climbed the ladder and painted them. Schaefer worked at night, with the door to the courtyard open. How moving it must have been to paint the night sky in gold leaf while the real night was all around him . . . Later my parents moved to Montreal, and my mother used to say that she started her garden there because she no longer had the stars. Almost immediately after they moved, her brother died in the air, flying at night. He was in the RCAF. My father said my mother always connected the two events, though she felt too foolish to confess it. The moment she stopped keeping watch over the night sky, he was lost. There were only the two children – my mother and her brother – and they died within three years of each other.

Avery and Jean walked under the stars. The floor of the lobby was marble and ceramic tile; ornately braided stone archways led to the lift.

– This is the first ceiling in Canada made of poured concrete, said Jean proudly. The paint is acid-proof with Spar varnish; the heavens will never crack or fade!

– No one would ever guess the whole of heaven was here, said Avery, inside this stone building.

– Yes, said Jean, it's like a secret.

They had driven for hours together, but the night fields had been all around them and, between them, through the open car windows, the cool summer wind. Now in the tiny lift they stood cramped and awkward.

Upstairs, Jean opened the door to moonlight and street-lamp light; she'd left the curtains open and the living room floor, covered entirely with plants, glowed, the light glinting off the edges of hundreds of jars filled with seedlings and flowers.

– Here are some good examples of indigenous species, said Jean. And she thought, Here I am.

———

They left Avery's car at the edge of the forest. The track was overgrown, not much wider than one's shoulders; how quickly the forest forgets us. There was little to carry, a paper bag of groceries, Jean's satchel. The low canopy of leaves pounded with the sound of the rapids. Mist was caught between the trees, as if the earth were breathing. The cabin was still some way from the Long Sault, yet even here the roar exploded. A handful of cabins had once stood where now only one remained. Inside, a wooden table, three chairs, a bed too old to be worth the trouble of moving. A wood-stove. The forest-shadow and the river-depth had penetrated the cabin for so many years there would always be dampness and the memory of dampness. The same day Avery had found the cabin, while assessing the site of the rapids, he had moved his gear from the hotel in Morrisburg, purchased bedding, a lantern, a supply of mantles.

Stepping inside, Jean could hardly believe how loud the Long Sault boomed – it seemed an acoustical mirage – as if amplified by the small bare space. Immediately the coldness of the cabin and the smell of cedar and woodsmoke became inseparable from the crashing of the river. She felt she would either have to talk with her mouth against Avery's ear, or shout, or simply mouth her words. When Jean leaned toward Avery to speak, her hair touching his face felt to him unbear-ably alive.

– After a time, said Avery, the sound becomes part of you, like the rushing of your own blood when you cover your ears.

Avery lit the lamps. He built the fire. Jean unpacked their groceries; there was nothing fresh from Frank Jarvis's own garden, and the fact that there would never again be a garden and the reality of the almost empty General Store had unnerved her. They'd bought canned tomatoes instead, carried by ship all the way from Italy, and a long carton of pasta, a small jar of basil, and a shiny white cardboard box from Markell's, containing the same kind of sweet buns her father used to bring home to Jean when she was a girl. These she laid out on the wooden table.

Because of the noise of the river, neither spoke much; instead they felt intensely their every movement in the small room. Avery watched Jean push her hair from her eyes with her forearm as she washed her hands at the sink. She saw his discomfort as he scanned the cabin for embarrassing traces – the grimy rind of soap by the kitchen sink, his mud-stiff trousers hanging from the back of the door.

There was little room to move; the table was at the foot of the bed, only a patch of rug on the plank floor separated the kitchen from the bedroom. All was orderly, the axe in its leather sheath by the door, the Coleman water containers waiting to be refilled. A narrow shelf for a wash basin, the folded square of frayed towel. On the floor next to the bed, *Edible Plants*, *The Pleasure of Ruins*, *The Kon-Tiki Expedition*, *Bird Hazards to Aircraft*, *Excavations at the Njoro River Cave*. On the windowsills, the usual collection of stones and driftwood, but here organized by shape or colour, kept for their resemblance to another form – the stone shaped like an animal or a bird. It has always been this way, Jean thought, the desire for a likeness, for the animate in the inanimate. The whole cabin was organized as a chef might organize a kitchen, everything in its place for ease of use. Avery was acutely aware of how deeply the room betrayed his habits.

Jean added oil and basil to the tomatoes and threw salt into the boiling water. They ate in the sound of the rapids.

From the window there was only forest and this, too, cast its spell: the very invisibility of the overpowering river. As the room grew darker, the noise of the Long Sault seemed to increase. For the first time, Jean thought about the intimacy within that sound, the continuous force of water on rock, sculpting every crevice and contour of the riverbed.

After the meal, through which they had barely spoken, with nowhere else to go, Avery took Jean's hand and they lay down.

— If we're getting into bed, then we'd better get dressed, said Avery, and he passed her a wool jumper and a ball of thick socks. It's very cold at night and sometimes I wear everything I have, even with the fire.

The sight of Jean in his clothes almost broke Avery's resolve. But he remained quiet beside her.

He could smell the woodsmoke in her hair. And she, in the wool of his sweater, could smell his body, lamp oil, earth.

The lantern light, the fire, the river, the cold bed, Jean's small, strong, still hand under his sweater.

To claim the sight of her. To learn and name and hold all that he sees in her face, as he, too, becomes part of her expression, a way of listening that will soon include her knowledge of him. To learn each nuance as it reveals a new past, and all that might be possible. To know in her skin the inconsistencies of age: her child hands and wrists and ears, her young woman's upper arms and legs smooth and firm; each anatomical part of us seems to attain a different maturity and, for a long time, remains so. How is it the body ages with such inconsistency? Looking at her across the table, or looking at her now, his face next to hers, his limbs along hers, the yielding of her face as she listens, of one face into another and another, always another openness, a latent openness, so love opens into love, like the slightest change of light or air on the surface of water. Lying next to her, he imagined even his thoughts could alter her face.

After a very long time, Jean began to speak.

— My father brought me to Aultsville for the first time after my mother died. He said he was taking me to hear the 'talking trees,' to lift my spirits a little . . . I still have no word for that depth of sadness. It is almost a different kind of sight; everything beautiful, a branding. During the whole train journey he wouldn't tell me what the talking trees were . . . After his day of teaching we walked out to the apple grove near the station . . .

It was warm, pink, dusk. Shadows fell between the rows and soon it was not so easy to see the way. The path was woven with shadow. I remember holding on to his arm very tightly. He always rolled up his sleeves in the summer, above his elbows. I can feel his bare arm now. The wind shook the small silver leaves — that indescribable sound — and farther into the grove I heard the murmuring. I looked up and saw nothing, but of course in the dusk, the brown arms of the apple-pickers were hidden by the branches, were themselves like moving branches. They were women's voices, and the words were so ordinary. Sometimes a single word suddenly clearer than the rest — *Saturday*, *dress*, *waiting* — and it was the ordinariness of the words that was so moving, even as a girl I felt this, that such ordinariness should always sound that way, as if the wind had found its language. 'Voices sweet as fruit,' my father said, a phrase I'm sure he'd saved for me in his mouth the entire day. Another time, he took me with him in the middle of winter, it was after a storm and again we walked, this time in snow-white darkness. From the mill roof hung immense icicles, almost to the ground, a frozen waterfall, twelve or fifteen feet long; it made me think of a painting I'd seen, of mammoth baleen in the moonlit ocean . . . Always he would show me these things as if they were secrets, not just there out in the open for anyone to see. And it's true, hardly anyone ever noticed the miracles my father noticed. We took the train back to Montreal together in the dark, and I fell asleep leaning against his wool coat, or his cool short-sleeved summer arm, full of the day's beautiful secrets and the irreducible knowledge that my mother was not with us. That she would never see these things. And that is when I realized we were looking for her.

Children make vows. From the moment I saw my father sitting in the kitchen, her sweater draped across his chest, about a month after she'd died, I knew I would never leave him, I knew I would always look after him.

When I think of it now, only now, I realize we lived in a hush, as if my mother had been all the happy noise we'd ever known. After she was gone, our range of expression shrank — to the small, to the significant. I ached and longed for her. I've missed her every minute of my life. Each morning I woke up, I walked to school, I cooked our dinner, and I never stopped missing her. I remember the first day at school after she died, all the children knew and they avoided me — they were too young for pity, they were afraid. She left a small garden that

I kept tending – for her – as if one day she would come back and we could sit there together and I would show her how well her lilies had grown, show her all the new plants I'd added. In the beginning, I was afraid to change anything and it was momentous when I dug the first hole. Then planting became a vocation. Suddenly I felt I could keep on loving her, that I could keep telling her things this way . . .

It was hard trying to learn simple things like what kind of clothes to wear or what was expected of me by watching my schoolmates, seeing what they wore and how they behaved, listening to them talk. My father had one sister, much older than him, who lived in England and she visited us once. My aunt seemed so vibrant, so exorbitant in her habits – so free and at ease. She wore silk dresses and velvet hats and when she arrived she gave me a pair of bright red woollen mittens trimmed with tartan ribbon. I remember how frightened I was to wear those mittens in the schoolyard. What if someone said something to make me not love them as much? I thought everyone would laugh at me – something so jolly and pretty could not belong to me, could not be for my hands! It was wrong, gauche, a display of happiness above my standing. But of course no one noticed them at all. And those mittens had a kind of magic in them: they had not been ruined by words. Long after my aunt returned home, her gift continued to make me bolder and, very slowly, I began to wear what I liked, and be what I liked. And again, no one seemed to notice or care. I wore my mother's old-fashioned cardigans and her lace-up Clapp shoes, which she'd always called her 'house shoes.' There were our two birthday parties each year, just my father and me, always with an elaborate store-bought cake with heavy ropes of icing along the edges. The thought of those cakes makes me weep because he did not know what to do to please me, how to please me enough. All his love went into the choosing of a cake, the colour of the icing, the sugar decorations – almost as if it were for her. Jean was crying. Everything to do with our life together was painfully beautiful. Everything between us was remembering my mother. What she might have liked, what she might have thought. My life formed around an absence. Every bit of pleasure, each window of lamplight against the night snow, the drowsy smell of the summer roses, attached itself to the fact of her absence. Everything in this world is what has been left behind.

In my final year of school, my father suggested we move to Toronto so I could go to university there. There was never any mention of my going alone. It was unthinkable for both of us. Sometimes things change simply because the time has come, an inner moment is reached for reasons one cannot explain – whether grief takes six months or six decades or, as in our case, eight years. Something latent in the body awakens. Sorghum seeds can lie dormant for six thousand years and then stir themselves! It happens all the time in nature; we should not be surprised when it happens in human nature. When we began to talk about moving, there was a lightheart-edness in my father, and I began to feel that there could be a new life for both of us. But I think now, for him, it was the opposite, a way to recapture something.

He wished to return to Clarendon Avenue. We made one

trip to Toronto to see the flat together and later that evening we went to a concert at Massey Hall. Elgar's Cello Concerto, one of my father's favourites. After the concert, as we were about to leave, he hesitated, then led me by the hand back to our seats. 'Listen with me,' he said. Sitting again in the empty hall I found I could still hear the music, it was a kind of haunting. 'Your mother and I,' said my father, 'used to do this whenever we went to the symphony; we'd wait for everyone to leave and then keep listening.' We sat together while the music again unfolded, until the usher came and said it was time to leave . . .

My father died before we'd moved. This happens so often – death at a time of change – that I think there should be a word for it. Perhaps there is: betrayal, or violation; not stroke or aneurism . . . Our house in Montreal was already sold. There was nothing else to do but continue to pack up and to move alone. I took cuttings and seeds from every plant in my mother's garden, but there's no place for them. Now her whole garden is in pots and jars on my living room floor. That was two years ago . . . I think of the last gardens on the river, I mourn them . . .

The light of dawn was beginning to filter down through the heavy trees. Jean could see the outline of their limbs under the blankets, a faint seam of light around the window.

– My botany, my love and interest in everything that grows – at first it was for love of my mother, a way of living with my yearning, and then perhaps an homage, but gradually it became something more, a passion, and I wanted to know everything: who had made the first gardens, how plants had been depicted in history, growing up in the cracks of cultures, in paintings and symbols, how seeds had travelled – crossing oceans in the cuffs of trousers . . .

I think we each have only one or two philosophical or political ideas in our life, one or two organizing principles during our whole life, and all the rest falls from there . . .

I remember a day in the Hampton Street garden with my mother; we were having a sun-bath together – her warm skin and the sun lotion – I used to push my face into her and smell her like a flower – the fullness of my mother's black hair was held back by a wide white band and she gave me a huge blossom, an Asian lily, and I am reaching up my hands. I'm barely the height of her legs, perhaps I'm four years old . . .

Every morning, before my father left for work, he stood with my mother, their foreheads touching. Sometimes I joined in, and sometimes I just watched, finishing my egg or oatmeal with my slippered feet wrapped around the rungs of the chair. Every morning my father – as if he were going down to the docks to begin a long sea voyage and not just walking down the road to a stolid brick boys' private school, with a smile holding all the intimacies between husband and wife – spoke the same sweet words: 'Wish me well.'

The forest around them was the forest of a dream. The sound of the river embraced them, safeguarded Jean's words, a pact between them. She felt there was no other place for her than beside him, a man who could transform the world this way, transform the dark into this darkness, the forest into this forest.

– My mother was connected to a ventilator. My father wrote a note and strung it across the bed, across those futile, thin hospital blankets, from one bedrail to the other. In case she woke and we weren't there. He wrote it again – *I love you* – and pinned the note to his shirt, in case he fell asleep in his chair . . .

For days I sat next to my mother and listened to the ventilator breathe for her. Until finally I realized that this was what I had to do – breathe for her. What does it mean to breathe for another person? To take them in and give them rest. To enter them and give them rest . . . as good a definition of forgiveness as any . . .

Her name was Elisabeth, said Jean.

Then slowly, not to wake Avery, Jean reached down and took off her shoes.

Sometime after dawn, Jean woke. For several moments she thought she'd gone deaf.

Repeatedly the seaway engineers had tried to still the Long Sault. Thirty-five tonnes of rock had been unloaded into the river, but the current had simply flung these gargantuan boulders aside, like gravel. Finally they built the hexapedian, a huge insect of welded steel, and now this, at last, had pinioned the rocks into place.

The detonation of silence.

Jean lay next to Avery, unmoving. Even the leaves on the trees were mute; so absolute the stillness, all sound seemed to have been drawn from the world.

Avery did not know what Jean was thinking, only that there was intense thought behind those eyes filled with tears. It was not only her weeping that moved him, but this intensity of thought he perceived in her. Already he knew that he did not want to tamper, to force open, to take what was not his; and that he was willing to wait a long time for her to speak herself to him.

Jean felt she would give almost anything to hear the heart-pounding sound of the rapids again.

———

Every history has its catalogue of numbers. Six thousand people built the seaway. Twenty thousand acres were flooded. Two hundred and twenty-five farms disappeared. Five hundred and thirty-one houses were moved. The houses left behind were deliberately torched, exploded, or levelled by bulldozers. To accommodate the amalgamated population, nine schools, fourteen churches, and four shopping centres were built. Eighteen cemeteries, fifteen historical sites, highway and railway lines, power and phone lines were relocated. Hundreds of thousands of feet of telephone cables and wire fencing were rolled away on giant spools; telephone poles were plucked from the ground and carried off on trucks.

In clearing land for the new lake, thirty-six hundred acres of timber were logged, and eleven thousand trees more — the "domestic" trees that had grown up close to people, near houses, in the villages, including the more than five-hundred-year-old elm with a trunk ten feet wide that had overlooked the woollen mills and grist mills that had brought the town of Moulinette its prosperity. The elm that had survived the building of all the early canals.

A priest was hired, at a rate of twenty-five dollars a day, to oversee the exhumation of bodies from the graveyards; more than two thousand graves were moved at the request of their families. The thousands of graves remaining were heaped with stones, in order to prevent the bodies from surfacing into the new lake.

In each church, a last service.

───────

Thirty tonnes of explosives lay nestled into the rocks of Cofferdam A-1, the barrier that had kept the north channel of the St. Lawrence riverbed dry. On Tuesday, July 1, 1958 – Dominion Day – thousands of spectators gathered along the bank in the hot summer rain. Jean had taken the early train from Toronto to Farran's Point, where Avery waited to meet her. Among the crowd at the barrier, Jean recognized the little girls her father had tutored, now grown women. Soon it was apparent that all the mosquitoes in the county had also come for the spectacle, massing under the umbrellas, seizing their chance of skin. Jean stood among those who had lost their homes and their land and who, in a few moments, would lose even the landscape. Thousands waited in silence, holding their grief to themselves, not because of pride or embarrassment, thought Jean, but warily, as if it were the last thing they possessed.

All shipping had stopped. The gates of the other dams were shut. Everyone waited. From this single blast, one hundred square miles of fertile farmland would be inundated. At first it was just as the crowd expected; the river did not disappoint them. The water pushed past the blasted dam in a torrent. But very soon the flood slowed and narrow runs of muddy water slithered into the dry bed. The water seeped, two miles an hour, toward the dam, where it would become Lake St. Lawrence.

Then the very slowness of the rising water became the spectacle.

For five days, the water sought its level. The river climbed its banks, creeping almost intangibly, and each day more of the land disappeared. Farmers watched their fields slowly begin to glisten and turn blue. In the abandoned towns, the pavement began to waver with water. House and church foundations seemed to sink. Trees began to shrink. Boys from the villages amused themselves by swimming over the centre line of the highway.

Jean could not keep away. Many mornings before dawn, Avery drove to the city where Jean was waiting with breakfast for him at the flat on Clarendon, and they returned together to the river.

The men and women of the lost villages rowed boats out to where they had lived; no one seemed to be able to resist this urge.

Blackbirds went foraging for food, then could not find their nests. For several weeks they circled in unnerving arcs, a continuous return, as if they could bore a hole in the emptiness.

The air was saturated with water. The August wind was high and any moment the rain would come. Along the St. Lawrence, the milkweed had burst, for days its silk had filled the air, ghostly hair clinging to branches and stems. It floated on the water of the sinking fields and looked like ice between the stalks.

Jean took off her sandals. She felt the water-loosened grass under her bare feet and the milkweed silk soft against her calves. Then a cold shape bumped against her leg.

She stood still with revulsion. She saw what she had not noticed before, patches of darkness, not shadow, in the water – like clumps of earth that had broken away – but they were not earth.

Avery heard Jean's cry and then he saw too. She ran back to the car and sat with the door open, scraping at her legs with handfuls of grass. By the time he reached her, she had calmed herself and sat quietly, looking out at the field.

– I'm all right.

After a few moments, Avery walked back to the water's edge. He imagined the underground passages, many miles of narrow tunnels, where the moles, hundreds, had drowned. With their powerful shoulders and webbed paws, they had always swam through this earth; precisely as swimmers in water, displacing only the exact space of their bodies. Every movement above and below ground had been audible to them. Avery imagined what they must have understood: the sound of water creeping inexorably toward them through the soil, soil dense as bread with its wealth of bones and insect nests and dormant seeds and scattered stones. When Avery was a child, his father had "adopted" a mink for him – "the public had been appealed to," to help pay for the upkeep of the smaller animals in the London Zoo during the war: "sixpence a week for a dormouse, thirty shillings a week for a penguin." The larger, dangerous animals had been evacuated because of the threat of bombing. For more than half his lifetime, Avery had forgotten this. Now, over fields that were slowly becoming a lake, the hot wind was constant, the clouds were blackened with rain, and there, near to him, was the sunburned face of Jean Shaw. Her hair was blowing where it had escaped from under her cotton scarf. Her head, he was sure, was bursting with thought. He realized that this is what made him look at the field and think about the earth in a way he never had before, although he had watched engineered ground being opened countless times and had witnessed the burial of his own father. In the suffocating heat it seemed impossible that, in a matter of eight or ten weeks, the soaked grass at the rim of the new lake would be frozen, long yellow fibres encased in ice.

Jean stood near Avery at the edge of the field, unable to move. She was remembering the destitution of standing above a grave as it is closed, the destitution of standing above.

Avery and Jean drove past a church that had been moved to its new site, at Ingleside. They saw the priest outside and stopped. There was something Jean wanted to ask.

— The question of deconsecration is very . . . distressing, said the priest. A church, or the old site of a church, the cemetery, and church grounds cannot be deconsecrated unless they are first rendered redundant. A deconsecration ceremony is very sad and disturbing. It means that God will no longer be worshipped in that place.

— But surely God can be worshipped anywhere, said Avery.

— How can a place of worship become redundant? asked Jean.

The priest looked at them and sighed.

— There is such a thing as consecrated ground. In this case, when the congregation moves, the church must move with it. The first place must be deconsecrated so that it cannot be desecrated, even accidentally, by other customs.

— But why, insisted Jean, must flooded land be deconsecrated? Can it not remain holy even when it is covered in water?

At that moment the phone rang in the church office. The priest excused himself and did not reappear, though they waited outside for some time.

———

When Avery drove from the St. Lawrence to Clarendon Avenue those first weeks, Jean had a welcome always prepared. The little table was pushed under the open kitchen window and was set not only with dishes and cutlery, but with books and flowers, postcards, photographs – all the things Jean had put aside to show him. The eagerness, the earnestness, the innocence of the scene was so affecting that Avery felt a deepening bond each time he took his place at her table.

Sometimes he drove to her in the early evening, and he watched Jean as she cooked for him. She worked in the twilight kitchen until it was almost too dark to see and they ate in that near darkness, listening to the wind in the trees through the small fourth-floor kitchen window. Sitting alone with Jean, Avery felt for the first time that he was part of the world, engaged in the same simple happiness that was known to so many and was so miraculous.

He wanted to know everything; he did not mean this carelessly. He wanted to know the child and the schoolgirl, what she'd believed in and whom she'd loved, what she'd worn and what she'd read – no detail was too small or insignificant – so that when at last he touched her, his hands would have this intelligence.

– My mother kept a commonplace book, said Jean, a record of oddments she wished to remember: poems, quotations from books, the lyrics of songs, recipes (icewater shortbread, cucumber and beet chutney, fish soup with verbena). These yellow copybooks were also filled with cryptic phrases that I both longed to understand and was thrilled not to, their mystery increased their value for me. They sat in a square stack, fifteen of them, on the corner of her writing table. Only sometimes she dated her entries, and this I take to mean that my mother wanted to place a particular strand of thought, a loose thread of a quotation, next to a moment of particular personal potency, the here and now, say, of 22 November 1926 at 3 p.m., when Keats made her feel the keenness of things, somehow marked her place in the world, marked a secret event I would never know. One day, when I was thirteen, my father brought home a notebook for me, 'just like the ones my students use for their sums, and to mangle their maps of the world,' and he also handed me the packet of my mother's copybooks to keep, and a Biro my aunt had sent from England a few months before she died, of a sudden illness, a lung disease. I remember writing with that Biro in that copybook: *Aunt Grace died across the ocean.* I also remember thinking how strange it was that she had lived her whole life and had died in a place I had never seen, the kind of common revelation that, at thirteen, fills one with an aching wonder and a sorrow, an excitement and a disorientation, and the beginning of the very slow realization that one's ignorance continues to grow at precisely the same rate as one's experience . . .

All this Jean recounted to Avery in those moments that are the mortar of our days, innocent memories we don't know we hold until given the gift of the eagerness of another. They both felt the randomness of fortune, the unnerving shadow of what so easily might never have happened, as they sat next to each other in the kitchen on Clarendon, talking, listening to the night radio, Avery fingering Jean's hair ribbon that marked his place in an engineering journal, an article on steel, and that gave him the wrenching thought that some day, in the distant future, this ribbon might be discovered in this magazine by someone, a son perhaps, like one of Jean's mother's never-to-be-solved clues, connecting the future to this otherwise unrecorded moment.

– If my mother hadn't died, would I remember things so vividly? Long after you've forgotten someone's voice, said Jean, you can still remember the sound of their happiness or their sadness. You can feel it in your body. I remember my mother and I having a tea party in our garden one day, and looking at her and really thinking about her for the first time: this is my sweet mother who knows how to pour tea into acorn cups and make teacakes out of fir cones, who can make doll's hats out of maple keys and doll's dresses from leaves and flowers. And who knows just the right way to push seeds into the ground with her thumb. My father said my mother had a green thumb, but I knew it was brown, and her knees too, and that this was much better, the earth under her nails just like mine, the earth making the fine lines of our hands suddenly visible. I can still feel her hand over mine, her thumb on mine, and the hard little seed, like a pellet or a stone, under my thumb as we pushed together into the soft earth. She showed me how to plant for height and shape and colour and scent, how to plant for winter. She taught me that teasels attract goldfinches. If you plant the right flowers, the whole garden can become a bird bouquet. Every garden is like a living house, she said, you should be able to walk right into the centre of a garden and lie down . . . and watch the leaves move, like a curtain through an imaginary window.

– Please lie down next to me, said Avery.

He took Jean's hand and led her to the narrow bed, the

girlhood bed she'd moved from the house in Montreal, and they lay on top of the sheets in the heat.

—When my mother was in the hospital she asked my father to bring flowers, her flowers. Watching him cut them from her garden was the first time I understood how ill she was. That day my father wandered around the kitchen boiling eggs, boiling potatoes, making lots of toast. He didn't know what to do. He made the few things he knew how to cook. We ate in silence at that little red-and-white kitchen table, and everything tasted terrible. We listened to each other chewing and swallowing. Everything looked the same, the little square bumpy salt-and-pepper cellars with their red plastic caps, and the little bit of lace under the butter dish. But suddenly it was a different house, a replica of the house I knew, and when we left to take the flowers to my mother after lunch, I started to cry. And then my father started to cry too and he had to stop the car by the side of the road.

Avery could feel her tears through his shirt.

—There are so many things, he said quietly, that we can't see but that we believe in, so many places that seem to possess an unaccountable feeling, a presence, an absence. Sometimes it takes time to learn this, like a child who suddenly realizes for the first time that the ball he threw over the fence has not disappeared. I used to sit with my mother in Grandmother Escher's Cambridgeshire garden and we would feel that strong wind from the Ural Mountains on our faces. The wind is invisible, but the Ural Mountains are not! Yet why should we believe in the Ural Mountains that we can't see when we're sitting in a garden in Cambridgeshire and not believe in other things, an inner knowledge we feel just as keenly? Nothing exists independently. Not a single molecule, not a thought.

— 'A garden must have a path,' my mother used to say, and she was right. A path that has worn its way into the earth, sunken cobbles, grass beginning to grow through the cracks, said Jean, a path that has been set into the earth through constant use. The way stone stairs over centuries hollow out in the middle. Imagine mere boots being able to wear away stone — the way some stories bend in the middle after centuries of telling. The ground knows where we have walked . . .

At night instead of a bedtime story sometimes my mother and I would look at seed catalogues. She sent to England for some of them, just to dream, and she would whisper a garden for me. I would imagine it with her, every detail, the ivy, the bench beneath the willow, the snow of blossoms in the warm spring air. Until I fell asleep.

Avery stroked Jean's face. He leaned down and took off her sandals and drew the sheet up her bare legs.

— Let me tell you a garden story, said Avery, a bedtime story.

Jean closed her eyes.

— Each spring, said Avery, when my father was a boy, he waited for the sparrows to return to that garden in Cambridgeshire. By March he was brimming with impatience. Day after day, he faithfully threw the tea crumbs into the ivy. Finally, one morning, the wall began to sing.

Avery had already imagined, in those first months with Jean, what the chance to grow old with her would mean: not regret at how her body would change, but the private knowledge of all she'd been. Sometimes, his ache so keen, Avery felt that only in old age would he finally have full possession of her youthful flesh. It would be his secret, forged in all the nights next to each other.

In the flat on Clarendon, when Avery couldn't sleep, Jean whispered to him while he stroked her arm. She recited a list of all the native Ontario plants she could think of: hair grass, arrow-leaved aster, the heath aster, swamp aster, long-leaved bluets, foxglove, side-oats grama, the compass plant whose leaves always align on the north-south axis. The sand dropseed, turtlehead, great St. John's wort, sneezeweed, balsam ragwort, fox sedge, umbrella sedge, the little bluestem . . . and then sleep grew farther away still and he began to touch her with purpose.

———

The desert heat would not leave Jean; above the yellow sand the air was a shimmering liquid, a palpable transparency; by early morning forty-five degrees Celsius in the shade. Even during the frigid night Jean felt her bones baking, even when the surface of her skin was cool.

On the deck of the houseboat she stood in her clothes and poured night river water through her hair. For a few ecstatic moments the chill reached her brain and she felt her skeleton cold as metal. But the effect seemed to last only as long as she was under the water.

To comfort her, Avery told Jean about thermophiles.

— They're a single-cell bacteria that thrive in heat — in temperatures of one-hundred-and-ten-degrees-Celsius — in thermal vents heated by magma, liquid rock. They squirm with pleasure and swim gleefully in baths boiled by bubbling lava, gorge themselves on sulfuric acid and molten iron. They set up house in the heart of volcanoes and in flues of steam spewing from the ocean floor. When you're hot, you must not think of cool things, such as Emperor penguins or the McMurdo Ice Shelf — it just doesn't work, it makes you feel hotter. Instead, think of thermophiles!

— I feel better already . . .

Among the few books Jean and Avery brought to the desert — aside from reference texts and field guides — were Jean's choice of Elizabeth David's cookery book, *Mediterranean Food*, and Avery's, of Thor Heyerdahl's *Kon-Tiki Expedition*.

There was sense to reading, high on a hill in the ancient ocean of the desert at dusk, where whales with feet once swam, about the small *Kon-Tiki* floating in the expanse of the Pacific, "where the nearest solid was the moon." To prove that the ocean, a highway of predictable currents, might have connected prehistoric peoples rather than kept them apart, Heyerdahl constructed the raft, following in every detail the design on a petroglyph. Heyerdahl's vessel, at a fast clip, crossed the ocean in a hundred days. During a storm, the crew in its fragile craft climbed mountains and valleys of water, "uncertain where we were, for the sky was overclouded and the horizon one single chaos of rollers." Avery read aloud as the desert colours flamed hotter, radiant, and the air grew cold. "When night had fallen, and the stars were twinkling in the dark tropical sky, the phosphorescence flashed around us . . . and single glowing plankton resembled round live coals so vividly that we involuntarily drew in our bare legs . . ."

Jean soon learned how chronic Avery's insomnia; no matter the depth of his physical exhaustion, the mathematical possibilities of error continued to combine and recombine in his head. So she began to read to him, first about the fruit-bearing trees of the desert – which proved too interesting to put him to sleep – then about herbs, and finally from Elizabeth David, whose serene voice promising so much certain pleasure seemed to calm him. "There's nothing like a good recipe to make you believe things will work out fine in the end," said Avery. "Even the phrase 'Serves four' is hope distilled."

In the small cabin of the houseboat, books in the blankets, Jean read to Avery about cappon magro, "the celebrated Genoese fish salad made of about twenty different ingredients and built up into a splendid baroque edifice." She unfolded her legs along his while assuring him that "wooden herb bowls with choppers are to be found at Madame Cadec's, 27 Greek St, W1," as if they might just stroll down to the shop the following morning before lunch, as if the closest market were not seven hundred kilometres away through cataracts and desert. Avery drifted with strange possibilities of fulfillment whispered in his ear: "If by chance you happen to come upon a watermelon and some blackberries in the same season, try this dish . . ." He listened to descriptions of peppers sleek with oil. In his childhood, the only olive oil Avery knew was sold in chemists' shops in tiny brown bottles as an ablution (which his mother had used to clear his ears), and rationing meant that meat and fish and butter in the quantities Elizabeth David wrote of were absurdities (roast of whole hog browned on a spit). But in that absurdity was an ideal, and in the ideal a possibility, and yes, that every meal was planned for four servings contained hope — even if that hope was leftovers.

And, of course, Elizabeth David had married in Egypt.

Only after many months, with the delayed response we often have to facts too obvious to see, did Jean realize that their dear companion of the kitchen shared her mother's name, and that when she listened to Avery read in the desert about phosphorescent plankton clinging to the backs of dolphins, turning them into "clouds" and "luminescent ghosts," swimming beside the raft in such tight formation the sea was white and solid in the darkness, and of black rays the size of a room, she was also listening to her father's miracles, his voice quiet beside her on the *Moccasin*, riding home from Aultsville.

———

They were to meet again in Morrisburg; they had known each other four months. Jean had taken the train and was to wait for Avery at the lunch counter near the small station. Avery watched her walking there, in her loose sweater flowing almost to her knees and with her auburn braid swinging back and forth across her back. He drove slowly alongside her and rolled down his window.

— I have to go to Montreal for a job interview, said Avery. Jump in.

Jean looked at him.

— I know you don't have anything with you, but I can buy you things . . . you can wear my clothes . . .

The wind was high across the river, through the trees a continuous splashing of shadow and early autumn sun. Jean's bare skin was cold under her cotton skirt.

They drove for about an hour and then stopped by the side of the road. Avery took out a folding camp table from the car and placed it in a field. The tabletop seemed to float in the high grass. Jean set out the hard sour spy apples and the blackberries, the bread and the cheese, two tin plates and a knife.

Jean looked out at the swaying field and the hurtling clouds; she held back strands of her hair with one hand. Amid the wind, the perfect fruit lay still and solid on the table.

Later they drove into the suspended light of dusk, the sun falling in the miles behind them. She could not stop thinking of the stillness of the apples, the movement around them.

A still life belongs to time . . . And this day's stillness, she thought, this single day: it belongs to us.

They continued to drive north in the cool beginning of night.

— During the war, said Avery, while my father was away, I stayed in Buckinghamshire with my mother and my Aunt Bett and my three cousins.

Every Tuesday in London there were lunchtime concerts in the vacant National Gallery; hundreds came each week without fail to stand in the picture-empty rooms and listen. Because my mother wished us to understand the importance of this – of people converging to listen to music despite the threat of bombing – at 1 p.m. every Tuesday my cousins Nina, Owen, and Tom and I pretended to pay a shilling – a circle of cardboard with the King's head crayoned on both sides – at the door of the sitting room. Then my mother and my aunt performed for us, duets they'd practised all week. My aunt played violin and my mother, piano. When the sheet music ran out, we listened to phonograph records. Afterwards we had tea at the dining room table laid with a clean white cloth, the good tea set, and my aunt's real silverware.

Despite bombings – one fell into the gallery's small court-yard and didn't explode until six days later, ironically while the Royal Engineers Bomb Disposal Unit was at lunch – for six and a half years there was a performance each week: 338 concerts. My mother took personal pride at this, for our sitting room concerts must have been nearly as many.

When they drove together along the edges of the flooded St. Lawrence landscape, Avery sometimes stopped and took out his paintbox – smaller than a pocketbook, square, with a hinge lid, a gift from his father – which he almost always carried with him. It was not often immediately clear to Jean what had caught his eye, an isolated farm building, a tree, the clouds. While Avery painted, Jean took the time to look at things. She kept a plant diary. Jean was used to long hours outside, but this feeling of companionship across a field was new.

They unwrapped the meals Jean packed for them – Edwards cheddar, sunflower bread, McIntosh apples, whole-meal biscuits – and ate on the ground, or in the car if it was raining – and only a long time later, in the dark, driving home to Clarendon Avenue, would they would describe to each other what they, with their different eyes, had seen.

It was an engagement of mind that was almost shattering in its pleasure. Jean could not look at the world now without seeing hypars and span-to-depth ratios, wind drift, and vortex separation oscillations. She learned that a building must never sway more than 1/500ths of its height or the wind could create alternating vacuums that would start the building wavering as much as three feet from side to side. "Office workers," said Avery, "have been known to get airsick in high towers." He told her about bascules and swing bridges, Gauss's domes and steel whiskers, and how an entire bridge can be supported by half an inch of metal. He explained the difference between hundred-year winds and design winds; he explained that air rushing between tall buildings behaved just like water forced through a narrow gorge. He told her about soil mechanics and the strange case of the National Theatre in Mexico City, which had been built on a sandy foundation. The weight of the heavy stone theatre squeezed water from the sand and the building sank ten feet. But just when they'd constructed a new staircase leading down to the sunken entrance, the building started to rise again, and yet another staircase had to be built so theatregoers could now climb up to the entrance. All the newly erected buildings surrounding the theatre had squeezed the water out of their foundations too and had lifted the theatre back up again. The world, she now understood, was always on the verge of flying apart. The only thing holding matter together was the very fact that it had reached its limits.

Jean had her secrets of matter too. She told him of the shyest plant on earth, the colocynth or bitter gourd, whose seeds cannot bear even a flicker of light; a flash will send them back to dormancy and they will hibernate until they are sure of the darkness they need to sprout. This makes them perfect desert plants, for they need only a little moisture to establish a strong root system before growing to face the scorching desert sun. She told him of a fungus that eats through wood, turning entire buildings to powder, and lichen that is blown about the steppes into great heaps, where it is gathered and roasted like popcorn. Some plants have been cultivated by man for centuries; some, like the olive, are thousands of years old. The most extreme example is probably the seventy-two-hundred-year-old Japanese *Cryptomeria*, although some claim that the Seychelles double coconut might be more than fourteen thousand years old.

– I happen to know about the *Cryptomeria* tree, said Avery in the car somewhere in the September evening east of Kingston, because I've just been reading about temples, about the Ise temple in Japan. Two clearings lie next to each other in the midst of dense *Cryptomeria*; the forest itself is considered holy. One clearing is covered with shining white pebbles. In the other clearing stands the Ise temple. Every twenty years, for almost three millennia, the temple has been dismantled and burned and a new, identical temple erected in the clearing next to it. Then the empty site is covered in white pebbles and only a single post remains, hidden in a small wooden hut; this is the sacred pillar that will be used to rebuild the temple when its turn comes again, twenty years later. The temple is not considered a replica, instead it has been recreated. This distinction is essential. It is a Shinto belief that a temple must not be a monument but must live and die in nature, like all life, and continually be reborn in order to remain pure.

The fields glowed under the moon and the car was dark. Jean kept the window open and the night air on her bare legs was cold; she loved this cold, like being on the deck of a ship.

— Sometimes, Avery continued, when I'm looking at a building, I feel I know the architect's mind. Not only his technical choices, but more . . . as if I knew his soul. Well, no man can know the soul of another man — perhaps not his soul, but the state of his soul. I'm ashamed to say this, it sounds so simple-minded, but there are choices that strike me as so achingly personal, and there they are in stone and glass, for anyone to see . . . a man's mind laid bare in the positioning of each doorway and window, in the geometric relationship between windows and walls, in the relation between the musculature of a building to its skeleton, the consideration of how a man might feel, placing his chair here or there in a room following the light. I'm convinced we feel the stresses in a building when we're inside.

No one can take in a building all at once. It's like when we take a photograph — we're looking at only a few things, half a dozen or even a dozen – and yet the photo records everything in our frame of vision. And it's those thousand other details that anchor us far below what we consciously see. It's what we unconsciously see that gives us the feeling of familiarity with the mind behind a building. Sometimes it seems as if the architect had full knowledge of these thousand other details in his design, not just the different kinds of light possible across a stone facade, or across the floor, or filling the crevices of an ornament, but as if he knew just how the curtains would blow into the room through the open window and cause just that particular shadow and turn a certain page of a certain book at just that moment of the story, and that the dimness of the Sunday rain would compel the woman to rise from the table and draw the man's face to the warmth of her. It was as if the architect had anticipated every minute effect of weather, and of weather on memory, every combination of atmosphere, wind, and temperature, so that we are drawn to different parts of a room depending on the hour of day, the season, as if he could invent memory, create memory! And this embrace of every possibility, of light, weather, season – every calculation of climate – is also the awareness of every possibility of life, the life that is possible in such a building. And the sudden freedom of this is profound. It's like falling in love, the feeling that here, at last here, one can be one's self, and the true measure of one's life can be achieved – aspirations, the various kinds of desire – and that moral goodness and intellectual work are possible. A complete sense of belonging to a place, to oneself, to another. All this in a building? Impossible, but also, somehow, true. A building gives us this, or takes it from us, a gradual erosion, a forgetting of parts of ourselves . . .

They passed the dark miles in this way, the St. Lawrence, then Lake Ontario on one side of the highway, farmers' fields on the other; a landscape inscribed by a lover is like no other place on earth.

— This river where no one bathes, said Avery, this new St. Lawrence with its graves . . . I understand perfectly why Georgiana Foyle would rather row out to her husband's grave than move it. Even though she will now have to be buried alone . . . This torments her. But she's right. His body belongs to that place because his life belonged there.

— There is such a long human relationship with plants, said Jean, not just between seed and sower, but with the creation of the first aesthetic gardens. Who was the first person to desire certain plants for pleasure, to separate these plants from wilderness, the way prayer separates certain words from the rest of language? Why did the Egyptians use a palm leaf to symbolize a vowel? Before about 8000 B.C., wheat was just a kind of wild grass. But by accident, this grass was pollinated with goat grass, and the fourteen chromosomes of each combined to create twenty-eight chromosomes: emmer wheat. Then emmer crossed with another kind of grass and made forty-two chromosomes, and this is the wheat we now use for bread, the wholegrain we ate for lunch. But this was really a rare accident. Because the seeds of the new wheat couldn't easily transport and fertilize themselves, they would not spread. So man and plant needed each other. This tiny accident led to settlement, to the scythe, to the plough and wheel and axle, to the potter's wheel and the waterwheel and pulley, to irrigation.

— To water rights and land rights, said Avery. To canals, dams, and seaways.

— I've been reading about rain, said Jean. That utterly distinctive smell, when rain first starts to fall — two scientists have analyzed it. They've named it 'petrichor' from the Greek for stone and for the 'blood' that flows through the veins of the gods. It's the scent of an oil produced by plants partially decomposed, undergoing oxidation and nitration, a combination of three compounds. The first raindrops reach into stone or pavement and release this plant oil, which we smell as it is washed away. We can only smell it as it is washed away.

———

In the autumn, Avery packed his kit again and went north into the rock and darkness, the darkest green of northern Quebec, to work on the dam on the Manicouagan River. Many Saturday mornings, Jean and Avery drove toward each other. The highway motels had their own strange attraction, nothing more than a brick rectangle inserted among the northern forest, the front door to each motel room leading directly from the highway; and yet the chill, astringent air of the firs, the coldness of centuries of shade, seemed to penetrate even the bricks and cinderblocks with a clean, live joy. One would approach and see the other's car waiting in the gravel parking lot; that sight was sufficient to overwhelm each with happiness. Let us always meet in motels, Avery had said, even after we've been together for a hundred years. Jean drove to these meetings in her father's old blue Dart, often with her botany textbooks open on the passenger seat so that, after the first hour or so of daydreaming, she could glance down and memorize facts for her courses at the university. Thus the botanical lexicon attached itself to the miles, to small towns and gas stations: Esso and *Equisetum*, The Voyageur Restaurant and *Athyrium*, Greenville and *Gymnocarpium*, Ste. Therese and *Selaginella*, Pointe-aux-Trembles and *Thelypteris*.

And sometimes Avery drove south to the Holland Marsh, and they spent the weekend together in the white farmhouse with his mother, Marina Voss Escher.

Avery alone was one thing, a universe with loose shirttails and notes in his pocket, to be discovered slowly. And Avery and Marina together, another universe.

For Avery it had always been three, until his father died. For Jean it had been two, longing for the third. Now they were three, and each felt the rightness of it.

—When my father came to Canada to work on the seaway, explained Avery, my parents searched for a place to please my mother. She chose the black fields of Holland Marsh. They moved into an old farmhouse and my father built a painting room for her. The house is bright white and sits like a ship on that good, black earth. A canal flows at the end of the garden. The colours and grandeur of the vegetables in the fields can pop open your eyes. After my father died, my mother thought she'd remain only temporarily in that house; but the longer she stayed, the less inclined she was to move. She found work illustrating for a children's press in Toronto. She bought a rowboat and docked it in the canal at the end of the garden.

The isolation suits her . . .

History soaked the ground of Marina's story-forests. One could almost hear the earth in her paintings grinding up the bones. Armed with only a heel of bread, a small basket, a walking stick, or a song; without resources and with the handicap of one's innocence, a child met the terrors of the dense, dark, unhappy wood, the winding paths from which one must not stray yet lead to the inevitable terror.

Marina's illustrations were the colours of plant rot, rain-soaked earth, shadow-coldness. The colours that hide under stones. Peering closely into the darkness of her paint, almost invisible, one saw half-faces, crippled hands, mad eyes, desires exerting their will on the events of the story. Is a curse anything more than a monstrous will at work?

Jean looked at the strong, compact body of Avery's mother, in her cheerful striped apron, swishing hot water in the teapot, chewing a biscuit, and she blurted out:

— Where do these forests come from?

Marina answered without a moment's pause.

— From home.

When Avery was working up north, Marina took Jean into her studio, set up a table there, and gave her exercises in looking. Then she let Jean's hand go free. Page after page, fast sketches dropped to the floor. Then again slowly – a single drawing each morning. They went on walks, they cooked together. Marina made pronouncements over the sound of the water as she washed the vegetables. "What is the meaning of the kitchen in a children's story? It is the mother's body!"

– William was away for so much of Avery's young life, said Marina, that they did not really know each other. But after the war, William took Avery everywhere with him in his Norton Big Four. He packed Avery into his blue Swallow sidecar along with their gear and they rode up to Scotland and down to Wales for the hydro-electric projects, Glen Affric, Glen Garry, Glen Moriston. Claerwen Dam, Clywedog Dam. William was part of the first underground power stations in England, in Strathfarrar and Kilmorack. But always he envied his colleagues who were busy building the underground in London.

We met on a train in Scotland, on the way to Jura, continued Marina. William was travelling with his father. The island of Jura is long and narrow. It has only one road. It was no surprise that our paths would cross again, and they did. As he came closer, I saw that he was the same man I'd talked to on the train. It was not a real road in those days, just a track really and, on either side, the wet bog. I was suddenly so shy I didn't even think but jumped down into the verge. Of course the instant I'd done it, I knew he would think I'd lost my wits. I lay down in the wet and clutched my book to my chest and closed my eyes. William slid down next to me. He just looked at me and asked, 'What are you reading?' It was outrageously funny, but at the same time I realized very suddenly how afraid I'd been that his first question would be 'Are you a Jew?'

I was almost twenty-three. I'd answered an advertisement to be a companion to an elderly woman who could no longer live alone. It turned out that I was the only applicant because the woman, Annie Moorcock, lived in such remoteness. But that, to me, was the attraction. And I was not disappointed. It is a gorgeously desolate eden. The island is only twenty-nine miles long and seven miles wide, and on it, along with perhaps two hundred people, live thousands of red deer. I cooked and cleaned and I read to her. Annie Moorcock's father had worked on a ship in the islands and she told me sea stories and stories of Jura from when she was girl. But the real gift for me was that her hobby was painting. She taught me a little. I began to want to paint the rain — a sure subject on Jura. I painted hundreds of pictures of rain. The patient, grey hatching of rain on wood, on stone, on the bog, on the sea . . . This obsession worried the old woman and one day she brought me an armful of wildflowers — it surely cost her tremendous effort to pick them. She said, 'Here are flowers. Why don't you try to paint them,' and I said I can't paint flowers, they won't look real. 'But you're a good painter, you're already much better than me. It will be lovely — does it have to look real?' In those days I felt ferociously, that yes, it must look real. Then she held out the wildflowers and that's when something happened to me. I suddenly knew what I must do: not to paint the flowers, but the hand holding the flowers.

And so for weeks I drew and then painted the old woman's hands.

It was only when I'd heard she'd died that I understood that what I'd really wanted to do was to paint my mother's hands. Hands that I could not remember ever having looked at carefully, hands that I could not remember.

Some time after that day, I had a dream that I put cut flowers into a vase of water, and when I took them out of the vase, they had earth clinging to their roots.

While Avery was away, Jean began to spend her time at the marsh. She attended classes in Toronto, then drove the short hour to Marina's, each time grateful for the pleasure of driving toward a place where she would be welcomed. Often they spent the day walking the entire width of the marsh or its circumference, Marina stopping to sketch a detail of the fields, or of branch and sky that Jean would later recognize in Marina's work. They bought milk and bread from the neighbouring farm, and were invited in for coffee, an invitation Marina almost always declined. "It's just politeness on their part," Marina explained, "and it's politeness to refuse."

One evening, after a winter walk along the canal, which was still flowing, an erratic line in the snow, they sat warming their feet at the fire in the kitchen.

—This will interest you, said Marina. I read in the newspaper that there's a movement in Germany to expel the rhododendron and the forsythia, to rip them out of every public and private garden, because they are not indigenous and are therefore a threat to 'pure German soil.'

The newspaper said that the cherry came to Europe from Asia Minor and has probably been growing in Germany for more than fifteen hundred years, and that the potato came from Peru. Do you think the rhododendron-haters will give up potatoes in their stew? A German birth certificate will be forged for them, you can be certain.

When I went to England and left my family behind in Amsterdam, my mother wrote to me every week. Her letters were like little pamphlets, filled with bits of information according to her interests and her indignations. I loved those letters. To this very moment I cannot believe I took leave of her on the platform of the Centraal station so carelessly, with such a youthful disdain of fate. I thought I had all the time in the world to return to her, but it was the last time I would ever see her face or be held by her. Marina wiped her eyes on her smock and sat down at the table.

— Daughters don't stop crying for their mothers, Marina said, and I had ten more years with mine than you had with yours. We long for our mothers more, not less. Suddenly she jumped up and rushed to the oven. The seed biscuits had shrivelled to charcoal. She opened the window and the winter air filled the kitchen.

— It's like a spell, said Marina. Nothing eats away time like the past.

The rhododendrons reminded me that, just before the war, my mother who, like you, also loved flowers, wrote to me in a fury about a professor who connected 'primitive' vegetation and 'primitive' man. One of his examples was 'tundra man,' where the human species, he said, had clearly stagnated at an earlier stage of evolution. The only legitimate German garden, he said, was 'the blood-and-soil rooted garden,' 'der Blut-und-Bodenverbundene Garten.' I tell you all this for a reason. During the war, there were strict 'landscape rules,' enforced in all the occupied territories, especially in Poland. Not only were 'foreigners' to be expelled – including the Poles themselves – but also the soil had to be similarly purified. To this end, a botanical purge was ordered against the tiny forest flower *Impatiens parviflora* – and that's the meaning of the little flower you see hidden somewhere in every one of my paintings.

Soon after their conversation about *Impatiens parviflora*, Jean went back to look again at the children's books Marina had illustrated. The paintings were saturated with detail – animal fur glossy with oil, drops of water containing landscapes, ominous shadows in folds of cloth. In each face, painted with such empathy, a human moment poised – such desolation, such depth of joy – Jean felt her own eyes staring out from the page.

In every childhood there is a door that closes, Marina had said. And: only real love waits while we journey through our grief. That is the real trustworthiness between people. In all the epics, in all the stories that have lasted through many lifetimes, it is always the same truth: love must wait for wounds to heal. It is this waiting we must do for each other, not with a sense of mercy, or in judgment, but as if forgiveness were a rendezvous. How many are willing to wait for another in this way? Very few.

– We become ourselves when things are given to us or when things are taken away. I was born in Berlin, said Marina. In 1933, my father was so disgusted by the turn of events that he convinced my mother to move. For my mother, this was very hard, to leave behind her sisters, her friends. In Amsterdam, my father joined my uncle's business, a hat factory. Before they left, my father told us that perhaps it wasn't going to be so difficult to leave his professorship at the university – a job he guessed would very soon not exist anyway – because it wasn't so far from filling heads to fitting them. My mother did not find this amusing.

My sister was only thirteen and so, of course, she stayed with them. But I was nineteen, and soon after the move I made the decision to go to London instead and practise my English. I was happy to live in another language because the year before I had been foolish enough to fall in love with a boy who suddenly decided in 1933 that he couldn't marry someone of my 'kind' after all. A student of my father's had moved to England and said he would be happy to have someone who spoke both German and English to tutor his children. So I went to live in Twickenham for a year. Then my mother wanted me to come back to Amsterdam, but I wasn't quite ready to do that. So that's when I answered the advertisement and went to work for Annie Moorcock, off the coast of Scotland.

I took the boat from Port Askaig. Annie's neighbour, Mr. Muldrew, greeted me at Feolin dock and we drove slowly through the rain, past Craighouse and Ardfarnel. Mr. Muldrew clutched a rag in one hand – constantly reaching out the window to unfog the windscreen – while he steered and changed gears with the other hand, until we reached her rough stone house.

I was surprised to discover that inside all was refinement and proportion: fresh flowers on a polished round wooden table, a round rug beneath it, in a receiving hall of panelling and drapery. If I had been surprised by this elegance, I was completely unprepared to find, in this house on this secluded island of Jura, Annie Moorcock's library. There were fine fitted shelves from floor to rafters, shelves over the doorway, shelves spilling into the room beyond. There were tens of thousands of books.

Though not ashamed of her obsession, the old woman was nevertheless somewhat shy, as befits the confessing of any intimate pleasure.

'I can't bend to retrieve the books from the bottom shelves any more,' she said, 'and this makes me so mournful I cannot express it, those books as inaccessible to me as my youth.'

That first afternoon we sat in the kitchen and Annie took the measure of me, Marina said. I could see it would be all right between us, and perhaps even something more – an affection.

Her children did not approve of her living alone on the island, but she would not leave her library and could not bear the thought of moving it. Within an hour of my arrival on that rainy late afternoon in November, I understood that I had been hired not for the simple task of keeping an old woman company by reading to her and cooking and helping her dress and bathe, but for a secret objective all her own. Over tea she said, with a tinge of triumph in her voice, that I was to help her catalogue her books, and that she had been preparing for this task for some time. Indeed, she had a table overflowing with neatly addressed piles of folded paper. Over the months, we slipped these notes and many others into the volumes as we went along: messages to her daughters, her son, and her eight grandchildren. We compiled her list for divesting each book – which child or grandchild would benefit most from a specific volume – her hope, as she told me, to provide a moment of solace or guidance or respite for the one who would open it some winter evening many years hence. 'Though I hope my rosy-cheeked Thea' – who was only six at the time – 'might never need John Donne, there is something about her, a little shadow, that tells me she might feel the want of these words some day.' And so the weeks went by, in this most peculiarly tender way.

Annie had an astonishing collection of movable books for children, including several published by Ernest Nister in Nuremberg. She even had a copy of Meggendorfer's *Circus*, which her father had brought home from a trip to Germany when she was a child. With the outbreak of the First World War, British children's books were no longer printed in Germany, and Annie had some of the earliest movable books published in England between the wars, almost all the Bookano Stories and the *Daily Express* annuals from which animals popped out of their V-folds. I often regret that she didn't live long enough to see the work of Vojtech Kubasta, the Czech architect who studied in Prague and then turned his hand to children's pop-up books – I discovered these in London after the war – his *Sleeping Beauty* and *Snow White* among many others – where the eyes of dogs roll around in their heads, demonstrated Marina, and melancholic dwarves are suddenly restored to happiness by the agency of a tab, and where long, empty tables are, in an instant, magically laden with food, a particularly welcome device in those years of cravings and deprivations.

It was because of Annie Moorcock, the extraordinary random chance of our connection, that I was able to join together the two things she loved and gave me to love: painting and children's books. Sometimes I feel she would not approve of what use I have made of her kindness, rendering images that would have turned her head away in despair. But then there are other days when I feel her blessing as I work, because she was the most acute human being I have ever met and this gift of hers was overlooked by almost everyone who knew her, until her library spoke for her, with such eloquence and such love, after her death.

I met William and his father for the third time in three days, said Marina, at Mr. McKechnie's shop when I was picking up the post. They were collecting supplies for the arduous walk to Corryvreckan.

They invited themselves to tea. Annie took an instant liking to them. She knew William and his father were both engineers and, after they explored the library, she set out her collection of movable books on the dining table. The three of them fell into a discussion of paper engineering – pivot points, rocker arms, angle folds, closed tents, wheels, and fulcrums. In her face, a transformation, a restoration worthy of one of her magical books – complete fulfillment, as if she'd been waiting decades for just this single afternoon of conversation – as William and his father sat with their teacups teetering excitedly in their laps, bearing avid witness to her life's work. After they left, this enravishment lasted for some hours before beginning to fade. By the time the shadows had grown between the trees, Annie had taken to her room, subdued. I never again saw that same pleasure in her face.

Jean and Marina sat looking into the fire, surrounded by the smell of damp wool and turpentine.

– Later, William's father helped me find my parents and my sister . . . but they had already died, in Fohrenwald . . .

For better or for worse, said Marina, slowly rising from her chair, love is a catastrophe.

Whenever Avery came down from Quebec, Marina and Jean greeted him with a lovingly prepared feast, which he received gratefully: pies, sweet and savoury, soups and stews made of vegetables from the marsh, pumpkin mashed and baked with butter and maple syrup, served hot, with cream. Afterwards, they spent the night around Marina's table, listening to Avery's stories.

Once, while walking in the woods above the river, Avery had met a young man, a teenager, who was helping his uncles build pylons for the dam. Avery watched him running between the trees in a pattern, endlessly, the same course.

– He saw me watching, said Avery, and came over to me without embarrassment, on the contrary, lit from within with urgency.

'I'm going to be a race driver,' he told me. 'I won't always be pouring concrete. Someday I'll have enough money to buy my own car.'

He looked at me a moment and decided I would understand.

'There are drivers who dare death – those are the ones who won't last. Then there are the drivers who respect death – those are the ones who hardly ever win.' He began to sway back and forth, following with his eyes the circuit he'd just run. 'And there are drivers,' he continued, 'who have so ingested – *ingérer, gorger, s'empiffrer* – death that they no longer have a taste for it. These are the ones who are already ghosts.'

'How do you know this?' I asked him.

The young man in the forest looked alien, mushroom white, his eyes an artificial blue.

'Are the ghosts the ones who win?' I asked.

The young man laughed. 'Remember my name,' he said. 'Remember Villeneuve!' And he ran off, one arm outstretched over the steep edge of the gorge.

Jean and Avery lay together on the floor of the Clarendon flat. It was a cold autumn night, a rainy wind. Marina had painted paper lampshades for Jean, in copper, madder, and gold, which gave Jean in her living room the feeling of sitting in the last minutes of sunset. Avery reached over and closed Jean's book.

— There's a new project . . . A new kind of project . . . I want you to come with me, said Avery.

— You look so worried, said Jean.

— It's far away.

Avery took Jean's hand and opened it, palm up, in his lap.

— Please close your eyes . . .

Your thumb is the Atlantic, your smallest finger, the Pacific. Your fingertips are Egypt, and the heel of your hand is Africa . . . Your heart line is the Arabian desert, your fate line is the river Nile . . .

Avery and Jean were married in the house on the marsh. It was a civil ceremony with two guests to act as witnesses, Marina's neighbours to the east, who'd kept a kind eye on her in her widowhood. Jean watched through the window as they arrived, their boots trailing out a brown path behind them across the marsh, through the snow. They left their woollen scarves and leather gloves to dry on the radiator, and Jean, standing with Avery, waiting for the ceremony to begin, committed the sight of these to memory: symbols of kindness. Is there no one you wish to invite? Marina had asked, and Jean, in her aloneness, had felt ashamed. Never mind, said Marina, we have each other now. What shall you call me? Just plain Marina, or Marina-Mother, or how about Marina-Ma? — that last name both women thought extremely funny, and loved for the Japanese sound of it, the joke of it, the delicate orientalism that seemed so far from the squat woman with the short, frazzled grey hair, cut like a boy's.

— Your heart line is the Arabian desert, your fate line is the river Nile . . . Not to scale, of course . . . Here, he said, circling the mound at the base of her thumb, is the Sahara . . .

During the months before their departure, first to England and then on to Khartoum, Jean packed away her newly earned diploma, sublet the flat on Clarendon, and moved into the white house with Marina. Neither could conceal their pleasure in this arrangement. They spent long days in Marina's painting room, they walked companionably along the canal through the snow, together they sat bundled with blankets in lawn chairs and stared out at the marsh. Neither could believe their good fortune, their affinities so matched. For Jean, to

be so at ease with the older woman, mother and daughter —
she was almost drunk with the satiety of it.

The summer before, Jean had brought all the jars from
her living room to the house on the marsh and had planted
each seedling from her mother's garden on a section of
Marina's land. Avery had built a low white fence around it,
so Jean would feel that square of earth was hers.

— Here, said Avery in the lamplit twilight, circling the mound
at the base of her thumb, is the Sahara . . . And here, kissing the
middle of her palm, is the Great Temple of Abu Simbel . . .

The Nile breaks over rocks of greatest resistance —
creating fissures, foaming gorges, stone islands — these are
the impassable cataracts, said Avery, the gateway to Nubia.
Beyond this, the river is slow and its banks are cultivated —
fields and date forests. The hills here, Avery traced the line
down her palm, are gentle — terraces of silt, sandstone,
quartzite. Here, between the fate and the heart lines, the
Mediterranean collides with Africa — the desert is strewn
with the ruins of two cultures. In your hand you hold
Christian churches with elaborate frescoes, Coptic temples,
fortresses, Stone Age petroglyphs, countless tombs . . .

For thousands of kilometres east and west, between the
Red Sea and the Atlantic Ocean, the sand, without allegiance,
claims everything. Tiny grains of quartz, oblivious to religion,
royalty, or poverty, grind even the hardest stone
monuments into dust, and whole dynasties have been
abraded to invisibility . . .

The cataract at Aswan, and the fact that it was carved into the side of a cliff, secured Abu Simbel for centuries. The Sahara slowly climbed the cliff until only the very tip of the temple was visible . . .

The night unfolded, Avery explaining all he knew. Jean heard in his voice how hungrily he desired this chance, not to be the one building the dam but the one to salvage. At last, he looked to her for her answer.

— I don't have anything with me, said Jean, but I can wear your clothes . . .

———

They arrived in London in January. Avery's cousin Owen was away and they stayed in his flat, a fashionable idyll of darkly painted rooms, chandeliers and silk carpets; teak furniture, firesides heaped with cushions. Only the kitchen had never been renovated, and in the cupboards Avery recognized Aunt Bett's dishes — chipped and faded — from their childhood. It was a nostalgia Avery had not expected of Owen, and he was grateful for the discovery, as if the smallest details of their years together during the war had not been forgotten.

Dusk in Owen's bedroom, the window open to the rain, roofs black and shining, a crack of sunset. In this rainy blackness and this unexpected last light, the scattering of birds just before dark, both felt a new kind of desire, inseparable from the city. Inseparable from London, January 1964. The desire experienced in unfamiliar streets, one's body never more known by another.

During their last days in England, after staying with Aunt Bett in Leighton Buzzard, Avery and Jean drove through the valley of the River Usk. They stopped at a pub that hung over the rail line in the thick forest above the tracks. On the door was posted a warning: *We strongly recommend that you do not bring your children here after 9 p.m.* Jean was uneasy — what violence arose here and spilled into the forest at night? — but they had not passed another place to stop for many miles, and so they went in. Avery ordered a glass of beer and Jean, after noticing the barmaid herself was drinking a cup behind the bar, ordered a pot of tea. Still she felt uneasy. The dark forest was all around them; they heard a train passing through the valley. Then, on the wall above the bar Jean noticed a similar sign: *We strongly advise you do not bring your children here after 9 p.m., in consideration of the patrons who wish to enjoy the peace and quiet of this establishment.* The barmaid was watching her and gave her a wink. "Aye," she said, "people will bring their crying bairns in the evenings and no one can heft a pint in peace."

They sat quietly as the sound of the train faded into the forest.

— My father and I took the train from Rome to Turin, said Avery. We sat in a compartment with a young couple. The way they sat next to each other told their whole story, his hand on her thigh while he pretended to read the newspaper, her head on his shoulder while she pretended to sleep. The restless desire in them was so palpable it infected my father and me with an embarrassment that I was too young to understand and we kept getting up to pace in the swaying corridors.

At last we arrived at the huge train station in Turin. Since we each had only a small valise between us, we decided to walk the short distance to the hotel where my father was to have a business meeting. As we walked through the immense station, my eyes were suddenly caught by a small sign, which, if I had only been walking faster, I might have missed. There was a single sentence painted on a wooden board that stated that this station was where the deportations had taken place during the war and gave the number – in the hundreds of thousands – of those who had been sent to their deaths from the very place we stood. It was a small notice, barely visible, and to this day I cannot say why my eyes did not overlook it. When we walked out into the sunny street, within a few feet of the station doors, I tripped on the pavement and fell. I cut my head and I needed stitches. My father had to take me to the hospital and missed his meeting and that is the story of the scar on my chin. I wanted nothing more than to leave that place, said Avery. It seemed to me a city of utter dread.

Jean was quiet. He thought of her quietness, this now familiar quietness of hers, as her heart thinking.

– The countless places in cities that have known violent death, said Jean, not just places where terrible things have happened in wartime, but all the other misery that is always left uncommemorated – a car accident, some violence inflicted – how can we mark these places? One could probably not walk a block without stepping into a place of mourning; we could not mark them all.

Sadness descended. Avery took Jean's hand.

— Let's go, he said.

Outside, the wind moved through the high leaves. The small scar on Avery's chin disappeared in the bright afternoon sunlight.

— Before we left Turin, said Avery, my father, in the hope of cheering me up, took me to the famous old café, Baratti & Milano, with its glass cases displaying chocolates and nougats, the carved wooden tables and chairs and starched white tablecloths and heavy silverware. The trolleys of opera cakes and mousses, the petit fours, the phyllo pastry and lemon custards, the high cakes with designs trickled along the top. My father wanted to distract me, but the dark elegance of the place depressed me. I looked around at the waiters in their black-and-white suits carrying their silver salvers, and it seemed to me that the room must not have changed in fifty years. I could not stop myself from wondering how many children had drunk their last cups of cocoa in this place, perhaps in the very chair I was sitting in. I kept thinking, Would the city have felt ominous to me even if I had not seen that marker in the station? Would I have felt this foreboding nonetheless, this presence, this dread, this hauntedness we sometimes feel — inexplicable, ineffable — in certain places, in a cast of light? In any case, my father drank his tea, and I ate my chocolate ice cream from its ornate sweating silver dish. We left the hotel early the next morning, after a restless night — my father because he had missed his business meeting and I because of my apprehension — and we walked to the train station. My father — no doubt remembering London during the Blitz or other places I knew nothing about — said, 'Some places are drenched with sorrow.' I remember specifically he used the word 'drenched' and we walked for a while in silence, my hand in his. Then I thought, Some people are like that, drenched in sorrow, despite the expression on their face.

———

When Hassan Dafalla, the commissioner in charge of the emigration, read the results of the census on a May morning in 1961, he learned that all Nubian land – without exception – was registered in the name of someone who'd died centuries before. This statistic moved him deeply and, with the report still in his hand, he walked out of his office in Wadi Halfa to contemplate it.

Hassan Dafalla was a man given to reflection, and the Sudanese government could not have chosen anyone better suited to the task of resettling an entire nation. He was a man of feeling – of empathy, fairness, and an extraordinary patience for the meaningful detail. It was Hassan Dafalla who ensured that an extra ration of grain reached the bakeries before the journey, and who arranged that there be a birthing car with hospital beds on the train for expectant mothers. It was Hassan Dafalla who handed a parcel of shrouds to the train conductor, in the event they might be needed during the long emigration, more than twelve hundred kilometres from the villages of Nubia to the new settlement at Khashm el Girba, near the sluggish Atbara River. The Atbara was a seasonal river, which annually turned to dust. It was Hassan Dafalla who insisted that the names of the villages be posted in the new town instead of numbers, though his order was ignored. And it was Hassan Dafalla who stood silenced at the sight of the new houses, hollow blocks of concrete that sat in rows on the ground with no connection to it, like packing cases. It was he who felt the acute, breath-taking, shock of defeat; and saw that life can be skinned of meaning, skinned of memory.

The houses in the "New Halfa" scheme had sloping tin or asbestos roofs and rooms too small for the families assigned to live in them; thus, villages were split apart. And when Hassan Dafalla saw that there was not a single tree in Khashm el Girba, he returned with a gift of thirty thousand tree shoots. Eight hundred date shoots were planted along the main street in a tree celebration. It was a shamefully deficient gift, he thought, for the ones who mourned their groves by the Nile.

When it was certain the Aswan High Dam would be built, the census-takers from the Department of Statistics in Sudan were sent from village to village. They recorded the number of inhabitants in each dwelling, the number of live-stock, an accurate account of the burden of furniture for each family. Everything would have to be carried – by lorry, boat, and train – and the number of railcars and trains accu-rately calculated.

Hassan Dafalla had studied the numbers carefully. In the Sudanese area under his concern there were: 27 villages, 70,000 souls; 7,676 houses, with an average number of rooms calculated at 5.8; the number of residents per room 0.9 in the town of Wadi Halfa and 1.1 in the villages. Of the animals to be transported there were: 34,146 goats, 19,315 sheep, 2,831 head of cattle, 608 camels, 415 donkeys, 86 horses, 35,000 chickens, 28,000 pigeons, and, grouped together, 1,564 ducks and geese.

Each fruit tree would have to be counted and described, so that proper compensation could be determined. The date trees fell into the following categories: fruit-bearing female trees including young females of five years, non-bearing trees (males and older trees), independent shoots (three to four years old), small shoots (one to three years old), and the vulnerable baby shoots still attached to the mothers' roots.

Of all the villages included in the mass relocation, only the inhabitants of one village – Degheim – refused to cooperate, though, of course, the water would defeat them in the end. The women of Degheim, in their black *gargaras*, swarmed and shouted, "*Fadiru wala hagumunno Khashm el Girba la*" – We will die rather than go to Khashm el Girba – and created a great cloud of dust, throwing into the air the earth that was no longer theirs.

The first village to be evacuated from the Wadi Halfa district was Faras. The journey would take a biblical forty hours, an exodus of epic proportion.

Hassan Dafalla had requisitioned 20,000 jute sacks, 20,000 coils of rope, and 15,000 baskets for the journey.

Twenty lorries had been pressed into service to transport the baggage to the train station. More than a hundred porters were required to load lorries and then the fifty-five train cars, the sixty-six goods cars, and the two hundred and sixteen animal wagons and the wagons of fodder and water for the livestock; and before all this, the villagers on the west bank would have to cross the river by steamer. The inhabitants of the Kokki islands — deep in the narrow gorges of the Second Cataract where no boat large enough to carry their baggage could reach them — made rafts of logs and inflated water skins and floated their worldly goods to shore.

January 6, 1964. On the east bank of the Nile at Faras, the train was waiting, complete with hospital carriage for the ill and elderly and for the women who might give birth at any moment. On the west bank, porters began to carry the bags, mattresses, and baskets of every size that were heaped at the front gate of every home, down through the village to where the steamer was docked.

Hassan Dafalla watched as the Nubians took the great wooden keys from their locks and then disappeared back into their homes to look once more. He watched as they sat silently in the cemetery. On the steamer, every eye took in the sight of their departing village; surely, thought Hassan Dafalla, few places on this earth have been looked at by so many at once, with such common feeling. Yet he knew history was crammed with precisely such scenes. Crowding the train station were the villagers from Faras East who had come to wish their neighbours safe passage and who would very soon be making the same journey themselves. He watched as all boarded the train, straining to look back, and as the train driver fastened branches from the Faras date groves to the front of the locomotive, shouting, "*Afialogo, heir ogo*" – good health, prosperity. He watched as the train slowly started to move, until it disappeared into the desert.

They would follow the main Khartoum line to Atbara junction, then by the Port Sudan line to Haya junction, then south to Kassala and Khashm el Girba. At each village along the rail line, people crowded the station, waving and calling out their support and, wherever the train stopped, dispensing tea and gifts of food to the passengers: sacks of sugar, flour, wheat and rice, butter, oil, cheese and honey. "*Afialogo, heir ogo, adeela, adeela.*" At Aroma, all the tribesmen of the Hadandawa gathered on their camels; each with a sword, a lick of light, at their sides. Pointing their staffs to the sky they banged their copper drums to the word "*Dabaywa*" – welcome. And so it was the same, at Sarra East, Dibeira, Ashkeit, Dabarosa, Tawfikia, Arkawit, and El Jebel. At Angash station, at Haya, and Kassala, the farmers loaded the train with generous sacks of citrus and vegetables until there was not a centimetre of space left in the bulging cars. Night was falling. Suddenly, at the Butana Bridge, every passenger leaned toward the windows for a glimpse of the Atbara River. Those who had stopped weeping began again, at the sight of a river so sickly, so dirty and small compared to the Nile they had left behind. At the other end of the bridge in the distance they had their first glimpse of the row of white houses waiting for them: Village #33.

In mourning, the Nubian women removed their black *gargaras*, flowing as the Nile, and disembarked wearing the plain saris of central Sudan.

A few days after the evacuation, Hassan Dafalla returned to Faras to meditate upon all he had seen. The sun beat down into silence. He saw the holes where the decorative plates had been pulled from the walls. He saw the footprints of hyenas everywhere.

After several days sunk in thought, Hassan Dafalla journeyed to visit the exiled settlers at Khashm el Girba. "We had a mutual longing to see each other," he wrote later in his diary, "as if we had been parted for a very long time."

At 9 a.m. on the day of the evacuation of Sarra, Commissioner Hassan Dafalla had arrived, hours before the train was scheduled to depart, to find the village already deserted. He stood in shock, at the wild unreality of finding no one there to emigrate. The night before, all the baggage had been loaded onto the train; wagons and heavy trucks stood in the sand, braying with livestock. Yet in the morning there was not a single villager to be found. Commissioner Dafalla, at a loss for what to do, climbed the hill above the village to think. When he reached the top he was startled again, this time to find himself looking down upon a shining green pool where yesterday there had been only stones and sand. Now he saw that hundreds of palm branches, shimmering in the heat, had been heaped upon the graves of the cemetery. In a great circle around the grave-yard the villagers were dancing the *zikir*. For two hours longer, Commissioner Dafalla sat on the hill while the villagers of Sarra read and sang to their dead. Suddenly, the green pool bled apart and reformed as a river, as all of Sarra moved in a wailing line up the hill, carrying their palm branches from the graves to the train.

The very staples that the Nubians had so expertly cultivated would now have to be bought at market – lentils, beans, chickpeas, lupins, and peas. In the new settlement there were no terraces for the women to sit together, no Nile with its green inlets and islands where they could sail their feluccas and watch the steamers passing to and from Egypt, loaded with goods. Now there was only the steep gorge of the Atbara River, with its barren banks, the dry thorny acacia scrub, and the rainy savannah. There were no palm date forests and no limitless hills of the Sahara. The women per-manently gave up the elegant *gargara* because now it simply trailed through mud.

Their sense of time changed; the way they looked at sky and stars was now different. Their Coptic calendar was replaced by the Arab stellar calendar. They learned to predict rainfall, the fierce tropical rains, from the direction of lightning – lightning in the east brings the storm, but lightning in other directions turns it away.

They had to give up their beds lined with date branches and now slept in beds of steel frames and wire springs.

Several months before the inundation, a Polish archaeologist had discovered a buried mud brick church not far from the village of Faras. One wall bore a magnificent painting in coloured lime. Using a chemical solution to imprint the image on muslin cloth, Professor Michałowski began to make a copy of the painting when he was surprised to find another image underneath. Each time he copied the painting on the wall, another was discovered beneath. Eighty-six layers of paintings were uncovered.

The Nubians, who had given up everything for the hydroelectric power provided by the new dam, were themselves without electricity. The cables passed right by the new settlements; only some extra poles and wire would have been needed to bring electricity into their houses. But the Nubians had to wait seven years to turn on a light.

———

Many days Jean watched from the shade of the houseboat as the Nubian women came down to the river. The sight of their black robes seemed to slice through the heat, although Jean could not explain why she felt this, since they, too, shimmered like black water above the baking sand.

It excited her to watch them; that is, she yearned for them to see her.

She felt like a child in their presence, and in the presence of the desert within them. They knew intimately the space of the desert and the timelessness of the river — two distinct immensities. And the third immensity, the sky. Yet there was also understanding between her and the women, or at least the longing to understand. She watched them move with fluid grace and knew that they too would soon be shedding the *gargara*.

How much of a woman's body belongs to herself, how much the clay of a man's gaze. Jean could not explain her loneliness, the lack in herself. There was some mystery of womanhood, she felt, that would remain forever lost to her; this, she believed, was because she was raised by her father alone. She wanted to strip off her clothes and roll in the sand, to lose the smell of herself in the desert and so, for a few moments, to feel at home there. She wanted Avery to understand something she could not explain; she knew this and could not fault him for not understanding.

She wondered how long it could take for the heat to sweat the northern-ness out of her – evaporate the body-memory of boreal lakes and forests – a transformation as chemical as cooking. How can place enter our skin this way, down into the very verb of us? It did not seem possible, yet she felt it was true. She felt that if she stood naked next to the Nile women, that even a man blindfolded in the dark would be able to tell that she was a stranger.

The European engineers took no notice of their strangerness – they brought their slide rules into the desert and spoke the ancient language of builders – a numerical language older than the temples. The men who had first come to this bend of the river to paint the line across the cliff face, more than thirty centuries before, could stand next to these engineers, look over their shoulders at their diagrams, and comprehend their intent almost instantly. And so Avery, with the ancient Egyptian builder looking over his shoulder, could not feel Jean's disgrace, an unworthiness that she herself could not find a way to express. She knew somehow it was not petty, not even personal, though it felt that way too, and all the words she had to describe how she felt, reeked of the personal. Soon she left off trying to express it to him. She left off, as in midsentence, and he did not notice. And this not noticing, she understood, was his relief. How much of our not noticing is a kind of relief.

———

Sometimes, if it was simply impossible to improvise a broken part, the engineers played cards or drew lots to decide who would have the adventure of scouring the market at Wadi Halfa for screws and boltheads, pistons and wire. Avery was given a four-day working holiday and he flew with Jean from Abu Simbel to Wadi Halfa. They had made several journeys to the market, and to Jean it always seemed that a great wind had blown into that dusty town, depositing a world's worth, a century's worth, of detritus that had been caught in its force. Electrical plugs and batteries, tweed caps, tins of tooth powder, bundles of herbs and paper packets of spices, women's evening shoes with silver buckles, eggs, pipe tobacco, ice skates, soft perfumed mounds of figs and dates and apricots, smoking jackets, great heaps of textiles – from Turkey, Asia, the Soviet Union, nylon stockings from Italy, English wool, calico and gingham, and the long bolts of fine dark cotton cloth – dark as the cold shadow of a desert hill – that the Nubian women used to make their *gargaras*. Coffee-sellers with radios at full volume, everyone shouting to be heard, dogs barking at the meat-sellers, meat-sellers yelling at the dogs, the tinkling glass of the soft-drink vendors, mills grinding coffee and grain, the sound of beans and split peas pouring into sacks, the tea-sellers rattling their cups. Taxi drivers arguing over a fare, donkeys braying, the loud exhaust systems of small French cars, the shouts of a boys' football match, and, suddenly right next to one's ear, the soft Arabic of a girl reading to her blind grandfather as they sat together behind a table heaped with socks and buttons, two items for which desert-dwellers have no use. Jean thought about the old man's livelihood being dependent on Westerners with loose threads and how completely, foolishly, European clothing had come to depend upon the button.

The market at Wadi Halfa was a place where every human whim had found a shelf. It was a catalogue of desires, a market of the broken and the lost, haunted by the hopes of both buyer and seller.

Baskets of hardware both shiny and rusted, springs, screws, nails, pliers, hinges; parts of boats and automobiles, electric fans. "Spare" parts that had been liberated from machines where they had not been "spare" or from machinery abandoned as useless in the desert. And here is where Avery often found the size of bolt he needed, even if it meant buying all the electric fans he could find, to pillage them for the single part. And here is where the rest of the now useless hardware of the fan would find itself, back again in the Wadi Halfa market, with blades that had little hope of ever being attached again, unless someone in turn twenty years later pillaged Avery's engine.

Spanners, handkerchiefs, pencil crayons, steam irons. Soviet cigarettes and old newspapers, years out of date, from all over Europe. Shellac, perfume, machine oil, tissue-thin blue air-mail paper edged with mucilage . . .

Jean looked with fascination at this debris of time and trade. But quickly this turned to melancholy, for by what other means than tragedy or unconscionable neglect would an object such as an engagement ring or a child's doll arrive at its fate in the distant desert market of Wadi Halfa? The market seemed one consciousness, one body of memory, haunted by murderous betrayal and ill fate, inconsolable loneliness, entire lives scorched by a single mistake; and the softer regrets — wistful, elegiac. She stood with a girl's knitted hat in her hand, or a cardigan worn for many years by a man who Jean imagined must have sat with his elbows on the table while drinking alone, or an ornate brooch heavy enough to rip the silk of a blouse, given by a fiancé or inherited from an aunt, found in a basket overflowing with such tokens. The anonymous loss, the hardship or death that brought this ivory comb or this watch engraved *from your loving father* to a stall in Wadi Halfa oppressed her; the memories she imagined these objects carried, the sadness of things. Sometimes Jean would buy something simply in order to rescue it from what she felt was the painful apathy of its surroundings, the market where customers preferred not to know an object's history.

In the slow end of the day's heat, Avery and Jean lay on their bed in the annex of the Nile Hotel, the annex itself yet another example of an object scavenged for use in another context, kidnapped from one history to another, for their room was aboard the *S.S. Sudan*, an old Thomas Cook steamboat, permanently moored to accommodate guests when the main hotel was full.

They never tired of this, the claiming of a hotel room, the strange bed, the act of opening a satchel and bringing their few objects into a new story.

They woke the next day to the sounds of the railyard at Wadi Halfa, the hammering on steel, the shunting of cars, clanging and hissing, as the trains were readied for their long journey to Khartoum.

Jean felt the sweat in her scalp and under her breasts despite the slow fan that circled above their heads.

Avery lay a book with a moss green cover across Jean's hips.

— Rosario Castellanos, said Avery. He turned over the book and read:

'Because from the start you were fated to be mine.
Before the ages of wheat and larks
and even before fishes . . .
When everything lay in the divine
lap, confused and intertwined,
you and I lay there complete, together.
But then came the punishment of clay . . .

Because from the start you were fated to be mine
my solitude was a somber passage,
an impetus of inconsolable fever . . .'

A dog barked through the words of the poems.

'. . . I learned
that nothing was mine: not the wheat, the star,
his voice, his body; not even my own.
That my body was a tree and that the owner of a tree
is not its shadow, but the wind . . .'

— It was in the bottom of the first-aid kit we saw in the
market, said Avery, that banged-up tin box with a lid —
perfect for keeping wingnuts and bolts — and still filled with
eye-droppers and squeezed-up tubes of ointment, old packets
of gauze dressings.

— Poetry in a first-aid tin? It's too perfect, you're making
it up, said Jean.

— No, said Avery. And this was there too. He leaned over
the edge of the bed and handed Jean a thin leather book — a
diary. The book was curved slightly, as if the owner had
carried it in a pocket.

— Ah, said Jean, afraid to look inside.

— Someone had only just started writing in it, said Avery.
No date, no name. Will you read it to me?

Jean opened the journal; instantly, tears filled her eyes.
The writing was very small, blue ink; she could not tell
whether a man's hand or a woman's.

'We tear open the oranges, the figs, all the fruit we can no longer bear to eat alone . . .

'We've met in so many cities . . . the ports where sleep empties its cargoes into the bay, the night and day of love. We waste nothing in these meetings, not a breath to spare. A full hold in each direction – what each brings to the other, what we carry home. It will be a long time now until we see each other again. At night, feel my hands, feel my voice, carry me with you, in a muscle and in a word. And I will too, carry you . . .

'In a forest of stars and boughs, here is your face. In the garden, in the shipwreck, in sacred stones, in figs and roses. Through long nights of walking, what does not sing for us? Through long nights of waking, what does not sing for us? . . .

'Walking with your mouth inside my clothes, and all the possible days. The city in the rain: violinists wearing tuxedoes, the white stick of the blind pointing to the wet pavement, sheet-metal skows moving slowly across the river. The owned and the old, everything either lost or found. With you, here, lost and found . . .'

Jean closed the book. After a moment she said, I believe you could pluck the necessary book out of the air.

They lay next to each other, listening to the clang of the metalworkers.

— After the war, my mother and I moved back to London, said Avery. We had a tiny flat and our kitchen table — my father's huge wooden worktable where we ate all our meals — was in an alcove, surrounded by four walls of books. Without getting out of our chairs, we could simply reach behind us and, yes, pluck! the appropriate book off a shelf. That was my father's idea, so that there would always be active discussions at meals, and so that I or any guest could find a reference in a trice. My father loved to call out directions from his end of the table like a mad navigator on a small boat: 'A bit more to the right, nine o'clock please, forty-five degrees left . . .' Over the years, certain thick or oversized volumes became landmarks by which we steered: 'The grey cover two inches to the right of *The Child's New Illustrated Encyclopedia* ("new" about forty years previous), below *One Thousand and One Wonderful Things*, about ten inches above *Engines and Power* . . .' And when the book was retrieved successfully from the shelf, my father would let out a sigh, as if just the right unreachable itch had been scratched.

My father illustrated his explanations using objects on the table, becoming so absorbed that eventually any outsider risked impropriety and drifted away, leaving him in silent and solitary contemplation of a miniature Battersea Power Station with its four juice-glass smokestacks, or a liftlock that began with a slice of bread . . .

'Every object,' my father used to say, 'is also a concept.' If you place two or three or ten things next to each other that have never been next to each other before, this will produce a new question. And nothing proves the existence of the future like a question . . .

My parents, as you know, first met on a train in Scotland. They had both walked the same road to the same rural station, a road thick with dust, and my father's boots and trouser legs were covered with fine powder. He stamped his feet, frustrated by the dust that was determined to cling. He looked up to see a young woman watching him, amused. He thought that her skirt was spattered with mud, but upon closer view he saw that the material was embroidered with tiny bees. Her shoes were spotless and shining. Had she floated to the station? 'Don't be silly,' she answered. She told him that she polished her shoes with a special homemade varnish that 'repelled' the dust. It had something to do with static electricity. Hadn't he heard of static electricity? My father replied that indeed he knew quite a lot about electricity – he had started out as an electrical engineer, after all – but perhaps he hadn't given enough thought to shoes. 'That's not surprising,' my mother said. 'It takes a woman to put two such practical things together.' And that's when my father learned a piece of wisdom he was to follow the rest of his life and passed on to me: 'No two facts are too far apart to be put together.'

My father possessed an enviable equanimity. If he sat on something painful – if I'd left a toy in the crease of the chesterfield – or if he tripped over something I should have put away, he picked it up, ready to complain. But then, upon inspecting the object more closely, all blame was forgotten; he'd stand there wondering how it was made, by whom, and where; he began to ponder the kind of machinery necessary to mass-produce such a product, possible improvements to the design . . . He worked with machines all day and then at home continued to fiddle and ruminate; he penetrated mechanisms with a sixth sense. His hands were deft with nuts and bolts, circuitry, solder, springs, magnets, mercury, petrol. He fixed walkie-talkies, dolls, bicycles, ham radios, steam engines; he seemed to see into the heart of any machine at a glance. Children from the neighbourhood left their broken objects on our doorstep with a note propped up or shoved inside: 'doesn't ring' 'wheel stuck,' 'won't cry any more.' When the object was fixed, he put it back outside to be claimed by the satisfied owner.

My mother was deft in another way. Sometimes my father had fits of private despair, of professional disappointment, anger at a job poorly done. I was attuned to my mother's work of restoration – the plate of biscuits; the bar of chocolate on my father's worktable; a sealed note, the envelope painted beautifully with an architectural detail or a valve or a latch – and then the whole house seemed readjusted, like the hands of a clock. Chaos was restored to its rightful place, that is, once again left to me and, when they came to visit, my cousins – four children who liked to build things and then blow them up, or blow things up and then rebuild them. We worked best together when implementing morally questionable schemes, like the heist of the sweet shop that involved, among other strenuous tasks, the digging of a tunnel from the end of our garden out to the street. We'd progressed about five yards before winter set in. The tunnel caved in sometime during the spring rains and remained there, a muddy scar.

Avery reached for Jean's hand, the hand that had once

served as a map of the Sahara. Through the open window they could hear new arrivals at the Wadi Halfa station shouting for porters, and for a moment Jean thought of the huge clock that dominated the little waiting room.

— I loved when my father made use of my mother's hands when he ran out of useful digits on his own, during complicated demonstrations, folding her fingers into stress coordinates, said Avery. Years later, I remembered this habit of his and began to wonder if my father had used other parts of my mother in private demonstrations I never saw. I liked the idea that perhaps I was the result of an intricate equation.

It was in the Wadi Halfa market that Jean conceived of her compendium of plants with healing properties. It would be a present for Avery, perhaps Marina could be persuaded to illustrate it: a list of imaginary botanica to treat very real but elusive ailments. She was looking at a volume of Linnaeus — someone had written in the margins in Spanish — when the idea came to her. Balms, tinctures, ointments, teas, salves, compresses, inhalations, for those who are far from home or for those who are housebound, for those who are bedridden on summer days, in autumn, on rainy days. For those suffering painful nostalgias of weather accompanied by severe despond, regret, shame. For those who have not felt a human touch for two months, a year, for many years — a matter of dosage. For those who have lost everything because they were misunderstood. For those who can no longer feel the wind, even on their bare skin. An ointment made from the astringent torreya, for those who suffer from miserliness. Balms of moss for those who have become colour-blind, for those who cry too easily, for those who have lost perception, for those who have lost the faculty of empathy, of forgiveness or self-forgiveness. Brew the bark or, for urgent cases, apply directly without boiling first. Safe for children and other animals. Ineffective on men with long hair; results achieved instantly; reapply every hour; for those weakened by too much hope, for those weakened by too much despair, for those who are landlocked and crave the sea, for those who fear the sea, for those who fear opera. For those who fear music sung by low-voiced women who have lost everything. For those who eat too much chocolate, for those who do not eat enough chocolate. For those who have forgotten how to pray, apply to hands and knees the milk of the pod of *humilitas immensita*, a strong-smelling tuber for treating wounds to the eyes, heart, hands, ears, genitals, lips, spirit. For those experiencing the vertigo of loss, very potent – for one-time use only – do not operate heavy machinery or make important decisions while under its influence. *Illuminatus* leaves for those who are lost or mis-guided, choose only the small leaves near the stem that give off a faint glow, effective even in moral quagmires. With gaudy blooms . . . Plants with strong odours . . . Use only the inner bark . . . Discard seeds and pulpy matter . . . A good cooking substitute for those who cannot eat garlic . . . Use only the stem of the plant, boil in salt water, boil in sugar water. If it boils, you must begin again. To reduce swelling. Apply directly to affected area. Soothing oil for feet too long in ill-fitting shoes, for those who have waited for necessities too long in queues. To fade the appearance of scars. Milky pods, milky stems, leaves and stems that weep with a clear sap, "hair of the dog" nettles, spikes, brambles, thistles. Ointments for those who cannot stop feeling angry, salve for those who have lost feeling in their hands and other forms of corporal rigidity. Compresses for those who cannot stop crying, and also encourages tears in those whose eyes will not weep. Tea for those who cannot remember their dreams, or for those who cannot forget them. *Consolatum empathatum*, salve for eyes that have seen too much, or too little. Astringent of thorns for those feigning serious illness to elicit sympathy from others and who punish those who withhold this abused mercy. Apply directly to tongue. Apply directly to eyelids. Avoid eyes. Repeat until urge to dissemble is purged. Reapply at night. Dual – often directly opposite – effects, depending on the severity of the affliction . . .

Before dawn on the third morning of their stay in Wadi Halfa, they met, as arranged, their friend Daub Arbab in the lobby of the Nile Hotel. He had flown from Khartoum, where he had collected an order of Novello one-handed chainsaws and 25mm-toothed Sandviken handsaws, used for the most fragile cutting. The shipment had gone astray once and Daub had been sent to oversee its safe delivery. This fell into accord with Daub's own plan, to seize the opportunity to visit Wadi Halfa as many times as possible before the inundation. This time he'd hired a truck to drive Avery and

Jean north to the Debeira pipe scheme. Avery wanted to see for himself the canal where the Nubians had set afloat their irrigation pumps on barges. "It is not far," said Daub, "and on the way back, we will stop to say our sad farewell to the most beautiful place on this earth."

They drove under the cold stars of dawn, north from Wadi Halfa to the now empty villages of Debeira and Ashkeit.

— In Nubia, said Daub, any dispute that arises is settled by the entire family, including women and children. Violent crimes are extremely rare, but in such a case, an exception would be made and only the men would meet to decide what was to be done. The guilty one would be shunned so completely that he would be forced, for his own survival, to leave the community. Cases are never brought to the police. In this way, Nubia has always protected itself, always kept its independence.

The economy depends on the division of ownership. This is a very satisfactory arrangement of real estate, capital, and labour. But often the distribution of the harvest is a complicated affair — because only the oldest women in the village can remember the tangled terms of the original transaction. These arrangements keep alive the history of each family. They ensure that even the labour exile will maintain his place in the village.

Here is a typical story of Nubia, continued Daub. Two men who shared an *eskalay* were quarrelling over the division of water. In order to irrigate the land of each man equally, the water had to be channelled from one ditch to the other. They were arguing over who was benefiting from the larger share when their uncle overheard. He arranged for a large stone to be brought and placed in the middle of the canal, separating the water into two streams, thus ending the argument. In 1956, when the hostilities erupted between Egypt and England over the Suez, the Nubians followed the events closely; they hurried back and forth from the field to the village, back and forth to gather around a single shortwave radio. An old man observed this rushing to and fro all morning and at last asked one of the young men what it was all about. 'Grandfather, the Englishmen are fighting Egypt for the Suez Canal.' The old man shook his head. 'Won't anyone put a stone in the middle?'

I will tell you another story, said Daub. My father was hired by the British army to train and serve as a translator. He was very young and very clever. One British officer saw how quick he was and helped him to come to England and to find a job. My father eventually married an Englishwoman. And so I was born and raised in Manchester. I worked very hard, studying for engineering. Then I decided to come to Egypt. My father was unhappy at this but also secretly pleased. He would say, 'Here in England you have everything, and there . . .' he would trail off. There, I knew he was thinking, enviously, was the river and the hills and the desert. And secretly pleased too, because part of every father longs for his own boyhood to be understood by his son.

From a distance Avery and Jean saw that, like other Nubian villages, Ashkeit had been built at the foot of rocky hills and a thick date palm forest grew down to the river.

And from a distance they saw that, like other Nubian houses, the houses of Ashkeit were luminous cubes — both sunlight and moonlight had soaked into the whitewashed walls of sand and mud plaster, smooth and magical as ice that never melts. Just below the roof, small windows were cut in the walls for ventilation — large enough to let in a breeze but small and high enough to keep out the heat and the sand. Each house possessed the wooden door of a fortress, and a one-metre-long wooden bolt, which would have held, before the evacuation, a giant wooden key. Behind the impressive entrance, Jean and Avery knew, would be the customary large central courtyard, with rooms leading from it.

Daub stopped a little way from the village. He turned to them. "There is something in both your faces," he said. "I saw it even the first time we met, that made me wish to bring you here."

Describe a landscape you love, Jean had asked Avery the first time they'd lain together in her bed on Clarendon Avenue; and he'd whispered the stone forests of his childhood; his grandmother's garden; the field at the end of his cousins' road in the countryside where he'd spent the war — there was a certain place, a fold in the hills that he could not stop looking at, a feeling he could never name, attached to that place.

Jean knew Avery's way of seeing, how he arrived some-where and made room for it in his heart. He let himself be altered. Jean had felt it the first time they met, and many times since. In the riverbed of the St. Lawrence and in the drowning counties; in Britain, standing in the rain at the edge of the world in Uist trying to name the moment the last molecule of light disappeared from the sky; in the Pennines; on Jura; and when they walked upon the absolute black of Marina's newly ploughed marsh. And when Avery looked at her in the dark, making room for her inside himself.

Now, in Ashkeit, Jean felt the blow, the disaster to a soul that can be caused by beauty, by an answer one cannot grasp with one's hands. The hunger for a home was much worse here, unbearable. For now it was to be found and lost. The village, the way the houses grew out of the desert – it was as if the need of Avery's heart had invented them. And, too, the kinship with those who made them.

The houses were like gardens sprung up in the sand after a rainfall. As if cut by Matisse's scissors, shapes of pure colour – intense and separate – were painted onto the glowing white walls. Designs of cinnamon, rust, phthalocyanine green, rose, antwerp blue, tan, cream, madder, lamp black, sienna, and ancient yellow ochre, perhaps the oldest pigment used by man. Each a shout of joy. Embedded in the whitewashed walls were decoration – designs of brightly coloured lime wash, bright as the eye could bear – geometric patterns, plants, birds and animals – with mosaics set into the plaster like jewels; and snail shells, and polished pebbles. Over the gates were elaborately painted china plates, as many as thirty or forty decorating a single house. They were like stones of a necklace set against the white skin – porous, breathing, cool – of the plaster. Here was human love of place so freely expressed, alive with meaning; houses so perfectly adapted to their context in materials and design that they could never be moved. It was an integrity of art, domestic life, landscape – a beauty before which one did not wish to prostrate oneself, but instead to leap up. When Jean saw the houses of Ashkeit, she understood as never before what Avery meant about knowing builder and building intimately even at first sight. And Jean knew that he would be thinking what she was thinking; that it was Ashkeit they should be salvaging; though it could never exist anywhere else and if moved, would crumble, like a dream.

Avery approached Daub, who was standing alone by the river.

– It will take all my life, said Avery, to learn what I have seen today.

But Jean took Avery's arm and gently led him off, for their friend Daub was weeping.

Jean and Avery waited for Daub at the edge of the village. They sat together in the twilight sand of Ashkeit. The air deepened. For a long moment this light was suspended, like the face of a listener at the precise moment of understanding. And then the new skin of starlight, like ice on water, spread across the sky. How remorselessly the sand turned cold, the surrounding coldness of thousands of kilometres of desert, an endless cold. Avery thought of his schoolteacher in England who had cut an apple and held one-quarter of it up to the class: this is the amount of earth that is not water; and then cut the quarter in half – this is the amount of arable land; and cut again – this is the amount of arable land not covered by human habitation; and finally, the amount of land that feeds everyone on the earth – barely a scrap of skin.

Like discovering latent knowledge in one's self while reading words on a page, like a shape emerging from sculptor's clay, so arose their feelings of astonishment and inevitability as the village of Ashkeit had come into closer view. It was the same sensation that Avery felt when he first saw Jean, walking alone on the riverbank. Inexplicably, in that moment, he knew the place held meaning, for him and for her, as if his own heart had brought this to pass. As if he had caused the event – then and there. More, as if the place itself had given rise to her.

It was also the knowledge that they would be forever changed, their bodies already changed; attuned to each other.

He could almost imagine that the houses of Ashkeit rose out of the sand at the very moment of his sight, born from the intensity of his desire.

Jean watched as the white shapes of the houses dissolved into the twilight; she thought of the leaf of the sumach, which looks like six separate leaves but which is botanically only a single leaf. So, too, Ashkeit. Jean took Avery's hand. His eyes were closed, but because he felt her hand in his he also saw her hand in his mind. So it was with the houses of Nubia; no landscape alone could arouse such feeling. It was what he felt, looking as a child at that crease of hill in Buckinghamshire, in the fall of light, familiar as a face. This earth, this Jean Shaw.

At that moment he imagined he knew, his body knew, what Ashkeit and Debeira and Faras, all the villages, meant.

When he had sat in the Buckinghamshire hills with his father – though he had said nothing about his feeling for that place – he knew his father had felt it too. How could Avery explain it; it was as if what he experienced there could not have been brought to life anywhere else.

When the water came, the houses would dissolve like a bromide. But they would not even disappear into the river, which held a memory of them. For even the river would be gone.

Daub had come and Jean sat between the two men, between the earth and stars. She thought of the children who had been born in this village and who would never be able to return, never be able to satisfy or explain the nameless feeling that would come upon them, in the midst of their adulthood, perhaps waking from an afternoon sleep, or walking along a road, or upon entering a stranger's house.

– A human being can be destroyed piece by piece, Daub said, looking out at the abandoned village glowing in the sand. Or all at once.

Do you know the beginning of *Metamorphoses*? asked Daub. 'Now I am ready to tell how bodies are changed/into different bodies.'

They began the drive back through the twilight desert to Wadi Halfa.

Avery spoke of the despair of space that the built world

had created; waste space too narrow for anything but litter, dark walkways from carparks to the street; the endless, dead space of underground garages; the corridors between skyscrapers; the space surrounding industrial rubbish bins and ventilator shafts . . . the space we have imprisoned between what we have built, like seeds of futility, small pockets on the earth where no one is meant to be alive, a pause, an emptiness . . .

Avery imagined a time, not too far distant, when engineers' calculations could be so cleverly manipulated, that materials, tension, stress, and weight-bearing would have a new vocabulary; a time when buildings of such startling shapes would rise from the ground like the sudden eruption of a volcano; a time when bombastic originality would be mistaken for beauty, just as austerity had once been mistaken for authority.

— It is not originality or authority that I desire in a building, said Avery. It is restoration. When you find yourself someplace — he paused. I suppose I mean exactly that — to find myself, in a place.

— We wish our buildings to grow old with us, said Daub.

North of Sarra the road climbed to the top of the hills, and Daub stopped the truck. It was almost dark. Here, from the height, they looked out to the groves of the Nile and beyond, to the great Sahara. Jean suddenly understood that the colours of the limewash at Ashkeit were as startling as the green of the floodplain.

— Soon, said Daub, everything we see here will be under water. There is an illusion of peace. But there is trouble and like much of the trouble in the desert, it is caused both by the living and the dead.

My father had a habit, which I find I have inherited, of clipping articles from the newspapers. He used to form an idea about the world, a theory, and then he would happen upon all kinds of 'proof' in the papers — coincidental, of course, but it amused him. And it became a small obsession.

Once, he held up a newspaper photograph of a dark-featured child, her hair wrapped in a scarf or shawl, holding a bundle of cloth.

'What do you see?' my father asked me.

'A DP from the war in Europe?'

'A Palestinian refugee, 1948.'

He showed me another clipping, very similar to the first.

'And this?'

'Another Palestinian boy?'

'No. A Jewish boy who has arrived in Israel from a refugee camp in Germany. And this?'

He held up a photo of a line of people, weighed down with suitcases and satchels, clearly carrying all they owned.

'Immigrants to Israel?'

'No, Arab Jews forced to leave Egypt, also 1948. And this photo — a Polish boy, a Christian, in a camp in Tashkent; and this — a Yugoslav boy in a refugee camp in Kenya; and another in Cyprus; and in the desert camp at El Shatt in 1944; and here, a Greek child in the camp near Gaza, at Nuseirat, also 1944. Quite a few times,' said my father, 'I have found faces that are almost identical. These two — one is from a refugee camp in Lebanon; the other, from a refugee camp in Backnang near Stuttgart. When you see just their faces, nothing else, do they not look like twins? That resemblance is what caused me to begin this collection, photos everyone sees every day, from newspapers or magazines, refugees from every side.'

Did you know, said Daub, that the first plans for the High Dam were drawn up by West Germany to appease Egypt, after compensating Israel after the war? There is so much collusion, from every side, it might be possible to sort it out, if only a single soul possessed all the information.

Here I am, a British citizen, whose father was born in Cairo, and whose grandfather died in London in the Blitz, sitting in the Sudanese desert, with a Canadian and her British husband, talking about refugees in Kenya, Gaza, New Zealand, India, Khataba, Indonesia . . .

Daub rested his head in his arms on the steering wheel. The breeze lifted the hair from the back of his neck and Jean felt a pang at the sight; a place of vulnerability. One could live a lifetime, she thought, and perhaps never be touched there.

— I was in Faras during the first evacuation. I was working in Halfa then, said Daub, and I went to witness it. I saw a mother and daughter saying their farewells. They had lived in two villages that were side by side, a short walk from each other. The daughter had moved to live with her husband's family when they were married, but the mother and daughter saw each other very often, just a walk of short distance between the two villages. However, the villages happened to be on either side of the border between Sudan and Egypt, that invisible border in the middle of the desert, and so now the mother was being moved to Khashm el Girba and the daughter fifteen hundred kilometres away, to Kom Ombo. Everyone watching this scene knew they would never see each other again. After the daughter, who was very big with child, boarded the train, and the train moved off into the desert, the mother looked down at her feet and saw the satchel she had meant to give her, with family things inside, now left behind.

Daub looked at them and then looked out at the hills above Sarra. It was dark now, the sand pale under the stars.

— When I witnessed this, I thought of my father's collection of pictures. It goes on and on, as my father understood, like the detritus of the Second World War that ended in bits and pieces, leaving behind horror and misery in isolated places, these foul refugee camps all over the world, like pools of stagnant water after a flood . . .

The next evening they flew back to Abu Simbel. From above, the camp came into view, glowing with its artificial light, a conflagration in the wilderness; filling the tiny plane sudden as a searchlight. Jean felt regret for the darkness of the desert they had left behind: palpable, alive, a breathing blackness.

The forces within the cliff at Abu Simbel were balanced by steel scaffolding and the roof of the temple was sliced from the walls to relieve the stress. Nevertheless, it was not known whether the release of the first block — on August 12, 1965 —

would cause the temple to crack open. Avery had stood on the crest of the cofferdam. The stone had been so finely cut, the seam so invisible, that at first it seemed the winch alone was magically reaching into the stone to bring forth a perfect block from the whole.

But Avery had not felt simple relief as the stones were lifted; instead, from the very first cut of the first block – the eleven-tonne GA1A01, Great Temple, Treatment A, Zone 1, Row A, Block 1 – a specific anguish took root. As the ragged cavity expanded, as the gaping absence in the cliff grew deeper, so grew Avery's feeling they were tampering with an intangible force, undoing something that could never be produced or reproduced again. The Great Temple had been carved out of the very light of the river, carved out of a profound belief in eternity. Each labourer had believed. This simple fact roused him – he could not imagine any building in his lifetime or in the future erected with such faith. The stone had been alive to the carvers, not in a mystical way but in a material way; their relationship to the stone had affected the molecules of the stone. Not mystical, but mysterious.

The heat and weight of Jean were in his dreams. And at the beginning, memory blossomed in him, childhood images so strong he could describe to her in detail the objects on a shelf. But as the pile of temple blocks grew around them, even Jean could not dispel what quickly became in Avery more than anxiety – a dispossession.

He had expected the salvage to be an antidote, an atonement for the despair of dam-building. He had imagined a rite of passage, a pilgrimage, an argument his father could respect. Instead he felt that the reconstruction was a further desecration, as false as redemption without repentance.

—There are seeds, said Jean, coaxing Avery to sleep, coated in wax, that can survive in water without germinating; like the lotus, which has been known to survive at the bottom of a lake for more than twelve hundred years and then sprout again; seeds that can survive even salt water, like the coconut that will float across the ocean fully protected, a stony globe, and wash to shore where it will take root. There is a plant — a kind of acacia — that carries on even when all its seeds have been eaten and it is nothing but husk; after the ants have left it hollow, the wind rushes in, and it whistles . . .

The desert was one immensity, the river another. In the hills beyond the din of the camp, Jean and Avery looked up at the third immensity, the stars.

The importance of place: the worn garden path on Hampton Street, the dried-up riverbank, a hotel room. The incline behind Avery's house in Buckinghamshire, a view his mind still knew viscerally.

Jean led Avery a small way up the slope. They stood by a scattering of stones. Standing next to him, looking down at the river flowing in the white light of the generators, she said:

– This very place we stand is where you first learned we will have a child.

And she smiled at Avery's astonished face.

By seven weeks, one hundred thousand new nerve cells in the brain are being formed each minute, by birth, one hundred billion cells. Half of Jean's chromosomes had been discarded to form her "polar body." By eight weeks, every organ of their child existed; each cell possessing its thousands of genes.

Over the months, the baby continued to swell and tighten the entire surface of her; and Jean felt not only her body, but the shape of her mind changing. She imagined taking her place next to the Nubian women, her belly a white moon next to the beautiful, swollen blackness of the other mothers. Fatigue overcame her suddenly; once, she did not make it all the way to the camp shop but sat to rest in the shadow of the generator, thirsty enough to drink the sky. She fell asleep sitting up, leaning against the machine, her legs heavy in the sand. She was not asleep long – perhaps a quarter of an hour – and woke ashamed. She'd been indecorous, and was relieved to see no one near.

As Jean moved to get up, she found beside her a jar of water. Only then did she notice the long trail of *gargara* all around her in the sand.

The next day, a Nubian worker she did not recognize came to the houseboat; with him was a woman.

— My husband is not here, said Jean.

The man, too, was embarrassed. He nodded toward the woman beside him.

— I come because of my wife. She wants me to tell you that she has seen you and that you are not like the other wives. You are always alone. She wants me to tell you that she is the one who brought you the water yesterday when you were asleep. She sees that you will soon have a child. She wants me to tell you that when the child is born she can help you.

The young woman beside him was smiling unrestrainedly. She was young, at least ten years younger than Jean. The sight of her youthful spirit put tears in Jean's eyes. It took a few minutes to sort out the man's consternation at Jean's emotion, but soon it was set right and the young woman and Jean were speaking through her husband's translation.

— One week after the child is born, he is carried to the river. We must bring the *fatta* and eat it by the Nile, but not all — we must share it with the river. We must light the *mubkhar* and lift the child over it seven times. Then we must wash the baby's clothes in the river and bring a bucket of river water back to the house so the mother can wash her face. The child must then be held over the *rubaa* of dates and corn and everyone says the '*Mashangette, mashangetta*' and we pass the child over the good food seven times. Then — this is most important — the mother must fill her mouth with water from the river and pour it from her mouth onto the child. It is only when the river water flows from the mother's mouth over the child that the child will be safe.

— You would do all this for me? asked Jean, holding back her tears.

The woman looked very pleased and then suddenly sad. She spoke with her husband.

— Yes, yes, the man reassured her. She will be like your mother and make the child safe.

———————

Now Jean often woke restless, her body strange to her, in the night. Avery entertained her with childhood stories of his cousins and Aunt Bett. He kneeled naked on the bedcovers and dramatized.

— One morning with nothing to do but wait for lunch, we sat in the long grass and discussed Aunt Bett's brother, Uncle Victor. For some reason he held a morbid fascination for us, and it was usually Owen who started us off.

Avery imitated the haughty angle of Owen's head.

— 'They say he died when a book fell off his library shelf and knocked him senseless.'

'What book was it?' I asked him.

Owen sighed disdainfully.

'Who cares,' he said. 'That's not the point, is it?'

Owen, Avery explained, was disturbed that a man who had survived being a soldier in the Great War could die so unheroically.

'It certainly is the point,' I argued. 'What book would you choose to die by?'

There was a moment's silence while we all contemplated this question.

'The Bible, I suppose,' said Tom.

'Oh, don't be so melodramatic,' said Owen.

'I'd choose Browning's *Portuguese Sonnets*,' said Nina.

'Not thick enough,' I said.

Then we heard my mother calling and as usual Owen, being the eldest by almost eight years, had the last word.

'I'd choose *Grey's Anatomy* or a medical encyclopedia, just in case there was a slim chance of resuscitating me . . .'

Jean laughed.

– 'Now we can play Dessert Island,' Nina would say as she always did when the table had been cleared. We called it that, said Avery, because we played the game while waiting for the pudding, such as it was, in those days. 'I'm first,' said Nina, 'because I've been thinking and I've got a good one. If I could only take one thing to a deserted island, I would take knitting needles.'

Avery imitated the boys rolling their eyes.

– 'Only a girl would think of something so ridiculous,' said Owen. 'And what a waste of a wish.'

'What good would that be?' I asked Nina, not unkindly. 'The wool would get used up fast and then you'd have nothing.'

'What do you mean?' said Nina indignantly. 'You've got a good warm sweater or blanket and you've still got the knitting needles. And they could be used for lots of things –'

'Like a spear for piercing a wild boar,' Tom suggested. He was next youngest and always defended his sister.

'Or to dig holes for planting seeds,' said Nina.

'And for cleaning under your nails afterwards,' added Tom.

'But your nails wouldn't need cleaning if you used the knitting needles to make the holes,' I said.

My mother and Aunt Bett approved of these discussions. 'Now, that's sound judgment,' they would say encouragingly. Or 'Perhaps we might think that through again.'

'Or you could use them to pierce a souffle,' said Owen sarcastically.

'A souffle!' shouted Nina. 'Yes, there might be ostrich eggs on the island!'

'Haw haw haw!' all the boys laughed.

'All right,' said Aunt Bett. 'That's enough. Knitting needles are a very good idea, Nina . . . and there just might be ostrich eggs on the island.'

'Haw haw haw!' laughed Nina.

—Your family sounds like something out of a children's story, said Jean.

—That's just it, said Avery. I think my mother and Aunt Bett discussed it and decided we would all be children out of books. They were determined. We children were their war effort. Why not? You have all those other owner's manuals — Dr. Spock and all, so why not Arthur Ransome or T. H. White? It's bound to work. To raise brave, moral, thinking adults, all you need is to give them a common mission —

— And a slab of chocolate and a torch. Ah, said Jean, that explains everything.

— I thought everyone grew up in a family like ours, said Avery. It was a shock to find out it wasn't so.

— Did your Aunt Bett have a sad childhood? asked Jean.

— All childhoods are sad compared to mine, said Avery.

Then Avery told the story of Nina's eighth birthday.

— When Nina's birthday package arrived from her father, who was in the RAF and stationed in an undisclosed location, she held the jewellery box in her lap, watching the ballerina come alive each time she raised the lid. Then Nina sat still with her terrible longing. I used to imagine Nina was my own little sister. I tried to look at the box the way my father would have; he would have talked to her about who'd carved it, the hands of the one who'd glued the pink gauze of the tutu onto the long legs of the wooden girl, who'd wrapped the felt around the black lacquer. Who was the man or woman who had tapped the tiny brass nails into the wood . . . I took her hand and led her into the sitting room, where the radio was on. The evening concert was beginning. The London Symphony Orchestra. Nina, who was deaf in one ear, used to sit next to me, her useless ear buried in one hand and her good ear open to the sound. She hooked her hair over this ear, so not a strand would get in the way of the music.

'Here we are in the countryside,' I told her, 'listening to an orchestra from London and a violinist from Russia who are now actually in a concert hall in Holland. That's electricity. All of those musicians hundreds of miles away, playing to us from a little wooden box in our little house in the country.'

Nina sighed. 'Tell me again about Maria Abado.'

'Every nightbird can see the ghost of Maria Abado. If she is here, the birds will tell us. All over the world the birds remember her and speak her name. The cuckoos and the turacos, the colies, hoopoes, the shy trogons, cranes and grebes, tinamous, nightjars, frigate birds, and cassowaries. The avocets, hawfinches, snow geese, the starlings that migrate across the Mediterranean aboard ships. The storks of the Bosphorus, the spruce grouse, the button-quail of India, the African snipe. The African village weaver bird who builds a cave of palm leaves. The upside-down bluebird of paradise, the bird of paradise of the Aru Islands. Maria was born in a village on the other side of the mountain. She befriended the birds when she was a little girl, and by the time she died, she was their patron saint.'

'Was she really a saint?'

'I don't know, but the birds trusted her, in order to repair her broken trust.'

'Why was her trust broken? Was it a broken heart?'

'Only the birds know. But they say all birds sing her story, if only we listen.'

Jean, pinned to the bed by her fatigue and the heaviness of her belly, thought how fortunate their child to have such cousins.

— Despite how close we all were during the war, said Avery, I haven't seen them for years. Nina still lives in England, but Tom went to Australia where he does something in television. And I did meet Owen in London, not long after my father died . . .

We met, accidentally, on the Fulham Road. The last time I'd seen Owen was also accidental, at a matinee of a film. He and his wife, Miri, had been sitting a few rows ahead, but I couldn't bring myself to disturb them. They were so involved with each other, so passionate, it had seemed an intrusion even to observe them.

As always, Owen was impeccably suited, an expensive overcoat and leather gloves. Even when he was starting out, as poor as any of us, Owen's wardrobe had been the source of endless teasing. 'How many people do you meet in a day who will ever come to your home?' said Owen defensively. 'But the whole world sees how you dress. I can live with nothing, not a chair or a teapot, without even heat! But I'll dress like I have all the money in the world. That's something mother taught me, and I know what I'm talking about, you'll see, you'll see.' And Owen, corporate lawyer, showed us all.

'How is Miriam?' I asked. 'The last time I saw you together I didn't say hello, you looked so happy, I thought you'd escaped the children for a rendezvous and I couldn't bring myself to intrude. It was at *Anastasia*.'

The traffic surged around us, the pavement in front of Conran's was bulging with shoppers.

'At *Anastasia*, with Ingrid Bergman?' Owen laughed. 'The very day before we were to be divorced! Miri and I wanted to spend one last day together. It was perhaps the most beautiful day of our marriage – perhaps even more beautiful than the beginning, which is always fraught with such terrifying hopes. We knew the ending – which is much more secure than a future. Then we looked at each other, and it struck us. We were both so content knowing it was over, why upset the children with a piece of paper? The next day we cancelled the lawyers and went along just as before. All that haggling had completely cleared the air and we were perfectly free of wanting be together. Now we could continue separately without upsetting the children – it was a master plan. So Miri keeps on in the country house and I have my own flat to be "close to the office," and no one has to talk about anything disagreeable. When the children are home for vacation, I come to the house and then go "back to work." We've never been a happier family.'

'But what if one of you wants to remarry?'

'Avery,' he said patiently, 'that's all over with, isn't it? I'll always be married to Miri, I just don't want to have anything to do with her. I don't want to hear about what she thinks or what she does – I most certainly do not want to hear another word about her just causes. All that fundraising for this charity or that. I used to say to her, "Can't we eat just one meal in peace?" But,' he said, softening, 'she liked a good film, she really liked a good film, and so we spent a lot of time at the cinema; she was fantastic then, really clever, I could hear her brain whirring. She never, not ever, talked during a film.'

Owen smiled, now quite comfortable in his memories. 'Don't you see? I know her so well. The very things that used to annoy me to despair now delight me. There's nothing she does that surprises me – even when she's trying to catch me off guard. The very things that irritated the life out of me, now that I'm far away, amuse me, fill me with compassion, even affection. When I'm at the house, I look at her, I know her every gesture. It was the same with my father' – Uncle Jack, added Avery – 'if we went to a restaurant for dinner and there was a choice of potato – every time, every single time – when the waitress asked if he wanted boiled or mashed, roasted or fried, he would hesitate, take serious pause, as if he were really ruminating on the possibilities and, of course – every time, every single time – after a long, expectant silence, he'd say, "Mashed." As if there really was the possibility of him saying otherwise. For nearly twenty years this drove me mad. Now it is one of the fondest memories I have of him. And if you ask me,' said Owen, 'that is the greatest secret in life. That's what we're really saying when we're carping on about love. That's who he was, you see; that's who Miri is, you see? And it has nothing whatsoever to do with me!'

Owen was giggling, practically cackling with glee.

'When I think of how angry I used to be,' Owen continued, 'what a waste of time. And when Miri parts her lips to begin a harangue – against that bad taxi driver who offended her on the way to the shops two years before, or the bank teller or the woman in committee number one hundred and four – all the strangers who upset her so, and with whom she rarely crosses paths twice – when she begins to rant, now I feel flooded with love for her, real sympathy and affection, and I can shake my head and tsk-tsk and pat her hand to soothe her, knowing at last that's all she wants me to do – that's all she ever wanted me to do. Ah,' said Owen, giggling again, 'I'm so happy now!'

Then he scrutinized me. Avery leaned back and narrowed his eyes in imitation.

'It's just the same with you,' Owen said. 'All those years ago when we were students, whenever we met you looked at me so earnestly, so seriously, and you asked me how I was. It always unnerved me. Now I see that what you were really asking was not "how are you?" but "are you in love?" That's all you really wanted to know about, and you were right, it's the same question. Now I see it, I look into your eyes even now and I see you were right, twenty years later. And now, whenever I think of you that's what I'll remember and it will make me smile. That's all we need to do in this life – find the single feature in each friend, the one really essential quality and then love them for it. When my mother checked to make sure the door was locked, even after she'd already checked a dozen times, even when she was at last sitting in the front seat of the car, in her place in the passenger seat next to my indulgent father, still she always had to get out and check the door one more time – and it wasn't good enough to watch my father do it, she had to do it herself. How that set my teeth on edge, I'd wait in the backseat literally grinding my jaws together. But she'd grown up with nothing and now she had a nice house full of nice things – of course she would have to make sure the door was locked again and again. Who in their right mind would trust such luck? The important thing is not that she checked the lock, but that she was once so poor and she never, never forgot it. You'd have to have a heart of stone not to be moved by that. Think of all the anger I wasted on locks when I should've been thinking about poverty.

'But that's just the way it is with the truth, it's never in the same room with you, it's never in the backseat with you, it's never there when you need it. It always bobs up years later like a waterbird that dives in one part of the lake and pops up in another. You grab for the truth with both hands and it pops up behind you . . .

'And now I'm late. I'm meeting a woman at a restaurant in the country and it's at least an hour's drive.'

Owen got into his car and was about to pull away when I tapped on the window. 'How's Nina?'

'She's just the same,' said Owen. 'She cries for everything that doesn't have a home. And in spite of the fact she only has one good ear, she thinks she hears everything.' Owen nodded to himself, already considering the traffic.

'Yes,' said Owen, waiting for his chance to pull out, 'it's written on your face. When you ask someone how he is, what you're really asking is "are you in love?"'

––––––––

There were meetings now regarding the lighting and ventilation of the rebuilt temples, factors to be planned for in the construction of the concrete domes. The domes were to be cylindrical over the front of the Great Temple, gradually expanding into a sphere; no part of the dome could touch the temple, for fear that any pressure during the settling of the cliff would damage the fragile ceilings. Each dome would carry a cliff-load of one hundred thousand metric tonnes.

– My father and I, said Avery – sleepless with Jean in the night, the skin of her emerging belly dry and hot and smooth as clay – stood together in the Scottish rain, in our thick-soled boots; he saw the great achievement of engineering man where now I saw blunt, brute force and the submission of the river. This leaching of faith had been so gradual, I cannot tell you when it first started, but the moment shocked me. I loved and admired everything about my father, the solid sensual reality of him: his wet wool and his pipe-smoke smell, the bulk of him, his caps of canvas or tweed, his authority that, to this day, fills me with awe. And, deepest of all, although I hadn't the words for it when I was a child, what I came to understand was his complete engagement with all he saw – with every place he went and everyone he met. I watched him squatting down and digging into the earth, sitting at tables with businessmen or on the grass with children, soliciting the opinions of students, schoolteachers, farmers, mayors – and farm animals and birds! He had a curiosity about every living and inanimate thing, natural and man-made; in the great vales of Scotland, in the hill towns of Italy and India, in the marshes of Ethiopia and Ontario, at public rallies and alone in the desert, I saw he could find his way to belong anywhere. I watched him ruminating, sorting things out, as he observed various elements combine and recombine. He would unfurl maps across his knees, lay plans across camp tables, and I would watch as he altered the landscape with a stroke of his pencil, rerouting rivers and strangling waterfalls, bringing forests to the desert, and emptying entire lakes. Altering water tables millions of years old. And I wished I could snip the dams away like a stitch in a cloth, bring breath to the choked throat, bring all the water back with a single scrape of an eraser, bring back the houses, the graves, the gardens, the people. He would sit next to me and grab my arm with excitement. He brought me with him to the sites, to meetings in Quonset huts and expensive restaurants, to the first blasts of rock, to inauguration ceremonies.

My father looked at a bridge and he could hear it humming. He could hear the loom of forces, the warp and weft of stresses clattering in the span. It was instinctive, an intuition. But it's not that way for me, said Avery. I must work all the time. It's not in my skin. I'm like a pianist who must continually watch his hands. I have always wanted to feel what he felt. As a boy I craved to belong to him, to prove our bond. I felt I would always love him more than he loved me. I don't know why I felt this. He wanted me with him wherever he went; he wanted to show me everything, to teach me.

—You wanted him to be proud of you, said Jean. Perhaps you couldn't see how much he wanted you to feel proud of him.

— My father could really draw, he had such a brilliant hand. You could feel the structure inside the machine, feel how something worked. But when he tried to paint landscapes, my mother used to say she could feel the immense G.I. forces — gravity and inertia — but she also said there was something missing, something he could never capture — they weren't breathing somehow, is what she would say; there was no oxygen, no wind in his landscapes, as if they were under glass. He saw it too but couldn't ever seem to do anything about it. It's the same feeling one has looking at paintings of wild animals — somehow they never seem real, even when every detail is astonishingly precise — and well, that's because one could never be so close to such an animal in its own environment, we could never experience that kind of detail in reality. We feel their aliveness precisely because they are moving too fast or are too far away for us to take in those details. The convention has always irritated me – when I was young I was indignant about it – we could never be so close to a cougar, five paces away, in the wild; we could never paint it on its rocky crag from life. I used to yell on at my mother about it. As a portrait it was impossible because the relationship between the viewer and subject was impossible. A photo is possible, but not a painting. And well, though it seems I've strayed far from the point, somehow my father's painting always felt that way too – as if there was something not quite real about it, whereas my mother's paintings – well, they were too real.

Jean rolled off Avery and they sat together on the edge of the bed. She heard the trucks grinding up the hill.

– I was terrified to be in her studio alone, said Avery, yet I wanted to see. You can look at a few square inches of some of her forests for fifteen minutes and still not see everything that's there. It's hungry paint. A bottomless hunger. It was so distressing when I was small, to know that these images were made by my own mother, who otherwise was pragmatic and straightforward and so much fun – as if just to live – to walk around or do the washing or the cooking was a holiday . . . I could never put the two parts of her together. Only later when I began to learn the history did I truly understand this was not her nightmare alone, but the world's . . . and only then began to make sense of some things I'd heard about, and overheard, as a child . . . The first morning I was alone with my father, after the war, just my father and me, we sat in the hills and he talked for ages about abutments. Abutments! I loved the word, it was a liqueur, his liqueur – he was treating me like an adult, it was like having a first drink together, father and son. We sat in what had always seemed my private place, I had roamed those hills for hours, I had spent many, many afternoons alone watching the light moving across the landscape, the sun setting, in the rain, in the winter, and I knew every animal hollow in the grass. And now I was there with him, in that place, and I could show him everything and he could lie down on the ground and stretch out his legs with a great sigh and talk to his heart's content about abutments and Coade stone and pneumatic railways. It was bliss, that day. I was so excited to be with him, so shy of him, I wanted so badly for him to know me, and he looked so carefully at everything I showed him, took everything so seriously – the field mice, the clouds. It was a perfect afternoon. That was the first time I understood the war was really over. I thought it was going to be the beginning of many afternoons, but there never was another afternoon like that. That was the only one. We were in each other's company so much, and there were snatches of time alone together on his projects – a half-hour here or there, but never again an endless unfolding afternoon when I sensed he didn't want to be anywhere else but with me.

I want to feel what my father felt, Avery repeated, sitting on the edge of their bed on the Nile, what the *marmisti* know, what the blind man knows when he's on Ramses' knee. What my mother calls 'flesh-knowledge.' It's not enough for your mind to believe in something, your body must believe it too. If I hadn't witnessed this particular pleasure in my father when I was a child perhaps I wouldn't feel the lack of it. But I do. I can imagine what a chemist feels when he looks in a microscope, how his mind can practically touch what he sees. Or a physicist who can feel an equation tearing molecules apart along the shear, like tearing a handful of bread from a loaf. Or the tension in a meniscus. The closest understanding I have of this is when I look at a building. I feel the consequences of each choice; how the volume works, how the building eats the space it inhabits, even how it carries its ruins.

— I had a glimpse of what you're saying, said Jean, in Ashkeit.

At the mention of Ashkeit, Jean felt Avery surrender.

— I want to study architecture, said Avery. I feel like an apprentice who spends decades learning to draw a human arm or a hand before he is allowed to pick up a brush. You must learn to draw bones and muscle before the flesh can be real. The engineering is essential . . . But I want so much to pick up a brush.

My father was so pleased that I wanted to be an engineer, like his own father. It was as if it hadn't mattered that he'd been away all those years when I was a child.

— Well, said Jean slowly, you will still be an engineer . . . but an engineer with a brush.

Avery leaned back, his feet still on the floor. Jean saw the bones of his face, saw how his clothes pooled around him, saw the exhaustion that had penetrated him so deeply it was almost a smell. He held out his thin strong arm, muscle and tendon, and she lay down too, like him, across the bed.

She thought she would never be used to her luck, of lying beside him, this . . . scrupulous . . . broad-leafed . . . Avery-est Escher.

She heard the Bucyruses whining across the sand; a voice shouting in Greek, an answer, perhaps without understanding, in Italian. The whimpering voice of a child from a houseboat down the river: "*J'ai soif* . . ." The floodlights filtered down from the deck, a faint glow. The great desert factory never stopped.

— When he died, I sat looking into my father's face, said Avery. I held his hands. My mother lay with her face against his, and the side of him where she lay was warm. At first there was such a feeling of palpable peace in the room, a lightness so totally unexpected. And then, after a while, looking at his body that had not outwardly changed and yet was utterly changed, the simulacrum seemed to me blasphemous, a violation.

Avery looked at Jean. Her hair fell across her bare arms, a splash of shadow. At what moment had the transubstantiation occurred — at what moment during their years together had this woman, this Jean Shaw, become Jean Escher? He knew it had nothing to do with marriage, not even with sex, but somehow had to do with all this talking, this talking they achieved together.

— I want to build the room where I wish I'd been born, said Avery.

Jean felt the heat of Avery's arm beneath her back, a wire of heat.

— Perhaps it's not your father who hurts you so much, said Jean.

— My mother never wanted to let me into her workroom when I was a child, but sometimes I sneaked in — and I was always sorry afterwards. But it can't be my mother who's haunting me.

By the time Jean found a way to reply – the living haunt us in ways the dead cannot – the broad-leafed Avery Escher was asleep.

It was still cold and dark below deck, but Avery knew the men would already be talking around the fires and that he must soon get up. Jean, awake too, stretched beside him and drew the blanket up to her chin.

Avery leaned over her.

– Jean, what I said about sadness . . . what I mean is that a building and the space it possesses should help us be alive, it should allow for the heeding of things; I don't know even how to talk about it, what words to use; just that some places make certain things possible or even likely – not to go so far as to say a place can create behaviour, but it is complicit somehow. Is there a difference between making events possible and creating them? Does a certain kind of bridge create its suicides? I know that when I am in a great building I feel a mortal sadness, and it is so specific that when I leave the building – the church, the hall, the house – and walk back out into the street, I see everything around me with a clarity that only the experience of the building could bestow in me.

And what I said about building the room where I wished I'd been born, continued Avery, what I mean to say is that it would be a place to be reborn . . .

Jean reached for Avery's hand. She wondered where their child would be born: at the camp hospital in Abu Simbel, in the better-equipped hospital in Cairo, or in London, perhaps with Avery's Aunt Bett nearby. There was still time to decide, but perhaps London was best, perhaps Marina would come; for a moment she rested in the luxury of that possibility. But she knew that Avery would not want to be far from the temple, during the first months of the rebuilding.

Avery read the apprehension in Jean's face.

– Please don't worry, he began. And then, with a shock of panic: How will we manage.

———

After the evacuation of Wadi Halfa, the engineers turned to Aswan and to Khartoum for their supplies.

Jean and Avery flew back to the camp from Khartoum, following the Nile, its banks tarnished green where the silver river had overflowed.

At the village of Karina, the bright colour abruptly ended and, past the town, as if human history had stopped too, the eternal yellow sandstone of the Nubian Desert. They droned on in the clear air, no movement below except for the shadow of the plane and the ghostly circle of the propeller. The pilot turned slightly so Jean and Avery could look back. The floodplain spread behind them, long and green and generous. They headed farther into the desert known by the Nubians as intimately as their own bodies, and the bodies of their children.

Each time Jean had come to Wadi Halfa, she and Avery had disembarked at the aerodrome and followed the white, coarse sand road to the Nile Hotel. Past the brown hills, stony cliffs wedged with sand, blown by the winter wind for thousands of kilometres, thousands of years. The balcony of their hotel room had overlooked the railyards and they'd felt at home instantly in the incessant noise of the metalworkers.

But now they did not land, instead circled above, and saw that the town was as still as the surrounding hills. Their shadow fell on the houses, mottled the abandoned streets. So empty and so still was Wadi Halfa that Jean began to feel the city was not real.

Then, suddenly, the stones in the street seemed to jump, the sidewalk began to move, to slide back and forth, the brown ground erupted, bubbled, seethed, rock and sand burst to life.

— What is it? cried Jean. What is it?

The ground was moving so quickly it made her almost sick to look down.

— They must be starving, shouted the pilot. And now they'll be left there. The water will come and they'll drown.

He began to laugh, an awful, amazed, bitter sound.

Jean looked at him, frightened.

— Who? shouted Jean. Who will drown?

— It's dogs! he said.

Jean stared down at the seething ground.

— Just dogs! the pilot shouted.

There was a young boy in the camp; he did not belong to anyone. He earned the nickname of Monkey – the name was born of irritation and affection. He was everywhere, darting, hanging upside down, fingering tools and rope. The engineers had no patience for him, and the labourers swatted him aside. He jumped, dangled, squatted. The cook fed him so he would not pilfer.

Jean first saw the boy when she was in the camp store. He was hiding under a table, out of the sun. There was something wrong with him, with his bones. His back was twisted. But he was agile and graceful and he had a live, expressive face. The hair on the back of his arms and neck had a fine nap, the skin of a peach. His teeth were too large, a mouth full of stones.

From the moment she first saw him, Jean wanted to give him something.

– We do not like to think about children's fears, Marina had said one afternoon in the weeks alone with Jean. We push them aside to concentrate on their innocence. But children are close to grief, they are closer to grief than we are. They feel it, undiluted, and then gradually they grow away from that flesh-knowledge. They know all about the terror of the woods, the witch-mother, things buried and not seen again. In every child's fear is always the fear of the worst thing, the loss of the person they love most.

I come from a country where men begged not for their lives but not to be murdered in front of their children. Where people, ordinary in every way, learned what it is to look into the face of a man who knows he is going to take your life from you. Where people were afraid to close their eyes and also afraid to open them again. Of course this was true in many other places in the world. Afterwards, in Canada, a colleague of William said to me: you must paint these things. And I said no, I do not want to give them soil, another place to take root.

Even in horror, there are degrees. And that is where the details matter most, because degrees are the only hope. And that's what keeps a man alive until the last second. Knowing that if he's lost one leg, at least it's not two. Or lost all his fingers, at least not his arm. To live a moment longer. That's often what belief is – the very last resort.

After the war, I painted for children who saw nothing but terror in whatever I painted, no matter how innocent the scene. Once a child has known this, he cannot see any place, not a room, without terror in it. Even if it can't be seen, he sees it; he knows it is hidden. Now I paint for children who have not known this; I try to paint beautiful things, to arm them with images in case they'll need them. So that some of this beauty perhaps might become a memory, even if it is only a picture in a book. So that even if that child grows up to be the killer, he might suddenly recognize something in himself when another man begs to be taken outside so he won't be killed in front of his family.

I have so few seconds to capture a child's attention. I will not waste the chance.

Jean had been sitting still, listening, looking down at her lap.

—We make cuttings, said Jean. I think that is what we do. It is cuttings we take with us.

At the market in Wadi Halfa, Jean had found a wooden box — once, it had contained three cakes of Yardley soap — that now held an assortment of humble treasures that could only have belonged to a child: glass marbles, an acorn, a feather, a length of twine with a bead knotted at one end, a silver belt buckle, a penknife, some polished stones, playing cards, a key. It hurt her to hold it, the ghost of the child still owned it. But she could not bear to leave the little box of possessions behind in the rubble of the market, so she bought it.

Back in the camp, she took to carrying it with her, in case she saw Monkey.

Pah! said the boy and knocked the contents into the sand. He stood looking at her and made it clear he would certainly never stoop in front of her to retrieve them. One of the Egyptian engineers who had seen the little scene unfold came over to the boy and took him by the shoulder, but Monkey was strong and squirmed from under the man's hand and ran off. The man bent down. Jean would not let him kneel for her and she fell to the sand herself and gathered up the pitiful treasure.

— He's wild. He should be punished for his rudeness.

— No, please, said Jean. I didn't mean to offend him. I should have known such things would not interest a boy his age. It is my mistake.

– The boy acts too free. If he were my son – But my son would never behave in such a way.

Jean held the box out to him.

– Perhaps your son would like these little things.

The man laughed uproariously.

– My son is thirty years old!

And Jean, ruefully, laughed too.

———————

A child is like a fate; one's future and one's past. All the stories Jean told the child inside her as they walked by the river under the depthless sky . . . and the child took in nothing but the sweet sound of her mother's voice, a world entire. There was nothing Jean did not speak of those first months of pregnancy. She told her about Canadian snow and Canadian apples, about Egyptian boats, about techniques of grafting, topiary, and espalier. She told the child of her first weeks with Avery, and of Avery's excursions with his father, about the Newcomen atmospheric engine, "Fairbottom Bobs," that Avery as a boy visited near Ashton-under-Lyne and the River Medlock. The baby learned how Jean's mother made animal shapes in the soapy water of Jean's bath, and about Jean's father, who read to her *Milly-Molly-Mandy* and *Mrs. Easter* on the train. Everything was described, with wonder and longing, to the child inside her. The breeze from the river was different from the wind that came across the desert and they met in the potent space of the riverbank. Jean listened for the sound of boats crossing the water in the darkness; never a light, the sailors navigated by sound. Jean sat in the darkness, also without a light, and listened; the whisper of hulls, the weight of the baby, the map of stars.

She lay awake. Her fullness now pressed down on her spine. A mound of earth. She heard Avery on deck and in a moment he stood at the cabin door. Slowly he unlaced his boots and dropped them in the passageway. The sound held all his weariness.

He hesitated by the bed, calculating whether he had the energy to take off his shirt. He left it on.

Almost the moment he lay down, he was asleep. In his face Jean saw not just exhaustion, but despair. She took the pencil from his shirt pocket.

Jean woke with Avery and, after he left for the engineers' hut, sat alone on deck, still half asleep, watching the sun hesitate before breaking over the edge of the hill, the quivering before the river turned blindingly bright. For only a few moments each dawn the pomegranate sky was splayed open with its mesh of seeds still visible, the stars.

She heard a small splash. Something, some knowledge that fear gives us, suddenly made her look up and a little farther downstream. She saw the glow of his white clothing first, a dome of swollen cloth in the dark water. She ran toward it and then saw the undulating edges of soaked hair floating, and she grabbed at him, pulling his shirt, then finding his arms and pulling with all her strength. She was screaming; she heard herself screeching almost apart from herself, as if a terror she had always carried in her, unknowing, had at last come to its moment. She pulled until his dark head came out of the water, she could see it in her mind, could see herself pulling him out and pressing his belly until the water spurted from his lungs, she could see him opening his eyes as she pulled with all the animal power in her. Finally there were voices far away. She kept pulling, but the boy was weirdly heavy, as if someone were holding his feet and pulling him back into the water. She felt the strength suddenly go out of her arms and, weeping, she saw the child's head sink below the surface. So heavy. His lips over his teeth as if he had a mouthful of stones. Then the voices were right behind her and their arms plunged into the water and Monkey was pulled out of the river, long dead.

In the dream, it was clear that the boy had died even before he was in the water. And that Jean had been trying to save his corpse.

But what she also saw in the dream – the vision of his head rising from the water and of herself pulling him onto the bank – and the water pouring from his mouth and his eyes opening – this image was so vivid her mind could not put it away.

A few days later, Monkey was found at the bottom of the quarry. He had been goading fate for many weeks, swinging from a blondin across the chasm. Only after the grave was dug did they realize that no one knew his name.

Avery and Jean sat on the deck in lamplight, wrapped in blankets, reading – a bond of such stillness between them that Daub almost walked away without stopping to impart the news of Monkey's death. He stayed only a few moments, and afterwards, Jean pulled her chair close to Avery's, facing him.

– The boy died in my dream, whispered Jean.

Avery looked up from his work and saw her face.

– It's not your fault!

Jean stood up, a strange look in her eyes.

– Because you dreamed it, repeated Avery, does not make it your fault.

– Then what is prescience for.

Avery had no answer to this. He gathered her toward him.

– It's not my fault, but maybe I could have prevented it. Maybe both things are true.

Jean's logic hovered in the lamplight, and remained in the darkness as she lay in bed, and was still there the next morning and the next; many days afterwards, her first thought upon waking: maybe both things are true.

———

– It is not the heat, the doctor in the camp told Jean several days later. Sometimes, something goes wrong and the baby is not meant to be born. That is all.

Some mothers say they feel the exact moment the child stops living. Some sense something wrong, or dream of death without knowing why; others notice only later, when the movement stops – although even this is only a feeling, for when the baby is this large, it no longer has room anyway to move in the womb.

There is no safe way to induce the birth. It is best to let the body make its own decision, though this is a danger if labour waits too long. You may have to carry the still-baby for some weeks, perhaps even as long as a month.

Avery put his hand on her taut skin where he had felt movement for so many weeks and now felt nothing.

– Sometimes, the doctor said, it is simply not meant to be.

Avery could not help himself thinking: All the water inside her and our child dead.

– It is time to go to Cairo, the doctor said.

———

The young Nubian woman who had offered to bless the child in the Nile dipped palm leaves in river water and wrapped the cool greenness over Jean's distended belly. The leaves drew the heat from her skin. Again and again the woman did this for her, until Jean fell asleep.

No need of a translator between the two women now.

Jean understood that she must leave; await her time at the hospital in Cairo. But instead, for days, she remained in the darkness of the houseboat. And Avery, though anxious and afraid, could not deny her this right.

She did not know how to grieve; she could not separate the baby's body from her own. What had been a vulnerable ripeness, her shape, she now felt as deformity. The earth-weight, now a child cast in stone.

She remembered a middle-aged woman from her neighbourhood in Montreal who walked everywhere backwards, her elderly mother always beside her, watching out for her. The resigned love in the mother's face as she looked eternally into the damaged face of her daughter. When Jean was a girl, this sight had frightened her. Now, twenty years later, a welt of pity rose in her heart.

She sat in the dark cabin and could not make out the difference between soul and ghost.

She remembered the young girl from Faras, on the train travelling on forever without her mother's satchel.

For hours working on deck, Avery heard nothing beneath him. But when he went below, he found it had not been the silence of sleep, but of a disappearance. Jean sitting up in bed, staring into the dark; a vigil. When he tried to come near, he felt it, her invisible shrivelling from touch. As if she had spoken aloud: My body is a grave.

The pilot stood some way off, waiting.

— Are you sure you must go alone? asked Avery.

—Yes, said Jean. Her face was stony, the tears leaking out. We don't know how long we'll have to wait.

He moved toward her.

— If you come close, she said, I won't be able to go.

A moment passes; with all its possibilities. All that love allows us, and does not allow.

Avery ached when he saw the pilot's hand touching her arm, helping her board the plane.

No one knows what triggers labour. Finally, simply, the wild hormones are released.

Clutching the hands of a stranger — a nurse she'd never met and would never see again — suddenly Jean did not believe the child was dead. She rushed toward the pain, each contraction proof that the child was struggling to be born. Within the pain Jean felt an unbearable purpose, almost an ecstasy. But the baby would not come out. All through the labour, Jean would not give up this new knowledge, the feeling that the child was alive. She felt the presence of a soul returned to her, overwhelming, feasting on the oxygen in her blood. Hour after hour she focused her belief directly into the pain — an animal force of will. She wept with gratitude and joy. And then an almost preternatural, shivering attention, a kind of praying. The child's presence filled the room, she could feel the certainty of the child's heart beating into her own blood.

The next morning, they opened her. The scalpel made a red seam beneath her belly, and they squeezed the dead child out.

Now the nurses swaddled the child, a daughter, as if she were alive, in sweet-smelling cotton blankets, and waited for Avery's arrival. Jean held the sunken head against her own face, she clutched the now weightless baby and would not let go; the embrace that no nurse or midwife dared to tear apart. With infinite tenderness, Jean cradled the perfect cheeks that death had pressed with its thumbs.

The nurses would not forcibly take the baby from her. They stood by – the nurses, Avery – in the face of Jean's suffering. They could not spare her; for different reasons, they could not fully share it. There was a hair, a thread of terror in their empathy.

The nurses came and went, impatient to take the child away. The room grew dark; they came in to turn on the light, still waiting.

Avery sat in a chair next to the bed. When at last Jean fell asleep, he took their daughter from her arms.

The moment Jean woke, she called desperately for a nurse to bring back her child, the child who had died twice. Then she saw the guilt, the wretchedness, the betrayal, in Avery's face.

Afterwards, Jean could not take care of herself; she remained in the hospital, so listless she could not brush her teeth. Her milk came in. Her breasts went hard. The baby was sent to Montreal, where Marina received her, burying her grand-daughter, Elisabeth Willa Escher, near Jean's parents, in the graveyard at St. Jerome. Jean was no longer in the ward with expectant mothers bulging with life. Now she was in a room with women waiting, at various distances from death; heart disease, kidney failure. In Cairo, the heat pounded against the windows of the crowded hospital ward. In Montreal, the dark, cold, spring rain. Marina wrote and asked if she could come. No, answered Jean, don't come.

For months after birth, a child remains in the mother's body; moon and tide. Before the child cries, the mother flashes wet with milk. Before the child wakes and cries out in the night, the mother wakes. Deep in the child's cranial vault, the mother's gaze knits up the dangling synapses.

And when the child is spirit, it is exactly the same.

———

For several days Jean had noticed an old man sitting on the steps as she came back from her slow walk around the hospital garden. Then, one day, she did not look away quickly enough to avoid his gaze.

— You're walking a little better today, he said. Please sit with me and rest for a few minutes.

Jean hesitated. Then she sat down on the step below him.

— No, here, beside me.

Jean sat beside him. They leaned over their knees to their feet, as one leans over a railing to look down into an abyss.

— I know about your child, he said. I asked about you and the nurse told me. But now I am speaking of that young boy, that Monkey. I couldn't help but overhear you, with your husband. I didn't mean to listen, but people always talk freely next to me, even though the old have the greatest need for eavesdropping.

Jean could feel the tremble in the old man's arms and shoulders as he sat beside her.

— Let us imagine you are right, he continued, and his life was somehow in your hands. You were sent to him and this was your purpose in coming to this country. Perhaps your whole life, every choice, was meant to lead you to the very moment of meeting the boy in order to save him. But, if that were so, do you think that after so many years of living in preparation, your destiny would have failed you, or that you would have failed your destiny? And of your own child? Perhaps what you live now is still your destiny. And you do not know the meaning yet.

— I did fail, said Jean. I feel it inside, in the very core of me. She began to weep.

The old man continued to look down at his feet.

— Emptiness is not failure, he said. His voice was so paternal, Jean could not subdue her tears.

Very gently, he said, you feel you have been punished for his death. You must decide: were you punished for your fear or for your faith?

He looked at Jean.

— I was punished once, for my fear, he said, and it destroyed me.

He leaned forward, frail and unsteady, on his stick. But she didn't see frailty, she saw obstinate strength; almost courage.

— You don't seem destroyed, said Jean at last.

— Some banishment is so deep, it seems like calm.

Jean felt pain in the core of her, as if he had laid his hand on her belly.

— I was born in Cologne, said the old man wearily. I came to Palestine in 1946. My father was a British soldier who served in India before I was born. My parents met in Zurich. I can say a prayer for the dead in English, German, French, Gujarat, Arabic, Palestinian, Turkish, Japanese, and Chinois.

— Chinese?

The old man looked startled.

— Yes, he said, but that's a different story. Please do not ask me to speak of it. That joy is the only secret I have left. And if I see something in the telling that I didn't see before? No, thank you very much.

— Don't be angry, said Jean. I misspoke. I'm sorry.

— I'm not angry. I've been thinking about what to say to you since I first saw you here. In fact, I've been thinking about it for fifty years.

In your misery you confuse fate with destiny. Fate is dead, it's death. Destiny is liquid, alive like a bird. There are consequences and there is mystery; and sometimes they look the same. All your self-knowledge won't bring you any peace. Seek something else. One can never forgive oneself anyway — it takes another person to forgive, and for that you could wait forever.

The old man rose unsteadily to his feet. For the first time, Jean realized that his back was bent; when he stood, he was still looking at the ground. She felt shame; sympathy.

— Thank you, said Jean.

— It's impolite to thank an old man for his sadness.

— I'm sorry! she cried. That isn't what I meant.

The old man nodded to the earth.

———————

Jean returned to the camp. She was pitied from afar. It seemed to Avery that he could not think, could not draw her close, without hurting her. She is below sea level, Daub had counselled, you must try. But Avery felt she could not bear even the weight of his gaze.

As the Great Temple was removed and the cliff face was emptied to a ragged chasm, in an almost symbolically inverse ratio, Jean's belly had grown. Avery was haunted, the desert was haunted, by the emptiness of the villages, by their destruction, by impotence and mourning, by the lie of the replication. And yet, all the while, the beautiful dome of Jean's flesh had somehow been a sign of possible redemption: all the Nubian children to be born. It was not rational, any more than Jean conflating her dream with Monkey's death, or Jean's mother's feeling she had abandoned her pilot brother when she left behind the night sky on Clarendon Avenue. He knew such thoughts were a need to bring order to tragedy, and that one must admit oneself such a need. But he also knew that his moral grief, his self-searching was nothing, utterly without meaning in the face of a daughter lost, a country lost. Yet, he could not prevent himself: when their child died, Avery felt Jean's suffering, and his own, in the ache of the cliff, in the silent villages, in

the new settlement of Khashm el Girba, in the heinous consolation of the rebuilt temples.

———

Hassan Dafalla arrived at Khashm el Girba for the first time
after the inundation and looked around for a place to sit. But
there was no shade. He and the settlers from Faras stood
together miserably, each overcome by his own regret.

Then a man spoke, as if giving voice to all: A nation is a
sense of space you will never walk with your own feet yet
know in your legs as belonging to you. Its heat is your heat,
its smells and sounds are yours – of water gushing through
a metal pipe, or flowing from the clay bowls of the *sagiya*,
dripping from the wet ropes, the dates warm in the basket on
your head. The sound of the felucca's hull passing close by in
the darkness, sailing always without lights through the long
room of the night river. You recognize your neighbour's voice
before you have opened your eyes, the voice of his young son,
almost a man, calling to his friend who is also on his way to
bring in the lentils and the barley. The shifting seeds as your
wife scoops her bowl into the sack, then straightens her arm
to cast them into the air, into the earth. The sound of the lentils
hitting the bottom of the pot. The wind through the small high
windows at night. But mostly it is the river that is in your limbs
as if you will live forever, as long as the Nile flows.

And so, who am I in Khashm el Girba? What is my body
but a memory to me? To come here is like growing old in
an instant, not to know your own body except as what it once

was. It was sudden like that, it was a madness, still to feel the hills, the sand, the river, even in sight of the ugly Atbara! You breathe different air, you smell different to yourself, and your wife smells different and your children. And the only time they feel truly familiar is when they're asleep, dreaming of home. Then I can smell the river in them.

I wish my son could see me, but he is in a stiff white shirt in London, a place I have never been. I remember his face with the hills behind, and I wonder what it would be like to see his face with London behind. When my son comes to bury me, I will be lying in a strange place; and my own father and mother will be under the waves.

I used to say to my wife: As long as you are in my arms, you are safe. But she is not safe now and my children are not safe.

———

Jean and Avery climbed the hill. Ramses was awash with light. Avery knew every square centimetre of the king's body by number – the storage code of each fingernail, each boulder of a knee, his nostrils and ears.

The illusion was immaculate. The sight before them was so immense and unequivocal that Jean almost staggered. The thin line across her own belly, the scar that was already turning white and disappearing into her flesh – thin as the line that had been sawn across Ramses' chest – this, she felt, was the lie, something inexplicable, distastefully personal. And instead, the gargantuan temple before their eyes – with all the lines of the saw now invisible – was irrefutable proof that the events of her body, and all of Nubia, had not happened. That the temple's purpose now had become this forgetting.

———

The expanse of desert that would soon become Lake Nasser lay emptied. In an area of more than three hundred kilometres, only one man remained, in Argin, in his thatched hut, and one family in Dibeira. They would stay until their houses were flooded. They did not know what would become of them, but the one place they vowed they would never live was the "New Halfa" of Khashm el Girba.

A few weeks after the Nubian villages were evacuated, a sandstorm struck the new settlement. It blew the roofs off Village #22 (the new Degeim) and the metal sheets and trusses flew as in a hurricane. A great number of the livestock, which had been so carefully transported, died in the sandstorm. The roofs and trusses had not been properly attached. The walls of the houses had not been anchored deeply enough in the ground.

And then, in a bitter irony, two months after the sandstorm, there was a lightning storm of such proportion that the whole resettlement of Khashm el Girba was submerged in water.

———

Hassan Dafalla waited. At last, just past 1 a.m., the Nile began to overflow in the harbour of Wadi Halfa. He watched as the railway station slipped away.

The water climbed the walls of the hospital, it flooded the houses at Tawfikia and Abbasia, then sped toward the Nile Hotel filling its bedrooms with its last guests — reptiles and scorpions. The gardens that had been withering for lack of water suddenly gleamed with lushness and vibrancy, only to die a day later of drowning.

The day before, Hassan Dafalla had posted a letter from Wadi Halfa, the last letter to bear the postmark of the town. On the last night he slept with his bedding trailing on the floor, so that if the water reached his room, his wet sheet would wake him. He saw the mosque crack open and watched the shops and mud houses "melt like biscuits." As he walked through the town recording all he could with his Rolleiflex, he saw rats fleeing with their babies in their teeth and, from all sides, he heard "the dismal roar" of collapsing buildings. He saw his own house split up the middle and crumble. Hassan Dafalla, the last man in Wadi Halfa, took his bags to the airport, but he could not keep away from the town as long as there was anything left to be seen and to record. It was necessary to chain his dog to a pole at the airport, fearing it might "return to the house, which was expected to collapse at any time. As a matter of fact, when the dog was tied up, I felt I needed a chain too."

When at last Hassan Dafalla departed Wadi Halfa, the only signpost to remain of the town was the tip of the minaret, floating like a stone buoy.

In the newly built towns of Ingleside and Long Sault, the inhabitants whose houses had been moved continued to wake and dress and eat each day; and although an observer would have said that everything about these houses was exactly the same, those who lived there – distressed, sleepless – knew that it was not. At first, one could not discern the cause; it was simply a feeling. Someone described it as the sensation of being watched, another as if the pages of one's mind were stuck together – that there was another, very different image beneath what was visible that one couldn't reach and, although the thumbnail of one's mind picked repeatedly at the sides of the thin page, it never separated. Another believed it was simply that the light was different, it did not fall across the table or across a book or through the curtains in the same way. Or maybe it was a trick of the wind, an unfamiliar breeze across one's face. Some felt it in the church that had been moved, stone by stone and, after the Sunday sermon, walking in the little graveyard, though in this case it was the feeling not of being watched, but instead the opposite, that no one was watching now, an abandonment. There was a feeling that the new towns were the ones that were "lost" and not the ones that had been left behind to be dismembered, burned, drowned. That postcards of "the lost villages" should depict instead the gleaming new subdivisions. It was an intuition, like that possessed by war pilots and navigators on the bombers, who had lost most of their hearing and yet could still, as veterans on the ground, feel the presence of a plane long before it could be seen. Some said it was like the difference between a man and his corpse, for what is a corpse if not an almost perfect replica.

Builders know that there is a grain in wood and a grain in stone; but there is also a grain in flesh.

———

Eighteen months after Avery's work on the salvage had begun, Ramses' face, with his one-metre-wide lips, was sliced just before his ears. He then suffered the indignity of a workman injecting him with a nasal spray of polyvinyl acetate. His visage, Block #120, held by the steel rods that had been inserted in the top of his head, was slowly winched into the sky.

Standing next to Avery, Jean could feel the heat radiating from his body and suddenly his shirt flashed into wetness only to dry instantly in the overpowering sun. Avery felt even the inside of his mouth was unbearably hot, felt even his teeth were sweating.

All work ceased as the huge head of Ramses slowly ascended on wires invisible in the sunlight. As thirty tonnes of stone seemed to ascend, hover, float in the air, the entire camp, three thousand men, stood silent and watched.

———

Avery finished writing in his shadow-book, just as his father had taught him, the personal record to be kept alongside the one maintained for his employer; their last night at Abu Simbel.

Every action has a cause and a consequence . . .

I do not believe home is where we're born, or the place we grew up, not a birthright or an inheritance, not a name, or blood or country. It is not even the soft part that hurts when touched, that defines our loneliness the way a bowl defines water. It will not be located in a smell or a taste or a talisman or a word . . .

Home is our first real mistake. It is the one error that changes everything, the one lesson you could let destroy you. It is from this moment that we begin to build our home in the world. It is this place that we furnish with smell, taste, a talisman, a name.

II

———

The Stone in the Middle

The Stone in the Middle

W hen Gregor Mendel — the monk who grew pea plants and became the father of genetics — was twenty-two years old, he was sent to study at the university in Vienna. Perhaps in the early mornings or in the long summer twilight, as he walked along the Danube, he first considered the succession and end of generations. Perhaps he sought consolation for his aloneness by sitting with the ghosts of the river-dead, whose bodies were interred in a small graveyard on the banks. Perhaps he felt it was a cruel choice of resting place for those who'd drowned, to be laid to rest within the sound of the river; those whose last wish — perhaps the last wish even of the suicides — was for the maternal embrace of land. So close were the graves to the river that again and again over the years, the rising water threatened the dead until finally the little cemetery was moved to a field behind the new dam, where there would be no danger of flooding. A small chapel was built and hedges planted. In the site of the old cemetery — where perhaps Gregor Mendel first contemplated the mechanisms of heredity — a small grove grew up among the nameless dead who were left behind. Today no one picnics in the thought-full grove nor in the grass of regret on that side of the river. Although there is no sign to indicate the site was once a cemetery, perhaps something in the light seems to forbid such pleasures. But if one wishes to visit the dead, one simply takes Tram 71 to the end of the line at Kaiser Ebersdorferstrasse. From there one must walk. It is not very far.

Jean stood at the gate of her mother's garden, flourishing now in the farmer's soil of Marina's marsh. The dahlias and peonies sagged with shaggy, weary fullness, drunken with heat and sunshine. Marina had taken care of everything; in Jean's absence, a young man had been hired to prune and tie and turn and tend; her tools had been respected, returned to hang on the wall of the shed in careful rows, their blades and prongs wiped clean.

Jean opened the gate. She wanted nothing more than to dig, to blacken her hands. She asked herself what it meant, this desire; it was not to lay claim, she was sure. Perhaps a way to offer herself, as one stands before another, asking to understand. The soil was wet and cold.

From the back porch of the house, Avery watched Jean kneel – the bend of her back, her skirt stretched across her thighs, her hair piled loosely on top of her head, so the breeze would reach the sweat of her nape and shoulders. He saw how differently she moved now, as if she were used to stooping from fatigue, from futility; this new body, of which he had no knowledge. The loss he felt was so sharp he turned quickly and went back inside. Marina was working; her door was shut, the house was quiet. Avery sat with his bare feet cool on the tiled kitchen floor and closed his eyes.

What was needed was a mechanical advantage, he thought, block and tackle. He must become the fixed pulley.

He remembered the months he'd spent in Quebec, how Jean had repacked his rucksack after their weekends together, sneaking in letters for the weeks they would be apart, each to be opened at an appointed hour: poems, stories, photographs. It was a way to domesticate their desire in their apartness, to provide another tributary for that desire. He had believed then, opening those letters – *after dinner, at 3 p.m. on Sunday, just before sleep* – that somehow he and Jean possessed between them, unearned, and made possible only by the other, an aptitude, a calibration for happiness.

Now he would be as one who had witnessed a miracle and would not let himself forget; as a believer who clings to signs and portents; he would refuse doubt. He felt that his father would have understood. For William had taught him the commerce of invisible forces, ions in league across enormous distances and densities. He would continue to desire, to believe, until, as when suddenly one senses someone's gaze across a room, Jean looked up. He sat, in the misery of this resolve.

Jean turned to look back across the field and saw the empty porch and the shaded windows, closed against the heat. She could not explain how native her defeat, her desolation, as if all the years of happiness with him had somehow been only a reprieve, not meant to be hers. His pity: one kind of love unintentionally mocking another. She would work until her hands ached, until the low, intense glow of twilight spread across the garden. She longed for the first clarity of autumn, wondering if the cold could cleanse her. But she knew it could not. She had squandered all the time the child had been alive inside her; she had been beseeching the dead; her ache for her mother; her mother's, for her.

————————

From the window of her studio, Marina watched Avery and Jean, two slight figures slowly crossing the marsh. She saw the distance between them. Avery's loose shirt flapped emptily behind him in the wind.

Since their return, Jean had slept in the little room she'd once shared with Avery, and Avery on the pullout bed in Marina's studio. He felt faint satisfaction to see this bed, the evidence of his separation from Jean, disappear each morning into the sofa, as if all might so easily be restored.

Avery and Jean stood a little apart, always now there seemed space for another between them. Rows of bright lettuce stuttered above the black earth. The marsh was bordered by rain-soaked trees. They had been out of the desert for almost a month and still the smell of wet earth was sharp and strange.

Jean could barely speak.

— Are you saying you want your freedom?

— I'm saying we should both feel free, Avery said, until we know what to do.

In this perversity, he felt certain, was a kind of truth, an integrity at least. As soon as he spoke, he knew it was so. He did not know how to restore her, he was incapable. Jean's despair was as true as everything else about her. He knew one thing with certainty: nothing would heal this way, in this orbit of defeat, this brokenness.

She was so thin now, the only pouches of flesh left of her were her breasts, her sex. The sight of her moved him to the core.

Jean was thinking hard. At last she said:

— I see. Going back to school will be difficult, you've waited for this a long time, you'll need to work without distraction . . .

Marina was washing peaches in the sink, the window wide open to the night.

— Jean loves you, she said.

Marina waited, but there was no answer. She turned around and saw Avery, with his soup spoon halfway to his mouth.

Standing behind his chair, she held him. Not one mother-cell forgets the feeling, her child crying.

Marina sat down next to him, crossed her arms on the table, and lay her head there, waiting for him to speak.

———————

The flat on Clarendon was empty, the subleasers gone, and that is where Jean went. The return to Clarendon was terrible. She brought a suitcase of clothes, a box of books, a table and two chairs, a mattress for the floor. Everything else was left at Marina's house on the marsh.

Avery found a basement flat near the School of Architecture, where he was now enrolled, a graduate student. The first night on Mansfield Avenue, he sat at his table, incoherent with the risk he was taking, setting her free. He remembered a story Jean had told him of her parents, one of the first stories she'd told during their night in the cabin by the Long Sault. Elisabeth Shaw had come home late from grocery shopping. Looking flushed and guilty, she'd confessed to her husband that she'd been standing in Britnell's Bookshop in her heavy tweed coat and woollen hat for nearly an hour reading Pablo Neruda. She had no money to buy the book so she went down the street to a jeweller's and sold the bracelet she was wearing. She begged John, "Don't be angry." "Angry!" he said. "I can't tell you what it means to me that I've married a woman who'd sell her jewellery to buy poetry." Avery thought about what his own mother had said that very morning, standing at the back door as he'd left her house, "Grief bakes in us, it bakes until one day the blade pushes in and comes out clean."

It was almost midnight when he telephoned Jean. They lay together with the few city blocks between them, his voice in her ear. He talked about what he would learn: the meaning of space, the consequences of weight and volume. Then he hung up and remembered her. He had not said what he wanted: send me a signal across the river, by lantern light or

bird call, come under cover of darkness, I will know you by
your smell, come with the rain . . .

Jean did not understand what her botany meant to her now,
nor what to do with it. At Marina's suggestion, she enrolled
in the university part-time. Many days, instead of going to
her classes, she drove to the marsh to work in her mother's
transplanted garden. Then she would cook for Marina while
Marina worked. She would set out on the table thick square
loaves of bread, round cheeses, vegetables pulled from the
black fields. But she herself had no appetite. Marina did not
ask questions. Instead she talked to Jean about Avery: "He's so
much older than the other students. He keeps to himself.
Except for Avery and the professor, everyone else was born
on the other side of the war, and those few years have made
another species of them . . . Sometimes, Avery says, he looks
to the professor for brotherhood, but the man looks away,
ignores him completely, too busy himself trying to squeeze
into that lifeboat of youth. He says he feels alien, as if his
English were a second language . . ."

As Marina spoke, Jean could feel Avery, his concentration,
his earnestness, his self-restraint.

Marina told stories of Avery's childhood, about her life
during the war living with William's sister and the cousins,
the seclusion with William gone; and she talked about her
work, painting all night, with a magnifying glass, the woven
fabric of a child's winter coat against the bark of a tree, as if

it were the most important thing to make this imaginary child a proper coat.

Jean always drove back to the city just before dark. The windows of the houses on Clarendon were filled with early lamplight. Dusk was chill, no longer pale; the beginning of a deep autumn blue. If the lobby was empty when she came home, she stood and looked at the ceiling. The constellations continued to float, a golden net, in their zodiacal sea. Afterwards, she lay on her mattress on the floor, watching the shapes of the trees in the window. She imagined Carl Schaefer, painting the stars with the door to the courtyard open to the keenness of the autumn night; and her mother, twenty years old and newly married, coming home under those stars, in her long red coat with the black buttons that Jean remembered from her childhood. She thought about her father. "I adored your mother, I adored her." She imagined Avery, reading on Mansfield Avenue, his mechanical pencil dangling from his hand; and Marina taking her night walk on the marsh, trying to see in the dark.

Who was the last person to hold our child? Jean sobbed instead of driving six hours to the cemetery north of Montreal to find and to look upon — she did not even know whether in order to thank or to excoriate — the one who had dug the hole.

Avery, having given up on sleep, fell into naps, in the early evening, in the hour or two before sunrise, between classes. At the moment of waking he instantly plunged his mind back into work . . . Every building makes space, and great buildings

make room for the contemplation of death . . . He remembered parting the blanket to look at his daughter entire, and
Jean's face when she woke in the hospital, seeing in him the
one thing for which her tongue could find no word . . . How
careful one must be with a roof – the enclosing principle –
the line between a man and the sky . . .

On the way home from the university one afternoon, Jean
came across a man, perhaps forty years old, well dressed in
a good suit and tie, asleep on the grass in a public garden. It
was startling to see someone so nicely dressed sprawled on
a lawn; had he been alone, she would have thought he'd been
struck down. But he lay next to an old woman who must
surely have been his mother. The woman, also neatly dressed
in a light coat, lay on her back, one arm across her eyes, in
the sunlight. The man lay curled beside her, his back to her,
as if they were in a bed. Jean could only glance, so intimate
was the scene. She did not know what detail made her
imagine the woman had emigrated, left her home in the last
years of her life to join her son, yet Jean felt certain it could
not be otherwise. They were together in this foreign place
and he would face the responsibility of burying her far from
everything she'd known. When Jean returned some days later
to that patch of grass between the two flowerbeds, she could
not look upon the spot where they had lain without feeling
it now belonged to them. It was then that she began to feel
a purpose; it was then that her plan first came to her. Very
early the following morning, she returned to the spot and

planted, quickly, a trespasser, in the existing beds, cuttings that would grow unnoticed except for their fragrance. If she had known their homeland, she could have planted with precision, flowers that would have reminded them of Greece, Lithuania, Ukraine, Italy, Sardinia, Malta . . . so that if they came back there to sleep on the grass, familiar scents would invade their dreams and give them an inexplicable ease. But she had not heard them speak and so had no idea from where they had come. So she planted wild sorrel, which grows in every temperate country, and which is both edible and medicinal.

At first, Jean planted in the ravines, then in laneways, along the edges of parking lots, places without obvious ownership, overlooked for years. Then she grew bolder, planting at night in the selvage between curbs and pavement, between pavement and front lawns; rims, crevices, along civic fencing.

She kept track in a notebook and sometimes returned to investigate the progress of her work. One might think this gave her pleasure. But after a night of planting, she was stunned with loneliness, as if she'd been tending graves.

———

It was not yet completely dark, but already even the streetlights above the thick trees revealed little. This was the dimness Marina painted with such knowledge, before the first real starlight, or even the shadow of the moon. Jean kneeled.

She felt the damp soil of the small city park staining her legs. There would never be a time now when the coldness of the ground, no matter how black and wet, would not remind her of the desert. She parted the soil with her trowel and, one by one, drew rough round bulbs from her bag and slipped them down after the metal blade. She worked steadily, her hands found their way. She felt her fingernails fill with earth. From a distance, her trowel, a flashlight tied to it, was a firefly bobbing erratically a few inches above the ground.

Jean dug, wishing she had acres to upturn with only a trowel; the meditation of lifting the earth one scoopful at a time, submerged in thought, for hours moving toward an understanding that is at first merely visceral and then becomes conscious knowledge, as if only such physical action could bring the thought into words. She would sink her mind into an image, something she perceived in someone's face in the street, or something Avery had said, or a sentence read while standing in front of the bookshop shelves like her mother, with no money to buy the book so that later she had to finish the thought, sometimes even the whole story, in her mind.

This night she was thinking about Avery's father, about dying slowly, in the kind of pain Nature metes out; and Avery's story of his father swimming in the cold lakes of Scotland and Northern Ontario. It was William Escher's ceremony and it never varied. He waded in slowly – ankles, knees, hips – all the while calling out to Avery, who waited on the shore: "I'm not going in! It's too cold, I'm not going in!" until he was up to his chin, still calling out, "I'm not going in!" and then plunging his head under water. Avery watched as the body-wake of his strong arms and legs led to the spot in the middle of the lake where his father's head would reappear, shouting, "I'm not going in! It would be lunacy to swim in such cold water!" Jean thought about Avery's boy-body in the lake up to his knees, watching, shivering in his bathing trunks, while his father opened the lake with his arms. And she thought about Avery remembering that story in the hospital, sitting next to his father when all the tubes had been taken out. "I'm not going in, I'm not going in."

— What are you doing?

Jean jumped.

— Do I have to be afraid of you? the man said, pointing to her glowing trowel. Are you a madwoman? Don't you know this is public property?

Now Jean could see he was amused. He was large — tall and bulky. He was older than Jean, but she could not tell by how many years. He wore paint-smeared overalls and a tool-belt with paint brushes. A worker. From one hand dangled a lantern. Though it was now quite dark and the park was empty, Jean, strangely, did not feel afraid. There was paint in his hair, a swath where his hand had pushed it from his face.

When asked a direct question, Jean was usually forthright, a child.

— I'm . . . planting, she said.

The man took in this information.

— *Scilla siberica*, said Jean, less firmly.

The man saw that nothing further was forthcoming. He thought a moment.

— Don't you know this is public property? he said again.

Jean quickly gathered her things.

— I'm just leaving.

— Wait, said the man, it's meant to be! Tonight I also broke the law of public property. I was just wishing I had someone to witness it when I saw your little light hopping up and down in the grass like a bird. This guarantees our solidarity!

— For a criminal you're shouting awfully loudly, said Jean. She looked around. She smiled slightly. The neighbours will open their windows and throw shoes at us.

— Shoes. The man nodded. Now that's a serious subject.

Don't be frightened. I've been working hard, he said, and I'd just like to show it to someone. I may not get another chance. Look, we can walk twenty paces from each other.

He moved off, to indicate his good intentions.

He walked through the gate and waited beside the fence of the small carpark, holding the lantern high above his head. He studied the fence, slowly swinging the lamp back and forth in concentration.

Jean saw that what he had painted was not a sterile replica, but had taken its life from the fence itself. The broken boards, knotholes, peeled paint, the stubble of old posters, graffiti, nailheads, cracks, industrial staples, every feature — man-made, weather-made, time-worn — was integrated into the textures and forms of fur, hooves, eyes, horns. In this way not only the animals of Lascaux, but the decrepit fence itself leaped into life. As if the Canadian fence had been waiting for someone to see what was hidden inside it, which happened to be cave paintings from Cro-Magnon Europe. Horses strained against the current of the stream. Bison on thin legs, their eyes wild with the chase. The animals leaped into the light. The work was fast, uncanny. She thought of Matisse: "Exactitude is not truth."

At last Jean turned to him.

—You're the 'Caveman'!

He nodded as if his collar was too tight.

—You know me, he said, disappointed.

— Not yet, said Jean.

At that, the Caveman looked happy again.

—There's a café right here, two steps away, he said.

Jean knew the place, though she had never been inside. It was a narrow storefront with a square of cardboard in the window: *Coffee*, the sign warned, *and nothing else*.

The Caveman loped meekly ahead, looking back every moment or two to make sure she was following.

— This little coffee house is my friend Paweł's place, it's like my living room to me.

He held the door for her. The smell of roasting coffee rushed past them into the night. Inside the empty café, a man, slight and pale, in a wax-white short-sleeved shirt, was sitting behind a wooden bar, reading. Beside him was a music dictation book, the kind that schoolchildren use. On the antique cash register was taped a slogan in the same handwriting as the sign in the window: *I do not presume to tell you what your sight has cost you. Do not presume to tell me what my blindness has cost me.* Behind the bar, a wall of tiny windows like an automat, filled with gleaming beans, oily and aromatic.

— Paweł knows his coffee, said the Caveman proudly. He's a vintner with his vintages!

Paweł stopped reading and looked up.

— Paweł, I'd like you to meet — this is . . . a girl with a trowel.

Paweł looked at them and took in Jean's muddy knees, her canvas shoes, and her planting bag with the torch-trowel sticking out. He saw how the night clung to them both. He quickly closed his book.

— Ewa's home tonight. Stay as long as you like. Just lock up, Lucjan, when you go. Leave the light on over the bar so the mice won't trip.

Jean sat at a small table. Everywhere was mismatched furniture, wooden tables and chairs of kitchen vinyl, frayed upholstered silk, wicker, plastic netting.

—Would you like Brazilian, African, Jamaican, Argentinian, or Cuban? asked the Caveman.

— Or Polish, said Paweł, quickly closing the door behind him.

— Have you ever seen a man, said the Caveman, so happy to be going home to his wife?

—Were they just married?

— Paweł and Ewa? They've been married since they were children — at least twenty years now, said the Caveman.

—What's Polish coffee? asked Jean.

— Instant, said the Caveman. Without the water!

The Caveman sunk a metal scoop into the beans.

— I read about your paintings in the newspaper, said Jean. The anonymous 'Caveman' . . . they were praising your work . . . Someone offered a commission . . .

— Okay, said the Caveman. That's too bad! But I won't dwell on it. Never dwell on good news! He took another long look at her, smiling. And now, before anything else, tell me why you plant things secretly, a nun leaving a signal for her lover.

Jean looked down at the table guiltily. Then, the quick defiance to speak the truth.

— When I'm planting, said Jean, I'm leaving a kind of signal. And I'm hoping that the person it's meant for will receive it. If someone walking down the street experiences the scent of a flower they haven't smelled for thirty years — even if they don't recognize the scent but are suddenly reminded of something that gives them pleasure — then maybe I've done something worthwhile.

Jean looked at him miserably.

— But what you evoke could be something painful, said the Caveman. When you plant something in people's memories, you never know what you'll pull up.

He saw the look of dismay in her face. He thought for a moment.

— Maybe you should work in a hospital.

— Why paint Lascaux? Jean asked. But as soon as she spoke, she felt a twinge of understanding. He had found the life within the fence — using each scar, adapting the animals to their environment. She felt an intimation of something she would realize later, that this was not about Lascaux but about exile and the seizing of joy that will not come of its own accord.

— My husband told me about a church in a little town in the centre of Italy, said Jean. From the outside it's a dirty stone box, not a single ornament. But when you step inside, plummeting into darkness from the Italian sunshine, as your eyes adjust to the dimness, the scale of the place unfolds; the church grows in front of your eyes! The statuary leaps out. I think they must have all been after the same thing — the early Christian grottos, the painted caves — to bring the stone to life.

The earliest churches were just enclosed space, said Jean, I think what really changed Christianity was when someone first put a chair in that space. People no longer felt the ground when they prayed. And certainly those chairs must have meant some were more equal than others in the sight of God.

— The fence makes you think of all this?

— Yes, said Jean.

— What I worry about, said the Caveman, is whether all those bison will confuse the squirrels.

———

The Caveman, Lucjan, lived in a building that had been marooned. Over time, the tumbledown coach house had been cut off from the rest of the property and stood stranded behind other houses and without an entrance on the street. Nevertheless, it had its own parenthesized address: *(rear)*. It was surrounded on three sides by residential backyards and on the remaining side by an apartment building. Two days after their meeting in the park, Jean followed the narrow path that led from Amelia Street, accepting Lucjan's invitation to tea. She hesitated at his gate. The trees were thick with leaves of every shade of yellow, the sun illuminating the coach house like a cottage in the middle of a wood. She felt that if she turned around, she would see the city street retreating from her, like the shore from a ship, and she wished Avery were with her. She felt the lurch of banishment, for the first time feeling he had already forgotten her. The swaying leaves, captured sun, moved continuously in and out of shadow, a woven disquiet; this seemed to Jean to be as sad as the first waking instant of consciousness, sad as the single continuously disappearing moment that is a life. Sad as a hope suffocating in a collector's jar, too few holes pounded into the tin lid.

Inside, Jean discovered, Lucjan's little building had been renovated, piecemeal, over many years. It contained only half of a second storey that might, fashionably, be called a loft, though in truth it was half a floor, reached by a steep staircase. This is where Lucjan slept. He had painted an oriental carpet in the centre of this room on the bare planks – two weeks of work. The ground floor was a single large room, a kitchen against one wall, with an old, elegant claw-footed bathtub in the corner. The tub had remained because of the pipes and, besides, had been simply too heavy to move. At night, with a fire, Lucjan soaked and listened to music, which filled the open space like a cathedral. He'd cut and sanded a board and placed it across the tub whenever he needed an extra table.

Lucjan used the other half of the ground floor as his studio.

Every surface of the kitchen was bright white – sparse and clean. But the other half of the large room, the half used for work, was piled with sculptors' tools, scrap metal, pieces of wood, old cabinets, driftwood, lumber, canvas, broken fur-niture. Lucjan followed Jean's gaze.

– My friend Paweł says, 'Don't think clean and dirty, think conscious mind and unconscious.'

Jean sat quietly in Lucjan's kitchen while he searched for a drawing. She had noticed small stones here and there, on the tables and the low shelf beside the bed, and now she noticed the books, on the kitchen counter, on the floor, gaping in varying degrees, and realized Lucjan used these round stones as bookmarks, to prop open his place.

Jean carried their cups to the sink and rinsed them. Then she crossed the room and picked up the toy train she'd glimpsed on the windowsill. The silver paint was scratched but still bright; and she saw, on the side of the engine, a swastika and the double-lightning insignia of the ss. Immediately Jean put it down. She stood very still. From across the room, Lucjan watched her.

He looked at her and suddenly she felt a great fear.

– I'm sorry, said Jean. I think I should go.

– Then go, he said.

Jean put on her coat and scarf and stood at the door.

— Do you think I'm a simpleton? he asked.

She opened the door.

— That engine, said Lucjan, I've had it since I was a boy. I loved that train, it was my first real toy, something store-bought, not home-made, not carved out of an old table leg or stuffed and sewn from scraps. It came from Piotrowski's on Krakowskie Przedmieście, plucked right from the shop window. My stepfather and I saw it together. We went in and he bought it straightaway. He knew something was about to happen, and it was a reckless, extravagant thing to do, to spend the money on something that would surely have to be left behind. For a few days' pleasure. But he did. So those ugly letters, that ugly symbol means something to me, yes.

Jean stood quietly, her eyes on the floor.

Without looking at his face, she came back into the room and sat down on a kitchen chair, though she did not take off her coat.

— You're very beautiful, Lucjan said. I'm sorry you're so afraid of me.

He sat at the table. He reached across and slowly pulled her handbag from her lap and with a startling gentleness set it beside her on the table.

———

In the mornings, Avery was woken by the family that lived upstairs. He heard the children on their tricycles as they rode around and around the dining room table, their father shouting at them to stop, the running up and down, the thump of the front door slamming.

The laundry room was in the basement and Avery knew that, when their mother was sorting the washing, sometimes the children explored his flat. Often they left toys or books behind (once, Tibor Gergely's *Animal Orchestra* – "the grey seals barked and lifted their fins and tweedled upon their violins . . ."). Avery did not mind the children's idle browsing among his things; in fact, he was disappointed to come home and not detect their trail. Finding the children's possessions among his own seemed to confer permission, confirmed his place; there, where he did not belong.

Avery lay with the empty house above him. His fellow students were fervent about the design of museums, malls, skyscrapers, mixed-use piazzas, entirely rebuilt urban cores. They were ardent and combative about urban fabric and infrastructure, crowd management and traffic flow. Avery listened to the noise of ambition around him and found himself alone, aching to learn what simple humanism might be possible, against all odds, in an industrial building, Aalto's Sunila or the Olivetti factory at Ivres. He was beginning to realize what it meant to build structures of the humblest and most straightforward disclosure, frank and spare, without irony; capable simply of both sorrow and solace: a house that understands that the entire course of a life can be altered, for better or for worse, by someone walking across a room. A room able to focus all its stillness in a single pear, sliced in half on a plate by a window. A school classroom so beautifully formed and situated that it is an idea. Playgrounds that children could continually redesign themselves, with movable pieces to make forts and shelters. Office buildings with alcoves for reading aloud, and big work spaces (space to think). Why were schools in particular so ugly, so barren, so bereft of aspiration or inspiration, the antithesis of the qualities one would wish to instill in students; cinderblock walls, sickly linoleum, dead light, dreadful basements, institutional fixtures, without self-respect . . . He knew one could spend just as much money building something lifeless as building something alive . . . It was not enough to make things less bad; one must make them for the good.

Has evolution moved the bone in our throat to allow for speech, have we learned to stand erect, to measure, to worship, to plant and harvest, to manipulate the atom and explore the gene, to thread needles – philosophic and otherwise – with our prehensile, self-conscious brains, to utter the world in paint and language, because we have no destiny as a species?

These thoughts were attached to the sound of the children running up and down the stairs, to the brief moment of silence when he imagined embraces before they all flew out the door, to the insurmountable fact of the happiness of others, as innocent as a child's name carefully printed in the flyleaf of a book.

———

For almost a month, Lucjan drew Jean. The velvet dress, the heavy sweater. She did not know if she would take her clothes off for him if he asked, if he moved across the room to her; but he did not. He looked at the way material gathered or stretched, glimpses of weight and bones. The comprehension that exists before touch makes one blind.

Lucjan's glance was painful; at first, Jean could barely tolerate his scrutiny of each part of her, even though they were parts visible to any stranger in the street: her face, the soft places between her fingers, behind her knees, the curve of her neck. Each afternoon his eyes travelled the same passage, the next day and the next, with increasing depth of knowledge, and after a few days she began to look at him as he drew, making the same slow journey of his body.

To be made visible by the sight of another.

Many nights that first month, they sat across from each other at Lucjan's table, or Jean on the painted carpet and Lucjan on the edge of the bed, two travellers on two separate journeys, waiting together in an empty train station, encouraged by circumstance into an awkward intimacy.

— Do you know the story of Kokoschka and his life drawing class? asked Lucjan from across the room. His students were painting from a model. He thought their renderings pathetic, feeble, dull. How could he bring their sight to life? One day he took the model aside before class began and whispered in her ear. Partway through the hour the woman collapsed and Kokoschka rushed to her side. 'She's dead!' he cried. The students stared at the suddenly lifeless flesh in horror. Then Kokoschka took the model's hand and helped her to her feet.

She resumed her pose. 'Now,' said the master, 'draw her again.'

In return, Jean told Lucjan about Hans Weiditz' woodcuts, the first illustrations of plants in a printed book. Suddenly, throughout Europe, apothecaries, herbalists, doctors, midwives could look at the same plant and identify it indisputably. Perhaps the same could be said of the first drawing of a human face. And from then on, Jean said, botanical drawing became an art; da Vinci's meticulous studies of tree bark and the serrations and veins of leaves. Albrecht Durer's watercolours – so realistic – his irises, folds and flaps of papery purple skin . . .

– All flowers are watercolours, said Lucjan.

Lucjan made a late supper. He threw all the ingredients into one pan, the vegetables, the meat, the eggs; he crushed and rubbed the dust of the herbs over the puckering oil and afterwards tipped the pan, spilling everything onto two plates.

Jean watched him. No one had ever sat her in a chair and cooked for her, in all the years since her mother died. She had not known that this had hurt her. The first time they sat to supper together, she wept as she ate, ordinary food more delicious than she'd ever tasted, and he let her cry, only taking her hand across the table, as if it were the most natural thing in the world, this gratitude. To eat and weep.

After supper Lucjan said, Whisper in my ear.

– All right, little Jean – Janina, said Lucjan as they sat fully dressed next to each other on his bed. The first bedtime story. If we're honest, there is only one. You wish me to speak first . . .

There are many degrees of solidarity. One who risks his career and one who risks his life; one who risks because his friends have, who can't bear the shame and loneliness of being a coward. The friend who helps you when you need it, and the friend who helps you before you need it.

We must learn the value of each other's words, what they cost.

Under her sweater, on her belly, Jean felt the bandaid on Lucjan's hand, she felt the buttons of his shirt, she felt his watchband. Never again would she feel indifference to such objects.

—There were thousands of us, Robinson Kruzoes, living in the debris . . .

The silence of ruins is the breathing of the dead . . .

It was the first time I'd ever been woken by the feeling of snow on my skin . . .

We are born with places of suffering in us, history is the proof of them . . .

I can only speak if you are lying next to me, he said, as close as my voice, my words throughout the length of your body, because what I am going to say is my entire life. And I have nothing really but these memories. I need you to listen as if these memories are your own. The details of this room, this view from the window, these clothes heaped on the chair, the hairbrush on the bedside table, the glass on the floor — everything must disappear. I need you to hear everything I say, and everything I can't say must be heard too.

It is terrifying to listen this way, leaving everything behind. Maybe I ask something impossible . . .

Smoke forced people out of the cellars, pushed them through doors of fire. The sound of the 'bellowing cows' – the machines that cranked the mines into place – then the explosion. The rubble rats would say, 'Don't worry, if you hear the explosion, then you're not dead . . .'

A crowd stood at the edge of the ruins. No one had yet dared to step forward. High above them – their heads leaned back in disbelief – smouldered the frozen tidal wave of rubble. Somewhere a man said, 'Put one foot in Poland and you're up to your knees in horse dung.' The crowd, seething, craned necks to see who dared say such a thing and to take a swipe at him. But when people turned around they saw the old man was crying . . .

Within days of the German retreat, there were twenty thousand of us living in the ruins, and within weeks there were ten times as many of us Robinson Kruzoes; many, many children who knew no other place and were afraid to try their luck elsewhere, who needed to be where they last saw their mother or their father . . .

When my stepfather came back to Warsaw after the war, we were sitting with others on a heap of stones that was once Krakowskie Przedmieście, the same street where we had, it seemed so long before, bought that toy engine. He grabbed the arm of an old man, a stranger, and showed me the man's tattoo, because he was so full of pain himself and he had no scar to show for it.

It was as if the sky had been made of stone and had crashed to earth: an endless horizon of rubble.

Snow laboured down, through smoke and stone dust. No stars could be seen through the thick atmosphere. The black river flowed north over exploded bridges.

The snow fell peacefully on seven hundred and twenty million cubic feet of rubble. It clung to the masticated, wrenched, shattered till of wainscotting, roofs, glass, metal bedframes, entire libraries, on the remains of kindergartens and trees, and on ninety-eight thousand land mines.

In the midst of this devastation was the crumpled city square, Plac Teatralny, once the point of intersection for every major trade route across Europe – from the Baltic to the Black Sea, from Paris to Moscow. In the centre of that city square, a slender stone column still stood, untouched, its tip barely visible, an engraved compass needle upright among the incomprehensible debris, marking the place: Latitude 52 degrees 13'N, 21 degrees longitude. Warsaw.

The air was charged and solid; it shuddered, as if walls were rising out of the ground at an accelerated pace. After a few minutes of terrified observation, Lucjan realized the sun was rising and the spectral walls were merely the effect of dawn making its progress up through the smoke. Sunlight passed through walls of dust where real walls had stood only a few hours before; the city, an afterimage. When the dust settled, this glowing flesh dissolved, leaving only the skeletons of the buildings, sharp piles of stone, ventilator shafts, mangled iron beams, shredded wooden beams, cobblestones, chimney pots, eaves, shingles, pantry cupboards with their round wooden knobs, glass and metal doorknobs, different kinds of twisted pipe, electrical wire, disintegrated plaster, cartilage, bone, brain matter. Floating fibres of upholstery and singed hair floated in the January wind; scraps of wool dresses, melted buttons, and the greasy smoke of still-burning, avalanched bodies. The air glinted with infinitesimally small particles of glass.

The dead were invisible and pervasive; in another dimension where they would never be found.

Emerging from the wreckage were objects left astonishingly undigested by the toppling walls and the fires: a hairbrush, the wheel of a cart, a finger. A window frame jutted out, its curtain still attached; flowers of pale yellow cotton drifted listlessly in the air, searching for the vanished kitchen.

Cities, like people, are born with a soul, a spirit of place that continues to make itself known, emerging even after devastation, an old word looking for meaning in the new mouth that speaks it. For though there were no buildings left and there was waste farther than the horizon, Warsaw never stopped being a city.

In the darkness one could see tails of smoke twitching in the wind, rising from cracks between the stones. Then one knew there was a cellar there, big enough for an underground fire. Only at night could one see how many lived in the ruins.

Often the entranceways to these *meliny*, these burrows, these tunnels into the rubble, were marked with a pot of flowers. Geraniums. A blurt of red, a spurt of blood among the bones.

———

— Once, a woman, probably the wife of a journalist — there were crowds of them in the city during the first weeks after the war — offered me a square of chocolate, said Lucjan, wrapped in a scrap of foil. The scent of her face powder, from the inside of her handbag, clung to the shiny paper. I remember looking at it for a long time — for me, the first chocolate since before the war. When I finally put it in my mouth, I felt the heat shoot throughout my body and, looking at that woman with her fur coat and the golden clasp of her shiny handbag, I longed to rest my head against her softness. Instead, in return for her kindness, I gave her a good long look, as though I hated her, and moved off fast before she said a word.

I dug down to find a room almost perfectly intact and, while I was out looking for food, someone else took it for themselves. I lowered myself into a hole and found a man covered with blood — it was everywhere, you could even see his footprints. I stared at him. 'Don't look so worried,' he said. 'It's only a head wound.' Once, I fell asleep in a place I found just as it was almost dark. When I woke, I was lying face to face with a doll sticking up awkwardly from the stones. But it wasn't a doll . . . Once, I found a cellar of a shop still filled with cartons of shoes. I did some useful bartering before someone else discovered that cellar of shoes too . . . You have another pair of shoes or a second coat. You stand in the street and hold out your arms and you are a shop . . . I learned quickly that a hole with nothing to offer was best, and no one bothered me. I had a blanket, a bowl. Sometimes a head would poke down, see me sitting there, and disappear.

Once, a girl came. She must have seen my candlelight seeping from the cracks. I was already asleep and she shook me awake. She was, at the very most, twelve or thirteen years old. She asked if she could stay until morning. A large wooden cross on a string dangled over her narrow chest, the arms of the cross stretching over almost the entire width of her. Before I could answer, she was behind me, lying with her forehead against my back and her arm across me, and within one minute she was asleep. I was terrified by the touch of her. I could barely breathe for the pain of her thin arm resting on my coat.

Once, scrambling over the rubble, I spotted a piece of calico tied around a woman's throat. That bright piece of patterned cloth was saturated with life. Not the woman, no pulse in her neck; but the strip of cloth, red and blue in the snow. At first I thought her forehead was glistening with sweat. But it was ice.

As people returned to Warsaw there appeared, more and more often, sticking up here and there out of the wreckage, a branch with a piece of paper jammed through; marking the place where someone had thought their house or shop had been, where they'd last seen the person they were seeking . . .

Add to this the smell, the shrieking stink of the *karbidówki*, the carbide lamps that reeked each morning when they were cleaned out . . .

Once, I overheard an old couple making their accommodation in the scrap heap. The man was clearing a space for themselves when suddenly he called out: 'Look, a glass, unbroken – not a scratch. Incredible! Now we can drink!' 'No,' his wife said, 'let's put flowers in the glass. We can still drink from our hands.'

People have an instinct to leave flowers in a place where something terrible has happened, by the roadside where there was an accident, in front of a building where someone was shot. It's not like bringing flowers to a grave where the body has been laid to rest. Those flowers are not the same. Someone dies a horrible death and suddenly the bouquets appear. It's a desperate instinct to leave a mark of innocence on a violent wound, to mark the place where that last twitching nerve of innocence was stilled. The very first – the very first – shop to open up in the ruins of the city, during the very first days following the German occupation, perched on top of the rubble, in the snow! – was a florist's shop. Even before the abandoned half-wrecked tram that contained the first café, selling soup and ersatz coffee – there was the florist. All the foreign journalists marvelled at it – such a sense of life, such fortitude, such spirit – all the drivel those journalists spluttered. Blah blah blah! Etcetera etcetera etcetera! But no one said what was surely simple and obvious: you need flowers for a grave. You need flowers for a place of violent death. Flowers were the very first thing we needed. Before bread. And long before words.

The German soldiers had enforced a strict schedule of demolition, said Lucjan; each building, street by street, had been numbered with white paint. In this sense, the numbers painted on the sides of those buildings were like the tattoos on the arms of the camp inmates; one might say the numbers signified their date of destruction.

Across the Vistula, the Soviets waited patiently, while the Wehrmacht, with great efficiency, levelled the empty city. When the show was over, almost three months later, the Soviet army quickly threw a pontoon across the Vistula — the same river that throughout the uprising and the city's demolition they had declared "impassable" — and claimed Warsaw for themselves.

Suppose, said Lucjan, lying quietly next to Jean under the blankets, you wish to convince me of the colour of a man's hair. Would you show me a man who had a thick head of hair as proof? No, surely his hair could have been dyed, or the photo altered. No, instead you show me a bald man. You say, His hair used to be brown. We examine his complexion, his eyebrows. It is not so easy to tell. Finally, we concede, Perhaps, yes, the bald man's hair might have been brown. Some years later, you see the same photograph, the face looks familiar but all you can recall is that the man used to have brown hair . . .

Okay, said Lucjan. Suppose you wish me to forget the sig-nificance of a certain name . . . In a clearing in the forest near Minsk, the Soviets erect a national war monument to mark the place where the village of Khatyn had been razed by the Germans. Day after day, for decades, they send busloads of children to the memorial. Why is this site chosen for a national monument when there are so many other places where the dead outnumber those poor souls of Khatyn? Simply because there is a certain other clearing, in a forest near Smolensk, a place called Katyn. In this place, where one feels an invisible presence – at first one thinks it is just the effect of sunlight moving through the trees – hundreds of Polish officers were slaughtered and buried in a mass grave by the Soviets in 1940.

The Soviets tried to make the Germans take the blame for this, but in the end there was only one way to make us 'forget' Katyn and that was to make the war memorial at Khatyn. The events are confused until there is only one event, made true by the irrefutable evidence of one gigantic statue.

And when you sit down for a drink with that same bald man and he talks about loneliness, well, is it Russian loneli-ness or Polish loneliness, is it the loneliness of a Catholic or a Jew? Is it the loneliness of the true Marxist? There was even, incredibly, a Soviet boat docked at Warsaw in those years after the war called *The Fairytale* . . .

————

Often, Jean sat in the university library, waiting until it was late enough to walk to Lucjan's, 9 or 10 p.m., when she knew he would be finished in the studio. She emerged from the glaring brightness of the library stacks, from taxonomy, epiphytic genetics, Blaschka glass, and Minton wax replicas, into the dark November street, with its display of intimacies, amber windows filled with mysterious, ordinary, living. She and Lucjan had tea together, and if Lucjan had not quite finished working, he'd go back to it, rummaging for the right shape of metal, painting, soldering while Jean read. Then a last cup of tea, sometimes with a shot of something in it for Lucjan; and the climb to bed, where Jean lay in her clothes and each night for perhaps ten minutes Lucjan drew her face. There were now thirty or so portraits; quick, precise, loving. A record of his changing knowledge of her. Then the bedtime story that continued to unravel, both recognizing this for what it was, an agreement of trust. Egypt, Montreal, but mostly Warsaw, at Jean's entreaty. His words opened a dark radiance, phosphorescence in a cave. What was illuminated was not the world, but an inner darkness. Not the flower, but the tinctures made from the flower. Often they fell asleep still in their clothes, now not as if in a train station, but as if on a night flight; in the small bedroom window, snow falling like ash into the black Vistula.

One morning they woke and the house was cold, the windows feathered white. Lucjan went downstairs to start the fire. He used pages of old phone books as kindling, choosing a letter at random and declaiming names and addresses aloud before crumpling the pages. Jean watched, shocked.

—You feel tender even toward a phone book, said Lucjan. What am I going to do with you?

He squatted in front of the fireplace and looked at her.

—Why does it make you so sad?

— I'm not sure, said Jean.

She hesitated.

—Take all the time you need. We'll just sit here in the cold while you think.

I'm sorry, he said.

— It's as if there's a connection between those names that we'll never understand, said Jean quietly. As if something important is being disregarded.

Lucjan sat beside her on the floor.

— I remember my stepfather getting up early to light the fire in the sitting room where we ate our breakfast, said Lucjan. I never knew my real papa, who died before I was born. I was two years old when my mother remarried. She was so beautiful. Educated, refined, assimilated. She embodied an era, a moment, the first and last of the Jewish debutantes in Poland. My stepfather, who was not Jewish, stayed outside the ghetto and joined the Home Army because he thought it would save us. Those years when my mother and I were alone together, she talked to me all the time. We crawled under the blankets to keep warm and she told me stories, everything she could remember about when she was a girl and what it was like when she met my stepfather, always stroking my hair and making me laugh. After the war when he came back and found me, I could see the disturbance in his face — all the things he made himself do for us — for what. It was really only for my mother and now

she was gone. He'd hardly seen me in almost seven years . . .
We went through the debris, we carried half the city between
us in our hands, stone by stone. He refused to believe we
would not find her. He dragged me from place to place. We
stood in front of one pile of rock after another, day after day.
I was always crying. Until finally he shook me and told me to
shut up. I must have been driving him mad. He said he was
going to Kraków. He told me to wait for him. In the end I
don't know whether the Red Army picked him up before he
could return for me or not. For a long time I thought that
single fact mattered more than anything. But many months
later there was a moment when I understood he'd never
intended to come back. I was working in the New Town,
helping to empty truckloads of broken houses into the
riverbed. It was raining. A man was nearly crushed under a
load. He called out and his voice in the rain was the saddest
sound I've ever heard. If rain had a voice, it would be that
voice. At that very moment, soaked through, hearing that man
cry out and out, I felt something fly from the very centre of
me. My stepfather – the brave, noble, gentleman-soldier my
mother had persuaded me to love – suddenly I was free, perfectly free of him. I can't express the relief such despair can
be. Some time I'll tell you the end of the story . . . Don't look
at me like that – that look of pity.

– It's not pity, said Jean.

– Well, it looks like pity to me.

– Would you recognize a look of pity?

For a long time, Lucjan said nothing. He sat on the floor
in front of the fireplace, very still.

— No one has ever said that to me. You happen to be right. What experience do I have with pity?

— Please don't burn the phone books, said Jean. Perhaps it's foolish, but I can't bear to see those names burning. It's as if no one will be able to find anyone again. It's like breaking a spell.

Lucjan pushed the book across the floor into the corner.

— It's cold in here, he said.

— Come with me under the blankets, said Jean, please.

He climbed in and she drew his face close to hers. They lay quietly and after a while Lucjan said:

—You're right, Janina. All those names in a book as if they belonged together. As if the whole city was one story.

———

Avery's classmates, after their initial probing, lost interest in him. They turned their attention to intellectual domination in the classroom, the ascertaining of like minds, the acquisition of lovers; it did not bother him that he did not signify in any of these categories.

He felt ambition now. He had a keen memory for buildings he'd seen with his father and, from years of work, a pure, distilled instinct for stress, balance, shadows cast. Books towered around his bed on the floor. He slept with the lamp on and when he woke in the middle of the night he deliberately pushed the heat of Jean from his mind.

He lived on cereal, bread, and tea. For dinner, Avery set the teapot, the foil brick of butter, and the loaf on the table.

The weather, the light, would awaken referred pain, details of her. The feel of her forearm up his spine, her hand between his shoulders. The warm curve of her, mornings she'd woken before him, lying contentedly on her side reading, his awareness of her absolute gentleness, even before he opened his eyes. At these moments, fear pressed him to end the separation. But, like two halves created by a single blade, there was a second fear informing his actions, which compelled him to forbearance, the fear of wasting his last chance with her.

In late November, during an afternoon of high wind and winter rain, Avery waited for Jean at the Sgana, a tiny café in a parking lot at the edge of the lake. He sat by the window watching as the old kitchen chairs and tables that had been left out since summer toppled against one another on the patio. No one brought them inside. The lake slapped against the concrete embankment. The café windows were glazed with water, and the wind came through the edges of the glass. Then she was at the door, her coat dripping, her wet hair under a wet scarf. As soon as Jean reached the table, Avery could see – though there was no outward alteration, he felt it at once – that someone else, another man, had changed the very look of her, changed her face. He had wished for this for so long, the hopelessness to be lifted, drawn away, and now it had happened, or was beginning to happen, the thing he had been unable himself to do.

They did not say much or stay long. It was unbearable to be so close to her and to feel this transformation. Avery could not describe it to himself. She was more beautiful to him now almost than he could bear. It seemed as though she had taken off something invisible and was, in every part of her, new and incomplete. She waited for him to speak. She asked, finally, close to tears, "Can't you tell me, what is it, what is it we should do?" "Not yet," he said, "I don't know. No." The smell of her.

———

Often the nights when Jean was not with Lucjan, the phone would ring and she would lie with Avery's voice pressed against her ear. He would talk only about what he was learning. But he spoke as if there were not a handful of city blocks between them but a mountain, an ocean, time zones, making every sentence count. When they hung up and silence descended, Jean ached from trying to understand what was important, whose need was greater, an excruciating inability to grasp the moral imperative, her task, the organizing principle of this derangement and longing. Some gardens are organized by taxonomy, some by geographic origins, some by feature. She knew that anyone overhearing their conversations, so steeped in context, would understand nothing. Their urgency would seem, to a stranger, to be anything but; instead . . . almost desultory.

———

All through that autumn, Jean and Lucjan met late at night at the house on Amelia Street. Sometimes he undressed her in the doorway, at first, only for a moment, like a parent whose child has just come in from playing in the snow. His hands through her hair to release her beret, unwinding her scarf. Her sweater pulled over her head. Jean, who had known no other man but Avery, was compliant, resting her hands on Lucjan's shoulders as he rolled her tights down her cold thighs. The hot bath was waiting; music filled the darkness. When she stepped into the invisible water, it was like stepping into a voice. She did not know the names of the singers nor understand their words. But she felt the heat of it, women singing of love, every broken piece of it. The voice was the city, it was the Polish forest, complicated earth. It was the lanterns brought to the true grave at Katyn, it was a meeting on the fire-stairs, it was the silk that smelled of her, it was a hotel room in Le Havre, it was the last time. The almost unbearably hot water, the dark chocolate of a woman's voice. Lucjan's hands never asked any questions. He knew and he touched. He renamed her with her name.

The music was the boy with stones in his mouth, it was a woman on stage whose nakedness is her disguise, it was the black *gargara*, it was the ominous, body-sized, paper moth-bags draped over the arms of the sellers on Marszałkowska Street, the paper shadows, the paper souls, it was the smell inside a hat, the smell of gas leaking across the rubble, it was cloves and nutmeg before the bitter coffee, it was the smell of coffee in the dark, it was the stench of the *karbidówki*, it was the silk that smelled of her.

— I slipped down between the stones, said Lucjan, into a neat burrow and found an oilcloth on the ground and a whole loaf

of bread laid out on a wooden shelf. I picked up the loaf and
started to climb out when I heard a voice.

'I don't have much. Help yourself.'

The voice spoke without sarcasm. I turned around to see
a man sitting cross-legged on the floor in the dimness,
leaning against the wall. His generosity made me so ashamed
I wanted to knock his head off, knock him over. But instead I
tore into his bread right in front of him, crammed it into my
mouth, and left for him only a pinch of it.

Still he didn't move. He sat, watching me.

I really felt like giving him a clout. But I was curious too.
So I stood there and watched him. Finally he said, 'Are you
going to stay here all night?'

'What were you doing,' I asked, 'when I came in?'

'Thinking.'

'What were you thinking about?'

'The city. Nowy Świat Street.'

I began to climb out.

'Wait,' he said. 'You're as strong as an oxen – two oxen.
Why don't you help us? I'll make sure you get fed. A whole
loaf of bread and a coupon for shoes.'

I waved him off.

'Don't you want to help? We'll rise again, you'll see. Are
you so sure you don't want to help?'

He looked hard at me. And then suddenly he understood.

'Are you a Jew?'

We stood looking at each other – a long time, maybe a
minute. Until – disgusting! – tears came into my eyes. Tears
came into my eyes, but still I wouldn't let go my gaze.

'Ah,' he said and finally looked away.

And that's when I felt what power it is to push people away. It gave me satisfaction and a hair-tearing sadness to watch him lower his eyes.

'I'll have bread every day?'

'Yes.'

'Just for carrying things?'

'Yes.'

I came back into the room and ate the last bit of crust I'd left for him. I ate everything he had and left him nothing, not a crumb.

Those who had shoes worked in the debris. Those who didn't, helped to draw up plans. It was unspoken, yet everyone clearing the rubble and working on the reconstruction of the city felt it – that when Warsaw was rebuilt, the dead could return. Not only the dead, but mortal ghosts, ghosts of flesh and blood.

After the war it was decided that the oldest district, the Old Town, would be rebuilt – not just built up again but . . . an exact copy. Every lintel and cornice, every portico and engraving, every lamppost. You can imagine the debate. But in the end, there was agreement: even those who disagreed understood the necessity.

Biegański, Zachwalowicz, Kuzma, and the rest based their plans for this reconstruction of the Old Town – of the market and of Piwna and Zapiecek streets – on Canaletto's paintings of Warsaw in the eighteenth century, on photos, and on the drawing exercises made by Professor Sosnowski's students from the polytechnic. When Sosnowski died during the seige of 1939, the architecture school continued underground. Students crept into the streets to sketch a careful inventory of memorials, statues, and buildings. These sketches were hidden in the cellar at the university. And in 1944, when the university burned, the drawings were saved. They were hidden among a stack of legal papers and were smuggled out of the city and given over to the custody of the dead; that is, they were hidden in a tomb at Piotrków monastery. Professor Lorentz's students made night raids to the ruins of the royal castle and carried to safety anything with architectural detail – the panelled doors of the chapel, slabs of plaster murals and marble fireplaces, window frames – thousands of bits and pieces.

I know this because I was recruited. I was small and fast and I had no one who cared about me. Therefore, I was of some use. At night I went along on these scavenging hunts, and afterwards they fed me. I collected door handles, bits of ironmongery, and stone ornaments in exchange for bread and shelter. I learned a lot, listening to those students, about all sorts of things. Nobody paid any attention to me, I was only twelve years old. I overheard many conversations – about democracy and weight-bearing walls and what books to read and, 'if a woman is present she must always be offered the first swig from the flask.' There must have been a lot of useful suggestions about sex, if only I'd understood what they were talking about. When I lived among the students of the polytechnic, there were so many liaisons, the passions were so fluid, so messy, so adult; I watched it happening around me, only later, when I was older, did I take part in it myself. And much later, when I was in my twenties, I eavesdropped again, on Ewa and Paweł's theatre tribe – everyone trying to find a home. With the polytechnics, I usually sat in the corner listening and fell asleep as soon as they gave me my bread, and they never turned me out. I owe those students so much, many people whose names I never knew. They taught me everything. What to read and how to argue about what you read. How to look at a painting. An entire education.

But most important to me of all the polytechnics was a student named Piotr. His father was British, and everyone gathered around him to learn a few English words. I think everyone felt as I did – leaning forward to catch the scraps – hungry for a world outside. He taught us first of all the names of boats, because he loved sailing: skiff, yacht, rowboat, ferryboat, steamer. This was not Polish or Russian but a bitter, clean language of escape. One could pronounce almost any English word with one's teeth clenched. There were no jsz's and cj's or ł's to loosen one's resolve. Piotr's most valuable possession was a Polish-English dictionary. It was the size of a small brick, and everyone wanted to borrow it. He could have traded it for an exorbitant price – an over-coat, an apple. But instead he came to where I was sleeping on the floor and slid it under me. I woke to feel it digging into my back. In it a note, in English: 'Do not stop running until you learn every word.' When I went to thank him, he pushed me off, gently, like an older brother. He said, 'I want Polish now, only Poland,' and nodded in the direction of a girl. That glance was my first real stammer of sex, I felt it in him, the angry longing, the insatiable humility of it – insatiable: page 467. I memorized the page numbers of many words – a double assurance they would not be lost. Doubly remembered. A few days later, Piotr and his girl were killed in a raid on the castle, carrying a piece of stone between them. Another boy had been there too and had run off; when he returned to the spot, they were still there. He ran back to the hiding place and told the others, twisting his hands with guilt, '*dalej tam leżały, dalej tam leżały.*' At night the dead were strewn, scattered, '*still there, still there,*' sometimes in the darkness without a drop of blood visible, as if the moon itself had struck them down. Each day after that I read one-half of a page of that thick English book – a little memorial I was making. Every word I speak, every English word chipped off that brick of a dictionary – and so I try to take care – remembers him. It's in the drawer beside you, said Lucjan, leaning over to the bedside table and placing the dictionary in Jean's lap. At first Jean, deeply lost in the story, could hardly believe it was true – conjured like a magician's trick – but she held the solid book, with its broken spine and its ordinary, grimy, colourless cover, and felt the small shock of it – as if Lucjan had produced a branch of the burning bush or a stone from Nineveh.

– However, Janina, my point is this. Who is to say that the rebuilt city was worth less or more than the original? Is desire the only determination of value? I don't know. Certainly bread is less important to the man who has just eaten. It is like the disagreeable irony of those German firebombs that succeeded in exposing the walls of the medieval town along Podwale and Brzozowa streets, an archaeological site no one had known about until those bombs exploded.

When the rebuilding of the Old Town was complete, people trembled at the sight. At first we stared into Krakowskie Przedmieście from the periphery, afraid of walking into the mirage and being swallowed up. But after a few had ventured forward and had not vanished, the spectators, all of us, poured into the Old Town. There was numb silence at first, and then a humming and a roar of euphoria. A nervous howling of crying and laughter.

No one could climb the steep steps of the reconstructed Kamienne Schodki Street or walk through the arches on Świetojanska Street or look up at the immaculately copied ironwork clock and the iron dragon and the stone ships engraved on the reconstructed walls and not feel they'd gone mad.

The old streets – every doorway and streetlamp and stoop – was familiar, yet not quite; somehow almost more real than we remembered. Then there were things we didn't remember at all, and we felt some piece of our brains had been knocked out. Everyone wandered the streets the same way, vaguely afraid, as if the dead father or mother, the dead wife or sister might suddenly jump out from behind a doorway. And at the heart of it all, a civic pride, a jubilation, and an unspoken humiliation, our need so open, and so inconsolable.

In Warsaw during the 1950s, people were desperate with hope. They would make the most extravagant claims: 'For decades, physicists have been trying to figure out – if time can flow both into the future and into the past – why can't a broken eggshell become whole again, why can't shattered glass mend itself? And yet in Warsaw we are achieving exactly this! We haven't yet figured out how to raise the dead or regain lost love, but we're hard at work and if it happens anywhere it will be in reconstituted Warsaw!' And while people ran about proclaiming such things, I could only think that everything exists because of loss. From the bricks of our buildings, from cement to human cells, everything exists because of chemical transformation, and every chemical transformation is accompanied by loss. And when I look up at the night sky I think: The astronomers have given every star a number.

Lucjan tore a piece of paper from his drawing tablet and crumpled it into a ball.

– This is what the world is. A ball where everything is smashed together – collusion, complicity – those German plans for Egyptian dams you spoke of, and countless other examples . . .

He threw the ball of paper into the fireplace.

– I do not know, said Lucjan, if we belong to the place where we are born, or to the place where we are buried.

– You speak of the Old Town, said Jean, and of false consolation. That's what Avery could not bear about his work in Egypt – this false consolation.

She felt Lucjan's attention, felt the quality of the darkness change, though he hadn't moved. Whenever she spoke of

Avery, Jean felt him drawing in all the power of his listening.

— I want you to talk about him, whispered Lucjan, because it makes our lying here together more real, because you are here with me partly because you love him. And to know you, I must know him. Please, keep on.

Jean sat up and drew her knees under her chin.

— It repels him, the idea of false consolation. In the end, he believed that's what the moving of the temple was. Because so many already believed the dam to be a mistake.

— I wonder what it means to save something, said Lucjan, when first we make necessary its need to be saved. First we destroy and then we try to salvage. And then we feel self-righteous about the salvaging. And who is to say yet that the dam was a mistake?

— What was lost is more than what was gained, said Jean.

— Maybe. Lucjan paused. And maybe that's what you feel about your own life, maybe your marriage too.

The injury of this travelled through her.

— Don't be angry, said Lucjan. It's old fashioned, but let's say there's a hierarchy — of suffering. We could open a stock exchange for moral value and trade shares in human 'necessity.' If anyone were interested. Then we could really compare what things are worth, without the ambiguity of currency. Just goods. A pound of Paweł's coffee in Toronto and a hundred sacks of grain in the Sudan. A bottle of whisky in Warsaw and an English book in Moscow by an exiled dissident. A car, running water. A temple, fifty villages, thousands of archaeological artifacts for the price of a dam. The loss of one child and the loss of three million children.

Jean held her head in her hands.

Lucjan sighed. He pulled her toward him.

— Everything we do is false consolation, said Lucjan. Or to put it another way, any consolation is true.

During the Uprising, children delivered messages, helped in temporary hospitals, ran weapons from cellar to cellar. Courage came to us, said Lucjan, in the form of a fly, a speck of life, a parasite, landing on your bare arm. It came to us as hunger.

Everyone harvested what they could from the rubble – knitting needles, picture frames, the arm of a chair, a scrap of fabric – it was the market of the dead. There was a use for everything, someone was always willing to trade for something . . .

He held Jean close.

— I haven't talked about these things for a long time, he said quietly. Not since my ex-wife, Władka, and I were young, lying on the deck of her father's apple boat, buried in the cold fruit, with only our heads sticking out.

Your skin is so white. When you lie on top of me like this, with your legs all along mine so brown, and your tough little arms all along mine, you're like –

All her weight was upon him, and Lucjan felt her –

— Like snow on a branch.

There's a lot of work for children in a battle, said Lucjan. We were good at hide-come-seek, we felt we had nothing to lose. I darted down holes and found all kinds of things, all kinds of situations. Once, I found myself in the middle of a conversation among two men and a young woman.

The older man asked, 'Are you really a rabbi?'

'Now is not the time to pretend to be a rabbi,' said the young man with the faintest smile. 'Besides, that would be a sin.'

The older man looked down at the woman leaning against him, asleep.

'We would like to be married,' he said. 'Could you do this? Here and now?'

Here and now. My childhood was full of those little words — *zrób to w tej chwili*.

'Even in the dark,' the rabbi said, 'you need a canopy.'

The man took off his coat and asked me to hold it over their heads. Under his coat was nothing. His bare skin, his black hair. 'But you can't be married without a shirt,' I said. What a stupid thing to say, I don't know why I said it. The man looked at me with surprise and laughed. 'I think God knows what I look like without my shirt.'

Until then, the woman had said nothing. Then she said, 'You'll be cold without your coat.'

Everyone except the woman looked at his ghastly upper body, white as paper. The hair on his chest looked like black threads sewing his skin together. He handed me the coat and I held it as best I could over their heads.

Afterwards, there was nothing to eat or say or do. The woman was crying. The man put his arm around her. After a while, I fell asleep.

I remember thinking that I had fallen asleep many times to the sound of crying. I tried, as a method of falling asleep, but I could not count them all.

Within days of the Red Army's occupation of Warsaw, people returned. At their first sight of the city, many sat down at the edge of the rubble, simply sat down, as if suddenly forgetting how to walk.

I was hidden outside the ghetto when it was emptied, and when Warsaw fell I was running for the Home Army, and for Professor S., in and out of any situation where I could eat. In the end I left the city with the others, and returned with the first to return, days after the Soviets moved in.

I'd helped rescue fragments of Polish culture, architectural slag. Now I worked to rebuild the city, stone by stone. I was a child and a Jew: you could say it was not my city, not my culture, and yet you could say it was. When your arm is in the water, you are part of it; when you pull it out, there is no trace of you left behind.

We lived in the ruins and hauled the rubble with our bare hands, loading trucks and filling holes. The city was a cemetery wired with explosives – thirty-five thousand mines were dismantled in the first weeks. And in the first months, seven bridges were constructed, and hundreds of thousands of trees were planted. Every Sunday, wagonloads of volunteers, whole families, came to the city to help with the digging and the carrying. And every July 22, the authorities staged a public celebration to officially open a newly constructed section of the city, to ensure we understood this miracle was not an achievement of Polish muscle and sweat but a feat of Soviet socialism. I went to every one of those July spectacles: the opening of the Poniatowski Bridge, the opening of the East-West Thoroughfare, the replication of the Old Town . . . and the inauguration of the Palace of Culture – for which the Soviets had torn down the only buildings that had survived the war.

One day I saw, sitting amid the rubble, the chemist who used to run the dispensary behind his high marble counter on Nalewki Street; I recognized him because I used to go there with my mother when she bought her headache tablets and her hand creams. Now he was crouched on his small suitcase on the mountain of destruction, still wearing his white coat, the angel who had always cared whether you took your vapours or dissolved your digestive powder, or used the right-sized spoon for your cough syrup, or mixed the paste to the proper consistency for your poultice – always so courteous and concerned about every particular, the size and pressure of the dressing, each small ache. Always he seemed to know just what to say to the man with a toothache or sore joints or bronchitis . . . and now there he sat, looking at the broken ground between his feet, without a word of advice.

And, in time, sitting in the ruins, all the old habits persisted, the ordinary gestures: mothers smoothed down the hair of their children and tugged at their jackets; men took out handkerchiefs and carefully wiped the bomb-blasted dust from the tops of their shoes.

To Lucjan, Toronto was a place of used-up, worn surfaces for painting – hidden fences, old traffic barricades, the backs of billboards hanging over the edge of the ravine. On the "Caveman's" tour, he and Jean squeezed their way between buildings that opened into other passageways, loading docks, transit sheds, abandoned train stations, brick walls painted with faded advertisements for shops that had gone out of business forty years before, silos hidden among trees, railtracks ending in scrubgrass. Lucjan scavenged for materials as they roamed, his eye keen for castaway plastic and wire, masonry, wood. Old doors, broken chairs, the detritus of renovations. Once, they dragged home a six-foot beam still bearing children's heights and ages; once, a box of first volumes of thirty or so encyclopedias – *Encyclopedia of Mammals A–B*, *Geography A–B*, *British History A–B*, *North American Trees A–B* – a whole library of subscriptions cancelled after the first free sample in the mail. "Imagine only knowing the world of things beginning with A or B," said Lucjan, and so Jean did imagine – anemone, aster, basswood, box, bigtooth aspen – as they carried their finds back with them and piled them in the already crowded studio.

Afterwards, the dishwater still on his hands, Lucjan soaping her back under her straps.

Sometimes Jean or Lucjan would choose a painting in a gallery – Rembrandt's *Lady with a Lapdog* – or a specific book in a library – Chekhov's *Lady with Lapdog* or Grotowski's *Towards a Poor Theatre* – and meet there. Jean favoured meeting via

Dewey Decimal, like the coordinates of a map. Sometimes they would choose a building or a remnant of a building – the last Dominion coal chute, a small wooden door cut into the hillside for waterworkers to enter the reservoir, the church on Kendal Avenue that had been left unfinished during the Second World War, half a transept dangling.

They passed other sites of lost hopes, sites of amputations and scars; vacant lots strewn with the debris of a building that had been torn down so long ago the rubble was overgrown with grass, an abandoned bank leaning over the edge of the ravine. Lucjan was an expert at identifying Hydro Houses, small electrical power stations scattered throughout the city with false facades each built in the style of the neighbourhood – from the outside, perfectly innocent-looking houses, but if one opened the front door one would stand face to face with two storeys of gleaming machinery, dials, and coils. These houses were hard to detect, and gave themselves away only by a vague aura of uninhabitedness, windows permanently shut, a lack of a garden, no porch light. They explored an alternate city of laneways – sheet metal garages and wooden sheds. They sought out all the streets leading to railway tracks, where night trains rattled back-garden fences and the scream of light tore across bedroom walls.

– You had at least two good rivers flowing through this city and what have you done with them? said Lucjan. You've covered them over and siphoned them off and turned them into expressways. Instead you could have had boats to ride to work! And water markets and flower barges and swaying cafés and shops. You could have walked down your little residential street to your little neighbourhood dock and taken the ferry to another stop around the city – to work, to school. You could almost still do it . . .

One autumn afternoon, the trees bare and black against a white sky, they walked through the back door of a hardware shop and out into the silence of a hidden Catholic cemetery: the final destination of immigrants who'd fled the Irish potato famine, now a square of grass concealed behind storefronts. They had met there several times before, under the chestnut trees, amid fallen gravestones with names now melted, only an undecipherable indentation, Jean thought, like the line a finger makes in sand.

No noise of the street leaked into this hidden place; the long grass grew so thickly tangled around the plinths that, even if one were to fall, it would not make a sound; only the trees clattered in the wind. The ground was cold and wet but, nevertheless, they spread the square of blanket Lucjan had brought with him and they leaned against the shelter of a limestone wall of a small octagonal building – beautifully proportioned – with deeply set shutters, closed tight and hooked fast.

– When ground is too frozen for the digging of graves, said Lucjan, the dead wait in these winter vaults. There is always a dignity to these buildings – whether made of brick or stone with expensive brass fittings or just a humble wooden shed – because they are built with respect for those who will lie within their walls.

But in times of war or seige, he continued, when there are too many civilians for such vaults, other makeshift shelters must be found. In Warsaw during the bitter winter of 1944–45, the dead rested together in root cellars, in mine-blasted gardens, amid the rubble of the streets under sheets of newspaper. During the seige of Leningrad, along the road to the Piskarevsky cemetery, thousands were heaped, so high the ice-encased dead formed a tunnel through which one passed in terror. Crowded trolley cars stood immobile in the ice and snow, tombs that could not be moved until the spring. The dead were wound tenderly in shawls, towels, rugs, curtains, wrapping paper bound with twine. In cold apartments, bodies were placed in the bath, left in bed, lain on tables. They clustered the pavement, doused with turpentine. In the thirty-degree-below-zero weather, the ground was, like the hymn says, hard as iron, and a mass grave could only be made by dynamiting. The frozen bodies were then thrown, clinking together, into the pit.

The winter dead wait, said Lucjan, for the earth to relent and receive them. They wait, in histories of thousands of pages, where the word love is never mentioned.

Brown birds lined the eaves of the vault roof. They balanced on the edge, small dark stones against the sky, now marbled grey: dusk.

– It was January, Jean told Lucjan, when my mother died. My parents had once passed by a country cemetery on a drive together, north of Montreal, and they stopped to walk there. My mother remembered that peaceful ground and the name of the nearby village, and that is where she chose to be buried.

But the ground was too cold to dig the grave.

For almost two months, several times a week, my father and I drove past the fields, past forest, to sit on camp chairs by the door of the vault. And do you know what my father did? He read to her. Keats, Masefield, Tennyson, Sara Teasdale, T. S. Eliot, Kathleen Raine. The vault itself was quite small and the door huge, all out of proportion, thick, with ornate metal hinges. At first I could not bear the thought of my mother listening behind that heavy, closed door. But slowly, as the days passed, I began to feel that although her dear body was inside, somehow her soul was not. The sound of my father reading became a kind of benediction, an absolution. Often it snowed. We opened umbrellas and poured out flasks of steaming, milky tea and, as he read, I sat under my mother's old umbrella and looked out to the wet trees and the cloud-blackened sky between the bare branches. One horse always roamed in the field next to the graveyard, liquid black against the snow. During all those vigils we never met anyone else. The day we finally buried my mother was the last we ever visited that place together. I understood what my father felt, something we never could have imagined – that even a grave can be a kind of redemption.

They walked north from Amelia Street, through the leaves blowing across the empty streets. Jean's hair was loose, shining under the streetlamps and streaming out behind her, in the dark water of the October night. They came to a semi-circle of narrow houses whose front yards emptied into a city park. A ribbon of pavement, perhaps a foot and a half wide, marked where private property ended and the park began.

Lucjan pointed.

— That's where I earn my living, now and then, the last house in the row. Do you see the electrical cord leading from the house into the trees? My boss has wired half the park with tiny bulbs. It amuses him, and no one has complained. He's like you, Janina, taking charge of the world, though he's not as dangerous. You're a memory bandit. But who can be distressed by little lights like fireflies in the forest? The expressway they were going to build — it would have sliced right through this quiet place.

— Perhaps that's the reason he lights up the park, said Jean. To remind himself that what we take for granted already had to be saved.

Lucjan took her cold hand and put it in his pocket.

— He's still a fine bookbinder, but he's old now, and can't do all the work on his own. I like sitting with him at the big table, with vise clamps and glue and the smell of leather. Sometimes we don't talk the whole day. I can't tell you how much I like him, I like the way he touches the leather, I like that he's neat, every petit fers and mullen and marbling comb in its place, every pot of aqua regia and myrabolan tannin wiped clean after use, every endpaper cross-catalogued by colour and texture and age, and then filed away in square drawers — in a cabinet he built himself. I like that he keeps his letters from Edgar Mansfield close at hand in a wooden box on his worktable. He collects moss and mushrooms and photographs them. People come to his door with specimens, squares of moss in little boxes, like jewellery, or envelopes of fungi from all over the world – from Bolivia, India, New Zealand, Peru. He puts samples under a microscope and draws what he sees. Sometimes he uses the shapes in his designs, carving them into the leather of the books, a beautiful effect, almost marbled. When we sit together I feel even his silence is orderly, as if he says to himself, Okay, today we will not talk about what happened in 1954, today we will not talk about what happened when my wife went to the doctor, today we will not talk about Stalin and the way it was during the war, today we will not discuss the pain in my knee or the grief that bulges out suddenly sometimes from being childless, today we will not discuss Jakob Böhme, or spores, or what the rain reminds me of. It is a good feeling, to sit at a table with a man and not talk about specific things together. He thinks and I think, we keep each other company, and at the end of the day it is as if we'd had hours of intimate conversation.

———————

Marina found a part-time job for Jean, three afternoons a week, at Mumford's, a children's press she sometimes illustrated for, a tiny publishing house, literally a house, near the university, a working mothers' co-op press, named after a suffragette grandmother of one of the editors, Jo Mumford. Its nickname among the editors was Mum's the Word. Jean's job was to do anything asked of her: type invoices, deliver packages, make photocopies, brew coffee.

Marina had told them Jean could cook, so sometimes she did that too, in the tiny kitchen at the back of the bindery. She learned the hand-press and printed small runs of book-marks, a cult item in the battle for feminist supremacy with the University Press' bookmarks, which featured ironic drawings of dull domestic cuisine – the "baked potato bookmark," the "boiled egg bookmark." Mum's the Word countered with their own series of bitingly lacklustre symbols of domesticity – the "kettle bookmark" and the "vacuum cleaner bookmark."

Walking to the university or to work, city signs now revealed themselves as fonts. She thought about Lucjan marbling endpapers for the bookbinder-on-the-park. She thought about paper, the first sheets that could be manufac-tured in endless lengths, without seams, rolling off the machine in Frogmore in 1803.

Jean began to imagine a botanical typeface. She began with A and E, astor and eglantine. Avery and Escher. She could not render it herself adequately but could picture it in her mind in fine detail. She thought of asking Marina if she would illustrate a chapbook of Jean's remedies for imaginary afflictions if Jean were to set the type herself, a single copy for Avery, hand-sewn. Marina was illustrating a series of small, hardbound, classic adventure novels – *Treasure Island*, *Around the World in Eighty Days*, *The Time Machine* – each to be followed by a sister volume of the same tale told from the point of view of a female heroine. "Though of course I know the plots," said Marina, "I keep reading anxiously, in a fever, hoping things will go differently than I remember, each moment hoping for better luck, for a reprieve, hoping I can make a difference with all my hoping . . ."

Jean sat at her table with her seed books and a map of the city spread open around her, pen in the air, while sorrow moved from heart to head, a creeping paralysis. The wrenching sadness that she had not known Avery's father. Avery as a boy, afraid, in the café in Turin with the patch of gauze on his chin. Every detail and regret accompanied by the fear that her history with Avery was being erased by Lucjan's touch, Lucjan's stories. He'd lent her a book of photographs of Warsaw, comparing views of the same city blocks, before and after the destruction, a single tree or a single wall the only evidence that the photographer had stood in the same spot. She felt Lucjan, and what it was to stand in that place.

It was too cold now for planting, and Jean's plans for the neighbourhoods, for Chinatown, Greektown, Little Italy, Little India, Tibet, Jamaica, Armenia, would have to wait for spring.

She had an unexpected ally in her plans for the city: Daub Arbab. Over the months, he had been sending seeds and planting advice from the places he worked. And to Daub, Jean had confided a painful question. She hoped he would find words for her, believed in him since their journey to Ashkeit. And because when she'd returned to the camp from the hospital in Cairo, Daub had said, "You weep for all the daily reasons, you weep because you will never brush your daughter's hair."

Just as belief is visceral, so was this doubt. It had first formed in her when she stood before the re-erected temple and had felt her personal suffering to be almost unconscionable. What was personal loss in the face of universal devastation – the loss of Nubia, the destruction of cities. Her misery shamed her. And yet, her shame was not correct, she knew it was not. To mourn is to honour. Not to surrender to this keening, to this absence – a dishonouring.

'Your letter has reached me in Bombay,' wrote Daub, 'and tomorrow I begin the long drive, hundreds of kilometres, along a river, the first work for a dam. In the taxi from the airport, the multitudes pressed against the car, hands and faces pushed against the glass, they banged their hands on the bonnet and on the windows, which I'd kept closed, suffocating with the heat and the misery around me, as if I were in an armoured tank. Then guiltily stretching out on the hotel bed.

'If I had a wife, I would not be here, I would be somewhere close to home, building something harmless, a bridge or a school. But instead I wander, my loneliness sticking like a burr. Why is Avery not with you? If you were my wife, I would be by your side. If love finds you, there is not a single day to be wasted. I watched you walking through the camp, the last weeks before your daughter was born, your horror and sorrow, and I could not understand then, as I do not understand now, Avery's reticence. I believe always it is a matter of taking the one you love in your arms. But I know nothing of marriage and what silences are necessary. As for your inquiry, dear Jean, I have been lying here trying to think what to say to you.

'Perhaps there is a collective dead. But there is no such thing as a collective death. Each death, each birth, a single death, a single birth. One man's death cannot be set against millions, nor one man's death against another. I beg you not to torment yourself on this point. We were many months in the desert together and I know a little of how your heart works. Please sit quietly as you read this and hear what I say: There is no need to replace your grieving with penance.'

There's too much sand in the cement, Avery had said, and Jean had listened, lying next to him in the dark, at the limit of self-possession, cradling the stillness in her belly. It's not the workers' fault, he had continued, they'd been unsupervised. Cement is not hardened by the air, as most people believe, but by a chemical reaction . . . And now, in the kitchen on Clarendon, Jean heard Avery's desperation. The cement that would not dry.

———

Lucjan was working on a series of maps, sized to fit, when folded, into the glovebox of a car. He painted each detail with care, like medieval decoration on an illuminated manuscript. Every trade, he had explained to Jean, has its own map of the city: the rat and cockroach exterminators, the raccoon catchers, the hydro and sewer and road repair workers. There is the mothers' map marked with pet shops and public washrooms and places to collect pinecones, with sidewalk widths and pot-hole depths indicated for carriages, tricycles, and wagon-pulling. The knitters have their own map, with every wool supplier in the city marked. Lucjan made a map of exceptional tree roots, of wind corridors, and water runoff. He made a coffee map (with only one location marked), a sugar map, a chocolate map, a ginkgo tree map, a weeping willow map, a map of bridges, of public drinking fountains, of boulders larger than five feet in diameter. A shoe repair map. A grape arbour map, a map of kite-flying spaces (without overhead wires), a sledding map (hills without roads or fences at the bottom). Then there were the personal maps. The remorse map. The embarrassment map. The arguments map. The disappointment maps (bitter and mild). The map of the dead; the cemeteries built on vertical slopes. And the map he was working on when he met Jean — perhaps the most beautiful of all — a map of invisible things, a thought map, indicating where people had experienced an idea, a fear, a secret hope; some were well known, others private. An intersection where a novel was first imagined, a park where a child was dreamed of. The beach where an architect visualized his skyline. The bench where a painter had a premonition of his own death. "How does one paint what is not there?" asked Jean. "One paints the place exactly as one sees it," said Lucjan. "Then, one paints it again."

———

Lucjan's friend Paweł was a member of the Stray Dogs, a jazz orchestra of old men — old except for Paweł, the youngest by several decades. Lucjan was a silent member; he didn't play an instrument, but he was good at finding unusual things to bang on and, because he understood them, his advice was invaluable; sometimes he was called upon to settle a vote. The cornet, Janusz, was the second youngest and proud of his youth, introducing himself to Jean as "barely seventy years old in my stocking feet." Some wore an air of permanent, desiccated romance, while the faces of the others, including the leader, "Mr. Snow" himself, contained such ransacked grief one could barely behold them. Mr. Snow – Jan Piletski – had worked with his father in the fish market at Rynkowa Street in Warsaw before the war. From a block away, Lucjan explained to Jean, you could see the long trestle tables, glinting with silver, a shimmering lake hovering in the middle distance. But this was a mirage with a stench. When the wind blew, the reek of fish floated for a quarter-mile in every direction. Once a week, I went with my mother and we always watched a man who used to sit at his easel, painting the wares. His fish were true to life – every shimmering scale – even the stink. Jan's wife, Beata, had referred to the distinctive aroma of the market as the Piletski perfume, and Jan Piletski himself was nicknamed by the Stray Dogs after the herring fisherman in a song from the musical *Carousel*. Mr. Snow became Jan Piletski's stage name, and this was also in honour of his fish-seller father, who had died in the Uprising.

All the Dogs remembered the days of the Crocodile Club, the Quid Pro Quo, the Czarny Kot – the Black Cat – and the Perskie Oko – the Persian Eye. They still dreamed of the queen of popular song, Hanka Ordonówna, and referred to her long affair with "that old man" Juliusz "My little Quail has Flown" Osterwafor with disdain and jealousy. The Stray Dogs were united in age, in inexpressible misfortune, in exile that defined them so completely it was difficult to imagine for them any other destiny, nor in their synchronized swim of chordal progressions and bent sound. Uniting them too was the knowledge that one's life is never remembered in its vicissitudes and variety but only as a distillation, a reduction of sixty or seventy years into one or two moments, a couple of images. Or as Hors Forzwer – the emcee at Warsaw's Round Club – might have said, from juice to jus. For each of them, the concepts of "music" and "women" were inseparable, as inseparable as "music" and "loneliness." As ideas, "music" and "women" could not be disentangled, and in fact made an irreducible whole, like a molecule that is defined by its components and, if altered, changes into something unrecognizable. Just as "death" and "life" are meaningless one without the other, so "music," "women," "loneliness." All this was evident in a single note gnarled beyond recognition, in a single chord heavy as a woman's thigh flung across a man's chest in the night. They played a cellarful of abandonment, the guilty look in an offguard moment, the coffee ring hardened into enamel at the bottom of the cup, the nub of a candle burnt down to the china saucer. And yet, there was a kind of solace too, the solace of emerging from the ruins to find that at least you no longer had any hair left to catch fire or that, for the moment, your prosthesis was not aching. "We want our music," explained Mr. Snow, "to make people long to go home, and," he boasted, "if the place is even half-cleared out by the time we've finished one set, we're overjoyed. Because for once it will seem better to be home alone in all one's misery than to be out listening to us. That's the kind of happiness we're capable of provoking!"

The Stray Dogs – a.k.a. the Hooligans, the Troublemakers, the Bandits, the Carbon Club (the latter a reference to the final days of the uprising, when Home Army Second Lieutenant Kazimierz Marczewski, who happened also to be an architect and town planner, had stood in the middle of Warsaw while firebombs fell and mines exploded around him, famously sketching plans for the reconstruction of the city on carbon paper) – indulged themselves with strange musical obsessions including Broadway musicals that they mangled into something agonizing, precisely heartbreaking, taking all the sweet hope and earnestness and extracting betrayal and despair with what Lucjan called "emotional acupuncture." And they played Laura Nyro's "Stoned Soul Picnic" and "Kamienny Koniec" – "Stoney End" – because Nyro resembled – was in fact an exact physical replica of – Beata in her youth, whom they all remembered with great feeling. How beautiful she'd been – *Jakże była piękna*.

"I was born from love – *Jestem dzieckiem miłośći*," Mr. Snow growled, his voice singeing Jean's ears. "And my poor mother worked the mines – *A moja biedna matka pracowała w kopalni* . . . I never wanted to go down the stoney end – *do kamiennego końca* . . . Mama, let me start all over, Cradle me again."

There were of course the *zakazane piosenki*, the "forbidden songs," all the classics of the Chmielna Street Orchestra: "A Heart in a Rucksack," "Autumn Rain," "Air Raid," "In the

Black Market You'll Survive," and "I Can't Come to You Today." And, needless to say, Hanka Ordonówna's signature "Love Forgives Everything," which Mr. Snow sang with a voice of such rancid sarcasm Jean wanted to stop up her ears before her heart shrivelled. "He is the only person alive," said Lucjan, "who looks even at a kitten with disapproval." Mr. Snow sang, "*Miłość Ci wszystko wybaczy* — Love forgives everything, forgives betrayal and lies" and by the time he reached the final line "*Bo miłość, mój miły, to ja* — Love, my dear, is me" in his strangulating creak, one felt one would rather die alone in a ditch than fall in love again.

The Stray Dogs took each song apart, dismantling the melody, painstakingly, painfully, sappers dismantling a lie, and then turned each single component around so many times it disintegrated. Then they put it together again from nothing, notes and fragments of notes, bent notes and breaths, squawks on the horns and the reeds' empty-lidded beating of keys. By the time the melody reappeared, one was sick with longing for it. "At first," said Janusz, the cornet, "following Mr. Snow in a piece was like following the tracks of a jackrabbit — I never knew where he'd land. But after a while I could guess where his demented, sentimental mind might take him and one or two times over the years I even beat him there first. You should have seen the grin on his face — as if he'd opened a door and finally found himself home. I think that's the best thing I ever did for a man, taking away that loneliness for a bar or two."

Paweł (double bass) wore a buttoned-down shirt and a thin houndstooth sportsjacket, Tomasz (trombone) wore a shapeless cardigan that dripped into a pool at his hips; Paweł had long hair, Piotr had no hair. Tadeusz (saxes), who was called Ranger – short for arranger – always wore a plaid flannel shirt, winter and summer. Ranger had been in Canada the longest and had learned his erudite English from a professor of Slavics who considered herself to have had two great insights, first to have married Ranger and then to have divorced him.

The first time Jean heard the Dogs, they were rehearsing at Paweł's café, after hours, a broken-down dirge. It tormented the air with its clockwork irregularity, a mechanical breakdown of stops and starts, notes grinding, grating, surging, limping. It was the music of revellers too old to be staying out all night, too dwindled to walk another step. Impatient and sad. A tonal meagreness. One by one the players dropped away until there was silence. Jean listened, mesmerized, the way one watches a fallen bowl circle round and round on the floor, waiting for the inevitable stillness.

She thought of dangerous rocks cascading intermittently down a slope, of stalled traffic, of conversations that stop and start not lazily, but instead signalling the end of everything.

– At night, said Lucjan, I lay in my *melina* listening to the stone rain. Pieces of brick or plaster that had been balancing precariously somewhere in the ruined darkness would reach their moment to fall – by wind, gravity, a soldier's boot.

Gradually I became accustomed to it, there was no choice except to go mad waiting for the next sound that never came until I was almost asleep and was woken into waiting again. I used to feel how far it was from listening to the rain with my mother in the spring evenings on Freta Street, when I had only the problem of deciding which fairy tale to read before bed, or which dessert to choose that evening, apple cake or poppyseed cake.

— Now I understand, said Jean, what the Stray Dogs play . . . the stone rain.

The only (erstwhile and unofficial) member of the Stray Dogs who had not known the others from Warsaw was Jan, a Lithuanian from Saskatchewan who, late one summer night on his way home from playing lounge piano in a hotel, had come across Lucjan sitting on a curb contemplating a huge metal bedframe, wondering how he could transport it home. Jan offered to take one end and Lucjan took the other. They sat until daylight in Lucjan's studio drinking iced peppermint tea and vodka. Then Jan took it upon himself to spread green onions on the bottom of a pan and pour Lucjan's last three eggs on top of them. "Thus," Lucjan told Jean, "are friendships sealed."

The Stray Dogs met regularly at Lucjan's to settle matters, financial and otherwise. They maintained they met there on the first Thursday of every month, but the day was always changed at the last minute and so far, in ten years, it had never been a Thursday. That was as close to a schedule as they ever came – the Never-Thursday Schedule. "It's important to maintain delusions," said Lucjan, "for the sake of order."

Paweł always brought along to these meetings his little white dog with the pointed snout – a white cone ending in a black plug. Jean watched as the dog ate daintily from Paweł's hand. One certainly could not call Paweł his "master," for in every gesture the man revealed his solicitude. In cold weather the dog wore a dignified navy-blue knitted coat. In summer, Paweł carried a flask of water and he cupped his hand so the dog could drink.

It was this little dog, their mascot, for whom the men named their orchestra, also referring to a certain café in St. Petersburg frequented before the wars by outlawed poets. It was their sad little Soviet joke; another way of hiding; a dilapidated homage; a wave across the abyss. It sat uncomfortably, just the way they preferred things. For a time they considered keeping the name they were known by in Warsaw, the Hooligans, but in the end it made them too sad and they left, like everything else, the name behind.

———

Lucjan and Jean walked through the darkly glinting, rain-soaked streets to listen to the Stray Dogs at the Door with One Hinge, a club open only on Saturday nights.

— In Warsaw, said Lucjan, kicking along the gutters gleaming with wet leaves, Paweł and Ewa had their own theatre. It was in their flat, a show once a week, and they were raided all the time. That was before such incredible theatre companies as Pomarańczowa Alternatywa, Orange Alternative. Ewa and Paweł were the vanguard, with all their escapades – street theatre with entire plays that lasted only five minutes and dispersed before the police came, or epics that took place in a series of pre-arranged places throughout the city over the course of a day. Now Ewa designs sets for all the small theatres here. Sometimes I paint for her. Some people are outsiders, no matter how long they've lived in a place, and no matter what they achieve, and others simply find the current and step into it no matter where they are; they always know what's being talked about, who's thinking what, where the next thing is coming from. Ewa's like that – an iconoclast supreme. When Warsaw was being rebuilt at top speed, she organized a monthly beauty pageant for the most attractive building, a model of which was crowned the new "Mr. Warsaw" at a ceremony staged every month in their flat.

Ewa enlists not only her husband, Paweł, but all the Dogs to help her. For a production of *Godot*, we made more than fifty trips to the ravine collecting bags of autumn leaves; for days Paweł drove back and forth from the park to the theatre – a room above a printer's shop – his Volkswagen bug crammed full. Their children helped empty the bags onto the floor of the theatre and they ran about with hair dryers until the leaves were bone-dry and brittle. By the time the play opened, the theatre was waist deep and the whole room trembled with each step. An eternity of leaves from Beckett's two bare trees in the middle of the room. For Brecht's *Chalk Circle*, Ewa used stones that Paweł, the Dogs, and I hauled from the lake. All the small theatres love Ewa because her sets never cost them a cent.

Lucjan and Jean would start out at 10 or 11 p.m. to meet up with the Stray Dogs, who would be starving after a night's work. Until it became too cold, they liked to picnic on the bourgeois billiard-table lawn of the Rosehill reservoir, with a view of the city in every direction. They'd eat cold potatoes and cheese, sweet bread and sour plums. Ewa and Paweł would come after one of Ewa's plays, with Paweł's little dog, who darted, a firefly, through the dark grass. Platters of food were passed from hand to hand, flasks of tea. The men stretched out and looked at the stars. Jean lay there too, in the green chill of the grass. In the darkness she listened to the stories, the resentments, the regrets . . . the enticing glance a woman gave, in passing, fifty-five years before, on the train to Wrocław. The cold beer on the boat from Sielce to Bielany. The women, the women, the women: the shape of a calf as a fellow passenger reached for her luggage overhead on the boat, how that singer-from-Łódź's buttocks clenched with muscle under her silky dress when she sang the high notes; how many one-minute love affairs these old men had enjoyed, full, not of simple lust, but of complicated passion and promise, and never enacted, not so much as a wink, so there was never the burden of an unhappy ending. Never unrequited, always possible except "under the circumstances." On this particular subject, the wives had stopped listening to their men thirty years ago and they lay together, their dresses spread out around them or tight across their majestic flesh, talking about one another's children and grandchildren, the toothaches and remedies, the talents and accomplishments.

Jean felt a scarecrow among these women, the Polish harem, just as she had among the Nubian women.

She listened to the men's political close calls, the romantic escapades, the concerts in pigsties and coffee houses across Poland and France, as they worked their way to the sea. All this in the park at midnight, the men and women sprawled and still across the grass, "like the dead," said Lucjan, "gossiping on a battlefield." Jean listened with Lucjan's hand finding her; she felt he could touch every point of her at once, with one hand. He wound his thick belt around her waist, pulled it tight and buckled it. He pulled her hair taut until every part of her was aching upwards, her mouth open. All this in the cold night grass. The night was voices and in her submission Jean felt the murmuring of Lucjan's friends on her body.

———

Lucjan carried a watermelon; he'd painted it to look like a large white cat curled asleep. Jean carried a cappuccino pie – the Sgana Café's specialty – wrapped in ice. They came to a row house on Gertrude Street.

From Ewa and Paweł's front porch, Jean could see right through the narrow house and out again to the tiny back garden. The front hall was crammed with stage props, eccentrically decorated bicycles, children's toys, and oversized sketchbooks leaning against the walls. Even the street was cramped, cars lining both sides, houses split in half, sharing a single porch, a single front yard. Each owner had made his small attempt to distinguish his side of the property according to his superior taste. The houses were at the very limit of what one could make of them, inside and out. Before she had even stepped past the door, Jean felt the pull of a new affection.

Ewa and Paweł's living room was full of children and Dogs. Guests perched on the arms of chairs, in laps, sat cross-legged on the floor.

The wall in the hallway was covered in children's paint — butterflies, flowers, a big yellow sun.

—The children paint the wall any way they like, said Ewa. Then every month we paint over it and they can start again.

Ewa disappeared and returned with a tray of tea and cake. She gave it to Paweł, who offered it around.

Jean and Lucjan followed Ewa into the kitchen. Someone said, "It's Lucjan's girl," and then Jean was surrounded. The women fingered her hair and stroked her arms, they felt her appraisingly, as if she were fabric, or an expensive handbag or a necklace, or a prodigy on display. Jean almost swooned with their scents and their softness and, most of all, their cooing approval. Now she was sitting down at the kitchen table with a glass of wine in her hand and the women's voices a spell around her. She saw Lucjan watching, amused, from across the room.

— Lucjan tells me you recognized him by his work, said
Ewa. She laughed. He enjoys what the newspapers like to
call 'local notoriety.'

Jean smiled.

— I enjoy it, said Lucjan, only because no one knows who
I am, and I never face my public.

— Not unless someone catches you in the act, said Ewa.

— Yes. He frowned. That's why I only come out to paint
at night.

Ewa and Paweł's children, five and seven years old,
climbed into Jean's lap and began to have their way with her.
Jean sat still as they investigated her attributes, examining
her hair, poking with their fingers. They made cherry ear-
rings and hung them from her ears, where they bobbled like
plastic marbles.

— Do they want to be doctors or hairdressers? Jean asked,
laughing.

— One of each, naturally, said Lucjan from the doorway,
taking obvious pleasure in Jean's initiation.

Jean soon learned that at Ewa's parties there was always a
project on. Huge rolls of brown paper were unfurled and
everyone painted a mural; a sheet was tacked to the wall
and a film projected while the Dogs played, sewing together
a melody out of silence and the whirring of the projector.
Actors gathered in the middle of the living room and, with
nothing more than a spoon or a dishtowel, transformed
reality — having a Sunday row on a pond or floating in
a lifeboat on the North Sea; suddenly they were lovers on a
picnic blanket, or thieves, or children on a swing. Jean knew

these actors had worked together for a long time, a bodily history among them. She had seen Avery perform loaves and fishes with objects, with stones on the beach, with rulers and wooden blocks, creating bridges, castles, entire cities. But his magic was solitary and intellectual compared with the instantly complex communication between these bodies, the moment continually changing, deepening into humour or sorrow. And sometimes this pathos was intense, and a hole opened, and everyone watching from the edges of the room found their own sorrow pouring into it. Crack! the earth of the scene split open and down everyone tumbled together into the wreckage of memory. And then the actors melted back into the party, and the food and the bottles were passed around again.

Jean's hair was pinned up in a knot, gently unravelling. She had Lucjan's sweater over her shoulders.

—You radiate happiness, said Ranger.

Ranger sat down next to her.

— Does Lucjan talk to you? he asked.

Jean looked at him, startled.

—Yes, Lucjan talks to me.

Ranger stretched out his legs.

— I'm drunk, he said.

He leaned his head on Jean's shoulder.

— What if, Ranger said, the most important, the most meaningful, the most intimate moment of your life was also the most important, the most intimate moment for hundreds of thousands of others? Any man who's lived through a battle, the bombing of a city, a siege, has shared the same private moment with thousands of others. People pretend that's a brotherhood. But what belongs to you? Nothing. Not even the most important moment of your life is your own. Okay, so we understand this. But what about what happens between a man and a woman in the dark, in privacy, in bed? I say there's nothing intimate about that either. You hold her hand in the street, everyone knows what you do at night. You have a child, everyone knows what you did together.

Jean was silent. She felt the damp weight of Ranger's head against her, a terrible sadness. Then she said, in a gentle voice, Do you mean to say that all women and men are alike, that one woman is exactly like another? Or do you mean to tell me that Lucjan has had many women? If so, don't worry, he's told me himself.

— And what do details matter? continued Ranger. Her father, his father, her mother, his mother, the deprived child- hood, the happy childhood . . . Even the particulars of our bodies — at the moment of passion, at that precise moment, she is any body, any body will do.

— Have you never been in love?

— Of course I have. I'm seventy-four years old. But the experience of love — what you feel — it's always the same, no matter who the object of that love is.

Lucjan came with Jean's drink.

— Jean, is he scaring you? Ranger, I wish you wouldn't — that's my job.

Ranger bowed his head and held out his hand for Jean's glass.

— No, said Lucjan quietly. Language is only approximate; it's violence that's precise.

— No, said Ranger, raising his voice. Violence is a howl — the ultimate howl — inarticulate.

— No, said Lucjan. Violence is precise, always exactly to the point.

— It's just a philosophical argument, said Ranger. Have a drink.

— Are you mad? shouted Lucjan.

Lucjan took hold of Ranger's shoulders and was about to shake him. But he looked at Ranger's hopeless face and kissed him on top of the head instead.

— You make me sick, said Lucjan.

— Me too, said Ranger.

Suddenly Ranger turned to Jean.

— Fresh blood, said Ewa, nudging Lucjan.

— What do you say, Jean? You're my last chance.

— I have to think about it.

— Ha, said Ranger.

— No, she means it, said Lucjan.

So they gave her ten minutes' peace. Jean left the din of the party and wandered upstairs to the children's room and sat on a small bed.

Beside her on a little table was a box brimming with metal bottlecaps. There was a stuffed cat and a drawing of a heart with wings floating over the ocean. The heart also had an anchor chain that disappeared into the waves. It made her head ache to think about it.

Violence is a form of speech. Violence is a form of speechlessness. Of course it is.

—You still want to believe in something, said Ranger. You still think there are such qualities as selflessness, or neighbourliness, or even disinterest. You still think someone will step forward with a plan! You still believe a man's beautiful books or beautiful songs are written out of love and not a way to brag of all the women he's had. You still think that love is a blessing and not a disaster. You still believe in a sacred bond sealed during a night of soul-searching love, in tastes, scars, maps, a woman's voice singing of love, the hot kiss of whisky between her legs, a sax solo played by an old Pole in a sweater with a voice like a mistake. You still believe a man will join his life with a woman after a single night. You still believe a man will dream about one woman for the rest of his life. I believe in taking what I want until there is nothing left. I believe in sleeping with a woman for what she can teach you. I believe in the loyalty among men who know they will slip away from the others the first better chance they get. I believe you can only trust someone who has lost everything, who believes in nothing but self-interest. But you, he said, waving his hand across all assembled in Ewa and Paweł's living room, still step into the street with the possibility that something good might happen. You still believe you will be loved, truly loved, past all frailty and misjudgment and betrayal. I've seen a man say goodbye to his wife with a look of such penetrating trust between them you could smell the breakfasts and promises, the sitting up with the sick child, the love-making after the child has fallen asleep, the candy smell of the children's medicine still sticky on their hands – and then that same man drives straight from that bedroom to his lover, who opens her legs like a hallelujah while the wife scrubs the pots from last night's dinner and then sits down at the kitchen table and pays the bills. As soon as a war is over we revive the propaganda of peace – that men do terrible things in extremity, that men are heroic out of nobility of soul rather than out of fear or out of one kind of duty or another, or simply by accident. Men honour promises out of fear – the fear of crossing a line that will rip up their lives. Then we call this fear love or fidelity, or religion or loyalty to principles. There's garbage floating even in the middle of the ocean, thousands of miles from any land. Men shoot chemicals into a human corpse and put it on display and no one arrests them! When you take away the human body's right to rot into the earth or go into the air, you take away the last holiness. Do you understand me? The last holiness. People picnicked in the ruins. Poles stepped over dead Jews in the street on their way to lunch. We were afraid to open a suitcase in the rubble because it might contain a dead child, the infant a mother carried, the suitcase banging against her legs, all the way from Łódź to Poznań to Kraków to Warsaw, waiting to die herself. Children betrayed their parents to the state. Two filthy words: military occupation.

Ranger stood. Lucjan moved to take his arm and Ranger swerved from his grasp.

— I'm not as drunk as you think.

Ranger picked up his jacket and left.

Ewa began to collect the ashtrays and empty them into the bin. No one said a word. Jean looked at Lucjan, who looked away with a shrug.

— I'm going to bed, said Ewa, climbing the stairs. Throw yourselves out.

Jean took off everything, then pulled Lucjan's sweater over her head; the sleeves hung down to her knees. The wool carried his embrace and his shape. Then she cooked only in the small light of the stove, working alone in the dim kitchen. She would cook something that required slow, long heat, the flavours intensifying. She smelled the herbs on her fingers, his smell in her hair, the eucalyptus scent of her own skin. She watched the kale and onions and mushrooms turn soft and shrink with the heat. Love permeates everything, the world is saturated with it, or is emptied of it. Always this beautiful or this bereft. She crushed the rosemary between her palms, then drew her hands over his sweater so later he would find it. Everything one's body had been — the pockets of shame, of strange pride, scars hidden or known. And then the self that is born only in another's touch — every tip of pleasure, of power and weakness, every crease of doubt and humiliation, every pitiful hope no matter how small.

It was an early Sunday evening in January, snow at the windows. Jean carried a tray with Paweł's Jamaican coffee and thick slices of brown bread, a pot of jam with a spoon sticking out of it. Lucjan was lying on the bed with a book over his face.

— Talk to me, Janina. Tell me about a Sunday you've had, he said from under the book.

Jean poured and set the cup on the floor beside him.

She thought of Avery, a sudden, burning homesickness. What they knew together: black earth and stone trees, swathing forest, a glimpse of stars. The grasses of Kintyre swaying above their heads in a sea of air. Collecting stones from the hard winter sand and building houses from them, the largest up to her waist, the smallest in the middle of the square kitchen table in the cottage they'd rented in this Scotland they loved, their great gasp of cold wind before the heat of the desert. The blankets heaped on the bed, so heavy they could barely roll over in their perfect sleep together. No use to ask Avery if he remembered. She knew he remembered.

— One Sunday, said Jean slowly, an archaeologist suddenly appeared on our houseboat. He was hunting for Canadians; he was from Toronto and was feeling melancholy, and it seemed the most natural thing in the world to sit with him on the Nile on a Sunday evening listening to him describe a concert he'd heard by Segovia at Massey Hall.

At Faras, continued Jean, there were archaeologists from Warsaw, and a huge Soviet camp at the dam. Sometimes we saw them at the market in Wadi Halfa. The Russians especially looked bereft. They sat in the shade of the coffee stalls smoking and whistling songs by Yves Montand. The desert was filled with foreigners – from Argentina, Spain, Scandinavia, Mexico, France – and there was brisk trade in the small bitter cigarettes of each country. And wherever the archaeologists were working, the Bedouin shadowed the sites, watching and waiting just off in the distance, never approaching.

– Wait a moment, said Lucjan.

He jumped out of bed and she watched as he moved through the dusk, down the steep stairs and into the kitchen. For a moment the light of the fridge touched the ceiling, then darkness again.

She heard him, scrabbling about trying to feel his way through a stack of record albums. Then a man's voice floated upstairs.

Lucjan stood at the top of the staircase, remembering.

– Yves Montand . . . There was a time in Warsaw, said Lucjan, when, from every open window, you could hear 'C'est à l'Aube' or 'Les Grands Boulevards' or 'Les Feuilles Mortes' in the street. When Montand sang at the Palace of Culture, thirty-five hundred people listened. Fifteen minutes after he left the stage, people were still shouting for encores. The bureaucracy did not object because Montand was a man of the people; he was the man who stood up and gave a spontaneous concert for eight thousand workers at the Ukhachov auto plant. Khrushchev knew Montand filled every seat in the eighty-thousand-seat Lujniki Stadium. But in Warsaw, we liked him even despite these things; it was partly because he was singing in a language that was not the language in which we bartered for food or fought over a soup bone, or swore at our mechanic, or begged for a cigarette from the man standing next to us in the prison yard. His language was unpolluted by that 'h' in Khatyn, that drop of tainted blood that poisons the whole body. And we liked him even more when he spoke his mind about the squashing of Hungary: 'I continue to hope, I cease to believe.' When the Soviets went into Czechoslovakia, he told a reporter: 'When things stink we have to say so.' That last commentary was the final straw – overnight, Montand was banned. From the moment the words were out of his mouth, we had to hide our LPs and pretend we'd never heard of him – of Montand! – who up to a minute before was selling by the millions. And that's why my friend Ostap, who'd just woken up from a bender, disappeared and was never seen again – because he was absent-mindedly humming 'Quand Tu Dors' while he was walking down the street. These rules always change overnight and too bad if you're a heavy sleeper. This is just the way the map changes; like a man who decides to part his hair differently one morning: suddenly Mittel Europe is Eastern Europe. Even Mr. Snow respects Montand and the Dogs won't touch him. They listen to his songs and never mutilate them.

Jean watched the shape of Lucjan cross the room toward her, walking through the darkness of Montand's voice.

In the tub, listening. The water of the bath as hot as Lucjan and Jean could bear; soaking in every extreme of love – humiliation, hunger, ignorance, betrayal, loyalty, farce. Jean leaned back against him, her seaweed hair across his face. She felt Lucjan drifting to sleep. Jean imagined the love between Montand and Piaf, when he was very young, the affair that would shape the rest of his life. She imagined what it meant to listen to Montand in Moscow or in Warsaw. Soon Lucjan would get up and put Piaf on the turntable, and they would listen for Montand's shadow in her voice. And then they would listen to Montand again. Hearing all that biography in their voices.

———

Lucjan slipped his hands into the warmth of Jean's neck and unwound her scarf. He pushed his hands under her beret and loosened between the comb of his fingers her hair, cold as metal, from the winter street. Jean held up her arms and he drew her sweater over her head. Piece by piece, her winter clothes fell to the floor. She no longer knew which parts of her were cold and which were burning hot. She felt the roughness of his sweater and his trousers down all the length of her and it was this roughness that she would always remember — scrubbed in her nakedness by his clothes and his smell.

Night after winter night Jean and Lucjan met this way. Jean knew Lucjan would never have spoken of himself without the vulnerability of skin between them. As if, in a reversal of all she'd known, that vulnerability held them hostage to the deeper pact of words. Lucjan felt in her an acute listening and this above all, Jean decided, was his desire. Very slowly she began to feel the power of this searing, that led each night to her surrender in different ways, and to his words. She knew that this was her particular contract with Lucjan and that if she had not silently agreed she would have lost all the history of him.

She began to understand that this kind of intimacy was, in its own way, a renaming. An explorer reaches land; the discovered place already has a name, but the explorer puts another in its place. This secret renaming of the body by another – this is how the body becomes a map, and this is what the explorer craves, this branding of the skin.

———

Sometimes Jean came home to a phone message left by Avery in the night, a rambling dissertation on how the roofs of a neighbourhood can create a secondary horizontal plane for building, parallel to the ground, or how concrete can be finished to resemble marble. Sometimes he left for her a piece of music, something he knew she liked, Radu Lupu or Rosalyn Tureck, the sound of the lonely piano worn and battered by its journey through the answering machine. Perhaps twice a week they spoke, usually in early evening, sometimes even having dinner together over the phone. She could not define the content of these conversations. She knew they were a kind of code he meant her to understand, but all she heard was a heart-clenching formality, a courtesy, yet not this exactly; the painful decorum that rises out of the ruins of intimacy, just as intimate.

— A few days ago we had a critique, said Avery, for a train station. One student designed an elaborate complex for 'freshening up' after a journey – a boudoir with nooks and banquettes and mirrors, personal sinks and showers. He kept saying that this 'spa' would become a destination in itself. 'It would be immensely convenient,' he said. 'The train would take people directly to the showers'; he kept repeating this – 'the train would take them directly to the showers, directly to the showers . . .' He kept on about it until I felt quite sick. All I could think of were the trains from Amsterdam to Treblinka, and finally I said so. The whole class turned to look at me as if I were demented. I thought, Now I've done it, they'll think I'm cracked, obsessed. Finally a young woman asked, 'What's Treblinka?' . . .

Yesterday we were talking about bridges. I said that yes, I suppose a bridge could also be a shopping mall and a parking lot, but why should we disguise a bridge, its function? What is the essence of a melon? It's roundness! Maybe someday we'll breed a square melon, but then it will be something else, a toy, a mockery of a melon, a humiliation. They looked at me again like I had lost my wits. But then someone said seriously, 'Square melons, why didn't I think of that?'

Jean heard, through the phone, the sound of papers rustling and guessed that Avery had put his head on his desk.

— Today I was thinking, said Avery, that the moment one

uses stone in a building, its meaning changes. All that geologic time becomes human time, is imprisoned. And when that stone falls to ruins, even then it is not released: its scale remains mortal.

Avery started out across the marsh. There was no moon, but the ground glowed with snow. The blackness above and the whiteness beneath him made him feel that with each step he might fall over an edge. A marker glowed above the canal. He moved toward it.

He lay down by the ditch and the ground now seemed almost warm to him. There was no one for many miles across the marsh, the nearest farm a pinprick of light. He listened to the water moving under the ice. Shame is not the end of the story, he thought, it is the middle of the story.

With the frozen mud digging into his back, Avery found himself thinking about Georgiana Foyle. He wondered if she were still alive, and if she had chosen where she would be buried, now that her place beside her husband was gone. He thought of Daub Arbab, who, for the first time, Avery realized, reminded him of his father, a seriousness that expressed itself as kindness. He thought that the closest thing he felt to belief of any kind was his love for his wife.

The painter Bonnard, the day before he died, travelled hours to an exhibit of his work so that he could add a single drop of gold paint to the flowers in a painting. His hands were too unsteady, so he asked his son to accompany him, to help hold the brush. Avery felt that even had Bonnard known that these were his last hours, he would still have taken that journey for the sake of a single second of pigment. What a blessed life, to live in such a way that our choices would be the same, even on the last day.

He thought about what his father had said to him while they sat together that afternoon in the hills, after the war: There is only one question that matters. In whose embrace do you wish to be when you die.

The lights were on in Marina's house; she had left them on for Avery's sake; for navigation, to plough the deep.

When Avery came in, Marina was waiting for him.

—You use that marsh like the desert, she said.

———

For several days Jean had been helping Lucjan knot lengths of thick rope for a sculpture; ten or fifteen knots, each the size of a fist, in each length. She did not know how Lucjan intended to use these pieces of rope, awkward and bulging. They worked with the lamps on, the pale February afternoon light barely passing through the windows.

Often they asked each other to describe a landscape, it was a key to a door between them, a way to tell a story. Now, in Lucjan's winter kitchen, the floor and table laden with lengths of rope, Jean quietly described the desert at sunset.

—The sand turned the colour of skin, and the stone of the

temple looked like flesh. The first time I saw the stonecutters slice into Ramses' legs in that light, I flinched, as if I had almost expected the stone to bleed.

She added her coil to the others on the floor, the knots beginning to resemble a mound of stones.

—And these, she said, draping the rope over her lap, are as long as the reins of a camel.

—The closest I've ever come to seeing a camel, said Lucjan, was during the war, though I might as well have been on the other side of the world. I remember someone telling my mother and me that camels had come to Plac Teatralny, camels that kneeled down on the pavement so children could climb up for a ride. 'And I thought nothing could surprise me now,' my mother had said . . . After the war, I found out that, travelling right behind the German army, was the German circus. It was the same in every occupied territory. The big top came to town and gathered up the last coins from the losers . . .

They continued for a while in silence, the snow falling.

—They say that children find a way. Sometimes, said Lucjan. Not a way out, but a way. Just like bones — they'll mend by themselves but won't set straight. The rubble rats used to play a misery game — to see who could outdo the others: if you lost a brother as well as your mother and father, worse still. And a sister too? Worse still. Lost a part of your own body? Worse even still. There was always a 'worse still' — jeszcze straszniejsze.

My stepfather used to get a look on his face, that warning grimace, of someone who knows he's doing wrong but can't figure out what to do instead, and so keeps on, defiantly, as if he were right. Knowing he was wrong gave him a real air of conviction. When we first saw each other again after the war, we looked at each other, trying to understand how we were connected. Everything was said in total silence in those first few seconds. He was only my stepfather – 'after all' – *w końcu*. What had the war done to him? Like an animal in a trap, he had bitten off parts of himself to survive – mercy, generosity, patience, fatherhood. Most of my life had been lived without him. He had never once appeared when I needed him most. I remember staring at the skull-white parting in his thick black hair, and tried to imagine my mother having touched that hair . . .

A woman could hold Lucjan close for a lifetime and even if his desolation had shrivelled to the size of an atom of paint, that atom would remain, just as wet. Jean had ascribed many meanings to the work she was helping with; it was a giant's rosary, the knots of a prayer shawl, an ancient form of counting. And now she thought, perhaps the worst knot of all: mistrust bound with longing.

———————

– Names were stolen while we slept.

We fell asleep in Breslau and woke in Wrocław. We slept in Danzig and yes, admittedly, we tossed and turned some- what, yet not so much as to explain waking in Gdańsk. When we slipped in between the cold sheets our bed was undeniably in the town of Konigsberg, Falkenberg, Bunzlau, or Marienburg, and yet when we woke and swung our feet over the edge of that same bed, our feet landed still undeniably on a bedside rug in Chojna, Niemodlin, Bolesławiec, or Malbork.

We walked the same street we had always walked, stopped for coffee in the same corner café whose menu had not changed in years, although where once we'd ordered *ciasta*, now we ordered *pirozhnoe*, which was served in the very same crockery with the very same glass of water. The coins we left on the marble tabletop were different, the table itself, the same.

Then there were the places that had changed everything but their names. After their obliteration, when the cities were rebuilt, Warsaw became Warsaw, Dresden became Dresden, Berlin, Berlin. One could say, of course, those cities had not completely died but grew again from their dregs, from what remained. But a city need not burn or drown; it can die right before one's eyes, invisibly.

In Warsaw, the Old Town became the idea of the Old Town, a replica. Barmaids wore antique costumes, old-fashioned signs were hung outside shop windows. Slowly the city on the Vistula began to dream its old dreams. Sometimes an idea grows into a city; sometimes a city grows into an idea. In any case, even Stalin could not stop the river from entering people's dreams again, the river with its long memory and its eternal present.

Europe was torn up and resewn. In the morning a woman leaned out her kitchen window and hung her wet washing in her Berlin garden; by afternoon when it was dry, she would have to pass through Checkpoint Charlie to retrieve her husband's shirts.

And what of the dead who'd once been lucky enough to own a grave? Surely, at least, if someone died in Stettin, his ghost had a right to remain there, in that past, and was not expected to haunt Szczecin as well . . .

The dead have their own maps and wander at will through both Fraustadt and Wschowa, both Mollwitz and Malujowice, both Steinau am Oder and Ścinawa; through Zlín and Gottwaldov and Zlín again. Down Prague's Vinohradská Street, Franz Josef Strasse, Marshal Foch Avenue, Hermann Goering Strasse, and Marshal Foch Avenue again, Stalin Street, Lenin Avenue, and at last, once again, without having taken a single step and shimmering only through time, Vinohradská Street.

As for one's birthplace, it depends who's asking.

———

Over the course of the afternoon the coils of knots grew higher, mute and heavy on the floor under the table.

A soup was simmering on the stove. Ewa had brought a roast chicken to Lucjan earlier in the day and now it was crackling in the oven. The light was nearly gone. Lucjan made the fire and lit candles.

He sat on the floor in the "unconscious" half of the house, leaning against the wall, looking at the tangle of knots, their afternoon's work, from a distance. Jean was reading a textbook quietly at the kitchen table. With false drama, Lucjan whimpered:

– I'm hungry.

Jean looked up from her book.

— What are you reading? asked Lucjan. Is it edible?

— This chapter is about hybrid vigour. But, she smiled, you could say I'm reading about cabbage.

— That's more like it, said Lucjan.

He sat down next to her at the table.

— Did they teach you about the *koksagiz* widowers at school? When the Germans marched into the Soviet Union, they searched everywhere for rubber plants. Russian women and children were driven into labour camps to harvest the *koksagiz* fields so even tiny amounts of rubber could be extracted from the roots . . .

The big high-rise housing development in the southern part of the Muranów district in Warsaw was built on top of what had been the ghetto. There was so much rubble — thirteen feet deep — and we had no machines to clear it. So instead the debris was crushed even further, and the housing built right on top. Then grass was laid down and flowerbeds planted on this terrace of the dead. That's their 'blood-and-soil garden.'

A few blocks from the School of Architecture, where Avery was working at a desk in the basement, Jean sat with Lucjan and Ranger in the Cinéma Lumière, waiting for the film to start, *Les Enfants du Paradis.*

Lucjan handed Jean a lumpy bag.

— Baked potatoes with salt, said Lucjan.

Ranger leaned over Lucjan and put his hand into the bag.

– It's long, at least a two-potato film, he told Jean, already peeling off the aluminum foil. I remember going with Mr. Snow and Beata to the Polonia, so hungry we could barely sit still. There was no water and no place to live but, four months after the war, there was a cinema. The Polonia sat like a stage set in the mess of Marszałkowska Street. Many times I lined up to watch a film and then afterwards lined up again down the street to fill my metal pail at the pipe that spurted water out of the ground. People carried containers with them wherever they went. There was always a clatter just before anyone sat down anywhere, people setting down their jars and flasks and pails at their feet.

– The clatter was usually followed by the rustling of newspapers, said Lucjan, as people took their *Skarpa Warszawska* from their pockets, a weekly magazine, Janina, that kept us up to date on the progress of the rebuilding. After the war so many newspapers sprouted up – right away, five or six daily papers. We couldn't hear enough about how well we were doing – two hundred thousand cubic metres of rubble removed by the horse-drawn carts, sixty kilometres of streets cleared of debris, a thousand buildings cleared of mines . . .

– Comrades, said Ranger, work has commenced on the market square, on the tin-roof of the palace, on the church on Leszno Street . . . The library has now opened on Rejtan Street!

Pilgrims converged at the same locations, the same square metres of rubble, each person mourning a different loss. The mourners stood together in the same spot and wept for their various dead – for Jews, Poles, soldiers, civilians, ghetto fighters, Home Army officers – dozens of allegiances buried in the same heap of stones.

– How does a city rebuild itself? said Lucjan. Within days someone sets out pots amid the rubble and opens a florist's shop. A few days after that, someone puts a plank between two bricks and opens a bookshop.

– In London after the bombings, said Jean, willowherb took root and spread throughout the ruins –

– Janina, said Lucjan, this isn't a romance. I'm not talking about wildflowers, I'm talking about commerce – that's how you rebuild a city. You can have all the wildflowers you want, but in the end someone must open up a shop.

Lucjan took Jean's arm in the street. It had started to snow while they were in the cinema, in nineteenth-century Paris, and by the time they reached Amelia Street, all was white and quiet.

They lay in the bath together, watching the snow fall past the kitchen window.

– That's a wretched ending to a film, said Lucjan. A man pushing his way through a crowd to reach the woman he loves and, for all eternity, never catching up to her.

He looked at the piles of rope around them.

– It's almost finished, said Lucjan. When there's too much and it's too heavy to move, it will be done.

This makes me think of my grandfather, my mother's father, who was a cabinet maker. My mother once told me that he'd made a magnificent piece of furniture – the most distinguished desk ever created in the world, fit for an emperor – but the one thing he hadn't considered was the door to the room, which was too small, and they had to cut a bigger hole to fit it through. She said I was to take this as a lesson in humility. She also told me about an enormous, curved display case he'd made for a shop – the wood shone like amber, the top was heavy glass with bevelled edges that looked, my mother said, like the watery edge of ice forming, and inside were wide, shallow, velvet-lined drawers for stockings and lace and silks. Each drawer opened with a tiny brass knob. He'd boasted that it took ten men to lift it. The cabinet had elaborately carved corners – wooden vines trailed thick and lush to the floor. The drawers slid, smooth and soundless, and the shopgirl would pull out the whole drawer so the customer could see the small silk things shining like pools of coloured water on the dark velvet.

This cabinet brought my grandfather many commissions for custom work.

My stepfather's people were from Łódź; they owned a hosiery factory. He had been sent to Warsaw to distribute the family wares. It was for this shop that my grandfather built one of his famous cabinets and that is how he met my mother. She was so young; the milk and cinnamon of her soft skin and thick hair, the sweetness in her face. She was nineteen years old.

I remember a tram stop with a clock next to it where, before the war, my mother and I used to wait. The clock had little lines instead of numbers. It disturbed me so much that there were no numbers on that clock, just anonymous little dashes, as if time meant nothing and simply lurched on end-lessly, meaninglessly, anonymously. I used to try to predict when the minute hand would jump forward. I tried to count the seconds, to guess when it would suddenly seize the next little line, but it always got ahead without me. While we waited at that stop for the #14 tram, my mother would comment that it was really a very foolish place to put a clock because it always reminded you how overdue the tram was and how long you'd been waiting and how late you were. I remember the feel of her wool coat against my cheek as I stood beside her, her sure fingers around mine. That little hand on the clock jumping forward without me is the symbol for me of how my mother disappeared . . .

A wall does not separate; it binds two things together.

In the ghetto, a woman came to visit my mother. She was an old schoolfriend or a relative; I don't remember, yet for my mother the nature of this relationship would surely have been the heart of this story. I do remember her hat — a pie-plate contraption tilting over her ear — which she didn't remove all through tea. I waited for it to fall off and land in her cup. I sat on the chair in the corner next to a little wooden table with my cup of 'fairy tea' — hot water and milk. The woman gave my mother some photographs taken when they were chil-dren. After she left, my mother and I sat together and looked at them. The season in the photographs was summer, yet outside our window that afternoon it was snowing. I remem-ber thinking about that fact, the first time it occurred to me that weather was preserved in photographs. And because the sun was so bright, there were many shadows. In one photo in particular my mother's shadow was very pronounced beside her and I couldn't keep from looking at it, that shadow lying across the pavement almost as tall as she was. And in another, there was the shadow of someone who had obviously been standing near to her, but who was outside the frame of the picture. I couldn't stop thinking about it afterwards, that my mother had stood next to someone – a quarter of a century before – whose identity I would never know and yet whose shadow was recorded forever.

Photos from those years have a different intensity; it's not because they record a lost world, and not because they are a kind of witnessing – that is the work of any photograph. No. It's because from 1940 it was illegal for any Pole, let alone a Polish Jew, to use a camera. So any photo taken by a Pole from that time and place is a forbidden photo – whether of a public execution or of a woman reading a novel quietly in her bed.

German soldiers, on the other hand, were encouraged to bring their Kine-Exakta or Leica with them to war, to document the conquest. And quite a few of those photos survive in public archives, such as those of Willy Georg, Joachim Goerke, Hauptmann Fleischer, Franz Konrad . . . Others remain in family albums, photos sent home to parents and sweethearts: the Eiffel tower, ghetto streets, the Parthenon, public hangings, an opera house, a mass grave, gas vans, and other signs of German 'tourism' . . . These photos were sent home, where they were kept next to the family photos of weddings, anniversaries, birthday parties, lakeside holidays. Although there were certainly photojournalists whose job it was to shoot for propaganda, many of the photosoldiers remain anonymous, their snapshots part of the great pile of images that make up the twentieth century . . .

I used to spend many hours watching from the window in our corner of the ghetto, and, once, I saw an old man put down a wooden box on the pavement and painfully kneel next to it. An instant shoeshine enterprise. At first I thought this was as ill-chosen as setting up a kiosk to sell matches at a fire; who in all the starving city would pay to have their worn-out, barely held-together shoes polished? But incredibly he earned himself some supper that day. And he polished German soldiers' boots – they took a lot of boot-black and they took it for free. It made me hold my breath to see the soldier's boot so close to the old man's head.

The places where people were killed often showed no mark; within moments the bit of pavement looked exactly as before. From my window I kept looking for a trace of the old man's murder, but there was none.

My stepfather eventually found a hiding place for my mother and me – much harder to find someone willing to take both of us. There were holes in the ghetto wall for such transactions and people were killed halfway through, with their head or their feet sticking out. A few days before we were to make the attempt, I sat looking out the window to the street below where my mother was waiting to meet someone to make a trade for food. She was standing in the street because of me, to feed me. That is how my stepfather thought about it afterwards and why he never forgave me . . . That and the fact that my mother and I always had our heads together, leaning over a book or a drawing, laughing over something so small we could never quite explain it to him . . . I looked away from the window for a moment – no more than a few seconds – or maybe I was just daydreaming – and when I turned my eyes back again, my mother was gone, simply gone, just like that. I never saw her again. I still feel sure that if I hadn't turned away my eyes just at that moment, nothing would have happened to her.

A simple-minded, childish revelation – that we can die without a trace.

At the bottom of the ravine, a thread caught the light; the river had been peeled of snow and drizzled with water from a tin pail. One of the Dogs each day came to renew its frozen varnish. The gleaming ice of the river looked liquid in the lantern light, even reflecting the lanterns hanging in the trees, as if a spell had been cast upon the water preventing it from freezing. So unnatural was this mirage that Jean held her breath as she watched the first skater place his foot on the surface, as if he might sink in his heavy skates, swallowed without a sound by the river's enchantment.

– Go ahead, say what you're thinking – Breughel's peasants. Jean looked at Lucjan in surprise.

–You mouthed the words, smiled Lucjan.

– It's the deep colours of their jackets against the snow, I think.

Then Jean watched as Ewa appeared in her pink fake-fur coat, her pink scarf, her thin black legs ending in pink skates. Jean laughed.

— A flamingo, said Lucjan, who always seemed to know what she was looking at.

— Is it all right to say I love Ewa although I've only met her twice?

— We all love Ewa, said Lucjan seriously.

Jean saw Ewa pointing and knew she was shouting orders. A board appeared and trestles and in a moment the table was covered with pans of cake and flasks of every size. Jean smiled at the theatricality of the scene — the feast, the enchanted river, the ice-coated branches clattering in the night wind, the lanterns like drops of yellow paint between the trees.

Jean and Lucjan stood at the top of the hill, looking down at the skaters. The scene reminded Jean of Marina's palette, which was so married to texture — patches of woollen scarves, shawls, quilts, dresses, the fur of a wet dog; each colour — soil, night sky, northern lights, ice, figs, black tea, lichen, the bogs of Jura — each lick of paint a distillation of a thought, a feeling.

— In the dark of winter, the Robinson Kruzoes went down to the Vistula with lanterns and shovels. The frozen river was scraped clean to its grey gleam. Bone scraped of its marrow with a spoon. There were enormous skating parties. Street orchestras, children, dogs. Vendors selling coffee sprang up on the banks. Pastries in waxed paper. They even came from the nightclubs when they emptied at two or three in the morning, sobering up under the moon, in the sudden cold. That's where I met my wife, said Lucjan.

I met my husband on a river too, thought Jean. Though it was not frozen. And contained no water. And perhaps was no longer a river.

—A few nights after we met, Władka and I sat on the river-bank. There was a freezing wind. The Vistula was neither solid nor liquid; huge chunks of ice buckled and swayed, bumping open seams of black water, then sealing them shut again. Then we heard a huge cracking sound and right before our eyes the bridge near the Citadel came apart and began hurtling toward us, downstream, huge pieces of it banging against the ice, dipping into the blackness and bubbling up again. In an instant the two banks of the river were sep-arate. Władka said later that 'if the bridge had not fallen right before our eyes maybe we could have learned to stay together, but with a symbol like that . . .' Władka had a very peculiar sense of humour.

One night, years before Władka and the bridge, I was lying in my burrow, listening to the rats. After a while I blew out the candle. But, like tonight in this snow light, it was not quite dark. I could see my hand in front of my face. Was something burning? I got up and looked out. There was a dim haze of light. There was the noise of a crowd growing louder. But there was no smoke. I climbed over the rubble toward the glow. Targowa Street had electricity! Hundreds of people were wandering about, disoriented, like survivors of a crash . . .

Do you remember when we met, you told me about a church that seemed to grow in size when you went inside? I can tell you a story about a church that moved, all by itself, said Lucjan. I was working with a crew building a road, the East-West Thoroughfare, and someone looked up and noticed the dome of St. Anne's was smiling. We didn't think much about that first crack in the stone, but the next day there were many cracks and they were growing wider and suddenly the whole northeast end of the church wobbled and broke off like a baby tooth. All the crews rushed to reinforce the rest of the church with steel, and we even tried Professor Cebertowicz's electro-osmosis idea, but St. Anne's and the earth continued to move, the belfry bending as much as a centimetre a day. Eventually the earth came to a halt . . .

Jean and Lucjan began to descend the hill.

– What happened, asked Jean suddenly, to that architect, the one who gave you bread?

When he did not answer, she looked up and felt she had never before seen such cold sorrow in his face.

– People disappeared. Sometimes they came back, but most of the time they didn't. There were reports of *stojki* – 'standings' – for months, with a lightbulb burning an inch in front of the prisoner's open eyes, who was being kept awake with injections. When someone died from torture, they said 'he fell off the table.' Ordinary words, banal words a child learns to spell in first grade. 'The man fell off the table.' Perhaps that was not his fate precisely, but . . . Unsuspecting people were trapped in 'cauldrons' – anyone who happened to visit a suspect in their apartment was arrested – that's what the Germans did and that's what the Soviets did. He survived the war, but he didn't survive the Soviets.

The Dogs joke about the Thursday-night meeting, but it is an old habit, an old intuition, not to show up where you are expected.

They heard Mr. Snow's voice through the trees.

— Let's listen to Mr. Snow sing, said Lucjan. He has a voice like a hatchet. The Dogs saw and wheeze and when they pass on you can be sure they'll rattle their bones.

If I have learned anything, it is that courage is just another kind of fear. And, Lucjan said, slapping his abdomen, if you are anti-fascist, you must have an anti-fascist belly and not an anti-fascist head. An appetite is more useful than a fever.

Lucjan slung his skates over his shoulder like a hunter carrying home a brace of birds and strode back through the ravine. In the distance, in the darkness, Jean could still hear the sound of blades on the hard ice. The Stray Dogs were almost always there before them and stayed on, almost always, after them. Looking back, Jean saw their breath in the dark. The ravine itself glistened like white breath, enclosed by the snowy embankments, the snow-laden trees, and moonlight that softly circled their faces as they skated across the ice. The air was cracking cold, the ice glinting and hard. She knew there was heat inside their clothes from their swinging legs and arms, and painful cold on their faces and in their lungs.

Jean and Lucjan walked back to Amelia Street, stopping at Quality Bakery, where the ovens baked all night. The smell of bread inhabited College Street, turning the snowfall, thought Jean, to manna.

—You cannot entirely despair, said Lucjan, with your mouth full of bread.

One could walk through the back door of the bakery, step right into the kitchen, and pay cash for loaves that had just been taken out of the oven. The bakers all knew Lucjan and the Stray Dogs. The cake man, Willy, used to play piano with them until he got his job at the bakery and couldn't play nights any more. "The bakery has taken all the walk out of my cake walk," Willy complained.

Then Jean and Lucjan sat in the small park at the end of Amelia Street, with Lucjan's battered metal flask of tea between them and each with a paper bag in their arms. They scooped out soft-breathing handfuls from long sleeves of bread, Lucjan feeding fingerfuls to Jean. Sometimes, after a whole evening together with Lucjan and the Dogs, this was her first taste of him.

Afterwards, they sat in the tub in the dark, listening. And still Lucjan had not touched her except for the tips of his fingers to her mouth, full of bread. This was a kind of rationing, a valuing of each pleasure. Nothing, especially desire, was wasted.

Lucjan looked at Jean asleep beside him in the winter afternoon light. Her hair was tied back with a twist of cloth, her face smooth and pale.

What did she believe in? What mess of assumptions did she live by, what tangle of half-formed beliefs and untested deductions, from the moment she opened her eyes in the morning or, for that matter, even when she was asleep? What mechanics did she live by? Did she believe in Plato's souls, in Kepler's harmony, in Planck's Constant? In Marxism, in Darwinism; in the gospels, in the Ten Commandments, in Buddhist parables; in Hegel, in the superstition of black cats and Mr. Snow's stories of the Czarny Kot, in crumbs of genetic theory, in who-knows-what family tales and gossip; in the conviction that sprinkled sugar tastes better than salt on porridge? In reincarnation – a little, in atheism – a little in the Holy Trinity – a little. In Husserl, in Occam's Razor, in Greenwich Mean Time, in monogamy, in the atomic theory by which her steam kettle boils each morning for her cup of tea . . . She believed in humility, he knew, and in the wince of shame that guides us to the right action, though she would call this something else, even perhaps love. This net of assumptions – if Lucjan moved one or two or two hundred of his own assumptions an inch here or there, was he not the same person as she, or her husband, or most members of the human species? Lucjan put his hand on Jean's waist. He watched her breath fill her lungs; as she lay on her side, he saw the curve of her hips, the crease behind her knee, the loose weight of her calf suspended. For this we erect monuments, kill ourselves, open shops, close shops, explode things, wake in the morning . . .

Jean parked her car at the beginning of the long driveway and walked the last way across the marsh to Marina's house. All was white and blue and black, the snow and sky and winter-wick trees of a clear cold afternoon in March. She carried her grafting satchel, the same canvas backpack she'd used since the days on Hampton Avenue. Now she recalled with longing the expedition to the hardware shop with her father when she was sixteen, to buy her first grafting knife – just the right size for her grip, with a wooden handle – and her first tin of wax, and the small primus. And when she thought ahead to Marina's peach trees, and the simple cleft graft she would make, she also thought of Abu Simbel, the clean slit of the knife into that precious flesh; cambium to cambium, scion to rootstock, and the pang – of both eagerness and regret – of being the one to induce those multiplying cells, just beneath the bark, into union. And of Albertus Magnus, whose seven-hundred-year-old question had startled Jean to attention in a drowsy, overheated, undergraduate classroom almost eight years before: Does a fruit tree have a soul? She thought it was time to read Magnus again, the heart-stopping *De Vegetabilibus*, a book that imagined, centuries before Darwin, plant varieties developing from their wild ancestors, for Magnus possessed the prescience of all men who dive into a subject without defence, and with their intuition sharpened by humility. If fruit trees have a soul, what does it mean, man's tampering? Now she was at Marina's white house, which was almost the exact white of the snow around it, and Jean thought that, in a storm, one might walk straight into it and perhaps even pass right through those white walls, like a ghost.

She knocked and waited. She stood on the doorstep and kept knocking, until she truly accepted the fact that Marina was not there. Reluctantly, she decided to begin work anyway, having no need of anything except Marina's companionship. Jean walked around to the back of the house to her mother's transplanted garden, enclosed by its white fence, now also lost to the snow. Startled, she then saw Marina and Avery, on lawn chairs piled with blankets, sleeping in the frail light of the low winter sun. She saw, too, Avery's old leather briefcase, stuffed with books, in his lap; he must have come, like her, straight from his car into the garden. Jean stood at the gate. The flowered pattern of Marina's smock, which she was wearing over her coat, rose and fell. Avery's hair, at his shoulders now, moved peacefully in the small breeze. How true their bodies looked together. She thought of Lucjan as a boy with his mother. She thought of the ghetto, the sleeping and the dead lying next to one another on the pavement. She remembered the afternoon she and Avery had left their car on the bank of the road and lay down together in the wet scrub of the Pennines, and fell into the sky. She thought of the eyes of thousands of deer watching young Marina and young William, on the moss of Jura, his coat beneath her head.

Sometimes there was shelter in lying out in the open, sometimes there was none. She thought of the dispossessed making their way on foot back into the ruins of Warsaw, how they must have stopped again and again to lie down beside the road. The people of Faras East climbing from the graveyard to the village one last time. Always, somewhere in the world, people are carrying everything they own and stopping by the side of the road. To sleep, to love, to die. We have always lain this way on the bare earth.

Jean ached to lie down in the snow, next to Avery's chair, with the great warm hills of Marina protecting them both. But she did not dare.

How terrible if they did not want her.

This thought did not arise from shame, but from a deep dispiritedness, the belief that grace is the aberration, something one passes through, like a dream.

After a moment more, she turned away as if she'd been told to and walked back to her car across the marsh.

That night, Lucjan stroked her shoulder until she woke.

— It's one in the morning, he whispered. Let's skate.

She saw something in his face and, without a word, leaned down for her clothes. Lucjan stopped her hand.

— Just this under your coat, he said, handing her his sweater. And your tights, nothing else. I'll keep you warm.

They drove through the white city to the edge of the ravine. Windows of light glowed through the falling snow, there was no interior that did not resemble sanctuary after a journey. By the river Lucjan spread a blanket on the snow and they changed into their skates.

Jean strode, her face pink not with cold but with heat. She was sweating under her coat, the heat building; blood flooding every muscle. Lucjan drew her toward him. He unbuttoned her coat. He drew up her sweater and pulled it over her head.

At first gasp – her skin so hot – the cold air was hardly recognizable as cold. She could not tell if his tongue was hot or cold.

– I want to tell you about a garden, the great hunting park of an Assyrian king, Jean whispered later, in the darkness of Lucjan's kitchen. Fragrant groves of cedar and box, oak and fruit trees, bowers of jasmine and illuru, iris and anemone, camomile and daisy, crocus, poppy, and lily, both wild and cultivated, on the banks of the Tigris. Blossoms swaying in a hot sunlight of scent, great hazy banks of shimmering perfume, a moving wall of scent . . .

The earliest gardens were walled not to keep out the animals, but to them keep in, so they could not be hunted by strangers. The Persian word for these walled sanctuaries was *pairidaeza*, the Hebrew, *pardes*, in the Greek, *paradeisos*. Jean felt Lucjan's weight begin to pinion her.

The origin of the word 'paradise' is simply 'enclosure.'

And after, Lucjan and Jean in the bath in the darkness, until yes, it was true, one was sick with longing for the melody to return.

––––

– Please tell me about your daughter, said Jean.

Lucjan lay on his back next to her, looking out the small window above the bed.

– First of all, her name is Lena. Second, she is almost

twelve years old, almost a woman. Third, I haven't seen her since she was a little girl.

Jean knew that she must wait. A long time passed.

— Władka, Lena's mother, worked with her father on their apple boat. You could smell those fruit barges from five blocks away, the sweet cider smell on the river breeze. The barges, piled high with cherries and peaches and apples, docked at the bottom of Mariensztat Street near the Kierbedz Bridge, bringing all the fruit to town from the riverside villages.

I remember those first water-markets after the war, the first mountain of Vistula apples, hard, sweet, sour, softened by the sun, rotting, fermenting, the bees circling. Władka and her mother baked pastries crammed with fruit and sold them at a stall on the docks.

Władka was so young, even younger than I, and her strong arms when she rolled up the sleeves of her dress, smelled of apples — as white and cold, as wet and sweet — and I could smell apples between her breasts and on her breath and in her hair.

We were married in the Bristol Hotel. 1955. I was twenty-five years old. Władka's parents insisted on the Bristol, with its mirrors and chandeliers, velvet chairs and bossy waiters. When you ordered, the waiters disagreed with you and never brought what you asked for, but what they thought was best. Our wedding feast was stuffed roast duck, ice cream, fruit. I remember very clearly because I hadn't eaten such food in twenty years. I was crazy for Władka — the thought of sleeping with her night after night — but that food made me very sad. Suddenly I knew, really knew, such meals had always existed, even during the war, for some. A great big greed opened up inside me, sitting at that table. A big rage. Every succulent mouthful filled me with despair. I was eating the duck of fury. None of us had any idea if we would ever eat like this again. That food made us all very sad.

Lucjan pulled on his sweater and went downstairs. Jean heard him filling the kettle. Then he began to hunt through the papers on the large table, through notebooks and newspapers on the floor.

–There's a photo of my daughter . . . If I can find it in this mess. I don't like to keep it one place or even in a frame, to make it a shrine. I like to come across Lena's face when I'm in the middle of something; it's like looking up and finding her sitting in the room with me.

He gave up and returned to the edge of the bed.

– I'll find it later, he said.

And Jean felt humiliation – at her own need to be found.

———

–You saw it all the time, said Lucjan, people standing in the street, perfectly still, holding a suddenly useless object – his coat, her book – staring at the place where the one they loved had just disappeared. All through those years we stood on the street, arms full of useless things, while the car drove off, while the line marched away, while the train departed, while the door closed.

Jean reached over and put her hand on his. He lifted her hand and put it down gently on the bed between them.

— You wanted me to tell this, he said.

He was right to reproach her; she should not have reached out her hand. What could her touch mean against such facts; nothing. Someone else's touch perhaps, but not hers.

— There are people on this earth who can't even bear to hear the engine of a truck. And the fact that their memories are shared by thousands of others — do you imagine this feels like a brotherhood? It's just as Ranger said . . . Every happy person, said Lucjan, and every unhappy person knows exactly the same truth: there is only one real chance in a life, and if you fail at that moment, or if someone fails you, the life that was meant to be yours is gone. Every day for the rest of your life you will be eviscerated by that memory.

Jean lay meagrely next to him in the dark.

Soon she realized Lucjan was asleep. His stillness was large and solid, a fallen tree. But she could almost hear his brain, even in sleep, rampage.

———

On a clear blue morning near the end of March, Jean drove out to Marina's to examine the peach trees. Then she and Marina made lunch together. Jean was peeling carrots and Marina was folding a mixture of egg and onion into a pan, when Marina said,

— I've given Avery a little project.

Jean looked up.

— Nothing expensive, mind. Marina smiled. Something he can plan on a single piece of paper. In fact, that was a condition. If the design can't be folded out of a single piece of paper, he has to start again.

It came alert inside her, an almost forgotten feeling: anticipation.

— Just a small one- or two-room house, a hut, a cabin, he can put it anywhere, but I thought perhaps by the canal. A place to think, to drift. A little project for him to do with his bare hands and his brain, something he can make mistakes with.

And I've thought of something for you too, said Marina.

She steered Jean into the dining room. Fabric, folded in large, flat squares, was piled on the table. Marina began to open and shake them out, one by one, perhaps a dozen designs of such outrageous brightness Jean had to laugh, erratic geometrics or florals eight or ten inches across, clean and alive, poppy red, graphite, mustard, cerulean, cobalt, lime, anemone white, of stiff strong cotton that looked like it could be used for the sails of a fantastical ship.

— I discovered the Marimekko shop in Karelia's, said Marina. It's a revolution. Fabric like this was unimaginable when I was young. Women are wearing these brilliant, preposterous colours and designs and striding about the world. We are going to make you some summer clothes, big, happy, square frocks, loose and cool. With your lovely arms and legs sticking out of them, you are going to look magnificent.

— And would you wear one too? asked Jean. A big, square, loose Marimekko frock?

They looked at each other, and themselves; Jean's shabby turnout — in planting clothes, baggy black leggings, an old shirt of Avery's that hung to her knees and an old sweater of an unidentifiable shade, mud-coloured, also Avery's, with elbows worn through, falling loose from Jean's slight shoulders. Marina's plastic painting apron, her woollen trousers that looked as though they'd been made before the war, which they had been, nicely tailored (for they had been William's) but sagging and paint-stained.

— Marina, said Jean, you're quite insane.

Marina took Jean's hand, almost desperate to see happiness again in Jean's eyes.

— Not quite insane.

A few days later, Jean came again to the marsh and left her car, as she usually did, just off the main road, so she could approach the white house on foot; to take in the sight of it, among the trees, now winter trees of black paint, vertical strokes, thick and thin, at the edge of the fields. She knocked at the back door, then realizing it was unlocked, went in. On the kitchen table was a bowl of soup. Large wads of bread were crammed into the bowl, bloated with broth. At that moment she knew Avery had been there, perhaps was there still; perhaps he had parked his car in the field on the other side of the house. She had never known him once to leave the table without clearing up after himself, out of duty or habit, and certainly not in his mother's house. Jean stood in the doorway and looked at the bowl of soup thick with bread. A child's bowl.

It was her own vulnerability she felt, looking, and not his. She went back outside.

From the window of her studio, Marina saw Jean and Avery talking together, and past Jean's shoulder, Avery's glove in midair, pointing. And she knew that Avery was beginning to think about that single piece of paper.

———

Jean sat on the edge of the bed while Lucjan drew.

— I worked as a slave, said Lucjan, building that great Soviet project, the Palace of Culture. I did every sort of job the lowest labourer could pass on to me. Slowly the monstrosity rose, stone by stone; no one could believe the gargantuan proportions, which symbolized, right from the start, the torments inflicted by Stalin. The higher it rose, the more elaborate its decorations and pinnacles, its spiky stalagmites, the greater the depths of submission it represented. I detested this work, which also fascinated me. And it's there that I met Ostap.

I hated everything that surrounded us, but I did not feel contempt for him. There was something about him, in the way he moved his body, the way he met a load head-on as if he respected it, the way he shrugged off another man's comments invisibly, yet not invisibly, with his ears, with his hair. I have never met another man who was so sure of his independence, his inner disdain. I can't describe it adequately — even after all these years I find it difficult to describe this independence he possessed.

Ostap liked to quote Andrei Platonov, although such quoting was not too good for one's health. He would stretch his legs out as if he had all the time in the world and didn't have to leap to his feet again any second, and he would recite: 'For the mind, everything is in the future; for the heart, everything is in the past.' 'Life is short, there is not enough time to forget everything.'

Often, while eating together, this Russian Ostap would take from his shirt pocket a pencil, sharpened to a stub the size of his thumb – 'short pencils have long memories!' – and scrawl pictures to teach me the names of objects in Russian. At first they were practical words – *truck*, *stone*, *hammer* – and then he taught me words that were useful in another way – *anger*, *idiot*, *friend*. Instead of throwing away these bits of paper, he mortared them between the stones. There are many words hidden between the stones of the Palace of Culture, enough to tell some kind of story. In this way I also learned fragments of his childhood in St. Petersburg – a cat, a bridge, a flat on Furstadtskaya Street.

In return I used to tell Ostap stories of places in Warsaw I didn't know as a child, stories that I'd heard later among the students, and it was unaccountable but even as I told them, those anecdotes seemed to become part of my own memory – perhaps that is the precise reason I told them – until it was impossible to tell them apart, the memories that belonged to me and the memories that didn't, as if by virtue of collective loss they became collective memory. To keep everything, even what was not mine to keep.

Never has there been a man so loyal to his childhood as
Ostap. After everything was taken, even the little tea set he
and his sister had played with, the one with Lenin's portrait
painted on all the tiny cups and saucers, Ostap made a decision
not to forget anything. He especially remembered books he'd
read as a child, a story about a hedgehog and a tortoise –
Slowcoach and Quickfoot – which he compared with the
Soviet 'classics,' terrifying trains and trucks with their human
scowls, robots with squared-off mouths and knob noses, faces
made of gears and cogs, not quite human and not quite
machine. They reminded me of the trucks grinding down the
cleared-out spaces on Freta Street. He showed me one of
Tsekhanovsky's flip books, little movies with their shrinking
children and machines growing huge or locomotives bearing
down on small animals. When he was young he'd read
Chukovsky's translations of O. Henry and R. L. Stevenson;
Evgenia Evenbach's 'How Kolka Panki Flew to Brazil and
Petka Ershov Didn't Believe Him' and '100,000 Whys.' He
talked about his mother, who was very small, who used to
rest her head against his shoulder, even when he was only
twelve years old, and who now lay buried in the cemetery on
Stalingrad's Golodny Island.

He and your Marina would have a thing or two to say to
each other. He knew all about children's books, he never
grew out of them, or perhaps better to say he grew into
them, into understanding their secrets. He knew which
writers were *stopiatnitsa*, a member of the 105 club, one
who's forbidden to live closer than 105 kilometres from any
city . . . and who was in prison for writing a certain story

about a rabbit and a goat. That was during the reign of 'Queen Krupskaya,' whose personal campaign was the denouncing of fairy tales as 'unscientific' and therefore dangerous to the state. 'Do rabbits talk? Do goats wear clothes? The anthropomorphism of animals is not realistic, therefore it is a lie. You are lying to our children.' Perhaps the writer did lie, Ostap agreed. Because he wrote a story in which a stone is able to turn into a man . . .

Those Russians sent to Warsaw to build the Palace of Culture slept in a big camp by the river. In the months I worked there, fetching and carrying, comrades 'fell' regularly to their deaths and were simply left to be buried by the foundations. Such a fall was described as someone having had 'too much to drink.'

Lucjan stopped talking. Wait a moment, he said as he slid from the bed. Jean heard him going down the stairs and heard the old metal handle of the fridge close tight. She heard banging.

— Don't worry, I'm just crushing ice with a hammer!

He came upstairs carrying a bowl of snow drizzled with vodka. The cold went straight to Jean's brain.

— Is any single part of us inviolable? No. Everything can be carried off, picked away; carrion. Yet, there is something in a man. Not even strong enough to be called intuition, maybe just the smell of your own body. And that is what you base your life on . . .

Lucjan began to cover Jean's back with the blanket but then, at second thought, instead pulled away the sheet and looked at her.

He twisted the sheet between her buttocks. He saw that she would agree to anything. He let go of the sheet.

– Don't give in to me, he said.

There was another Russian I knew when I worked on the Palace of Culture. At lunch he would smoke with his mouth full of food – I've never seen anyone else do that. He used to lecture the young ones. All women are the same, take what you can before they rob you . . .

And muzak, do you want to know the origin of muzak, why we can't go out to buy a package of frozen peas without hearing a woman moaning in the supermarket over her lost love, while all we want to do is buy the peas and get out of the shop as fast as we can – why we can't buy our carton of milk or a pair of socks or sit quietly in a café? The origin of muzak is the loudspeakers in the camps, at Buchenwald, all the war-bling lovesongs that were shoved in their ears in the lineup, in the infirmary, while the dead drifted in and out . . .

There is one moment in every lifetime when we are asked for courage we feel in every cell to be beyond us. It is what you do at that moment that determines all that follows. We like to think we are given more than one chance, but it's not true. And our failure is so permanent that we try to convince ourselves it was the right thing, and we rationalize again and again. In our very bones we know this truth; it is so tyranni-cal, so exacting, we want to deny it in every way. This failure is at the heart of everything we do, every subtle decision we make. And that is why, at the very heart of us, there is nothing we crave more than forgiveness. It is a bottomless desire, this desire for forgiveness.

And I'll tell you something else, said Lucjan, covering Jean with the blankets, this truth attends every death.

Walking for the first time into the replica of the Old Town, said Lucjan, the rebuilt market square – it was humiliating. Your delirium made you ashamed – you knew it was a trick, a brainwashing, and yet you wanted it so badly. Memory was salivating through your brain. The hunger it tried to satisfy. It was dusk and the streetlamps miraculously came on and everything was just the same – the same signs for the shops, the same stonework and archways . . . I had to stop several times, the fit of strangeness was so intense. I squatted with my back against a wall. It was a brutality, a mockery – at first completely sickening, as if time could be turned back, as if even the truth of our misery could be taken away from us. And yet, the more you walked, the more your feelings changed, the nausea gradually diminished and you began to remember more and more. Childhood memories, memories of youth and love – I watched the faces of people around me, half mad with the confusion of feelings. There was defiance too, of course, a huge song of pride bursting out of everyone, humiliation and pride at the same time. People danced in the street. They drank. At three in the morning the streets were still full of people, and I remember thinking that if we didn't all clear out, the ghosts wouldn't come back, and who was this all for if not for the ghosts?

Jean moved closer beside him.

— Janina, keep your compassion to yourself. Do you want to hear this or not?

He stuffed pillows between them.

— After that I thought maybe it would have been better if we'd just loaded all that rubble onto trucks and dumped it somewhere far away where it couldn't be used for anything again.

—You could have built nothing, said Jean. But . . . building nothing is hard work too. Perhaps, sometimes, it's harder to build nothing.

— Pah, said Lucjan. You don't understand anything.

He pushed away the pillows.

—You might as well touch me, since you don't hear a thing I say.

— I do understand, said Jean.

— All right, I'm sorry. But do you think a few words will do the trick? Do you think perhaps I haven't thought enough about it?

He threw his drawing book on the floor.

— For six years the Poles ate their fruit and bread. The juice ran down their chins while a hundred metres away people lay dead from hunger — they may as well have spread their starched tablecloths right over the corpses in the streets and had their picnic there.

Jean leaned over and gathered her clothes from the floor.

— I don't know anything, said Jean. You're right, I don't know anything about it.

— I don't want your pity. Not your psychoanalysis. Not

even empathy. I want simple, common, fellow feeling. Something real.

She began to dress.

—There's hardly anything to you. From behind you're like a little girl. Just starting out.

He got up and stood beside her.

— Except for here, he said, pushing his hands between her legs. And here, touching her breast. And here, covering her eyes.

He wrapped his thick belt around her waist, twice, and pulled tight and buckled it. He looked at the flesh, the slightest flesh that stood out from the leather and kissed her there and began to draw.

He twisted the belt around her wrists and stretched her arms over her head and pulled her body across the bed.

— Does it hurt?

— No, I could slip out if I wanted to.

— Good.

He drew her with her hands tied behind her back, and with her arms tied and hanging in front of her. The drawings were very close, always the line of raised flesh pinched by the leather.

In one of Marina's paintings, a child's face is severed by the edge of the canvas; only now did Jean understand the meaning of it. The edge, a tourniquet.

—You wouldn't harness an animal so tightly, said Lucjan, because you want work from that animal. Only would you tie a man so tightly, a man whose life is not even worth being worked to death.

She lifted her head to Lucjan. He looked at her as if he were pleading, but it was the contortion of holding back tears.

Afterwards, he showed her the drawings. It was her flesh.

———

Talk is only a reprieve, Lucjan had said this more than once. No matter how loud we shout, no matter how personal our revelations, history does not hear us.

In Jean, the remnants of two rivers – rendings. The uprooted, the displaced. She remembered what Avery had written in his shadow-book from the desert. Soon, more than sixty million people will have been dispossessed by the subjugation of water, a number almost comparable to migrations caused by war and occupation. While the altered weight of the watersheds changes the very speed of our rotating earth and the angle of its axis.

Unprecedented in history, masses of humanity do not live, nor will they be buried, in the land where they were born. The great migration of the dead. War did this first, thought Jean, and then water.

The land does not belong to us, we belong to the land. That is the real homesickness, and that is the proprietorship of the dead. No place proclaims this with more certainty than a grave. In this century of refugees, it is our displacement that binds us.

The sun was already low, a pale crimson seeping from beneath the clouds. Jean's hands were cold, but she did not like to work with gloves. She made the first cut into the bark of one of Marina's peach trees and carefully began the graft. She saw, at the far end of the orchard, the pile of lumber Avery had had delivered, awaiting the realization of his plans: a small house, mostly windows, of proportions that Jean knew would be hidden by the fruit trees, and that would stand within the sound of the canal.

For five thousand years, humans have been grafting one variety of plant to another — the division, the pressing together, the conductive cells that seal the wound. And for more than five hundred thousand years — until evolution, chance, or aggression left *Homo sapiens* alone on earth — at least two species of hominid had co-existed in North Africa, and in the Middle East, abiding in the same desert.

There is a soul in the fruit tree, thought Jean, and it is born of two.

———

— Ewa and Paweł, Witold, Piotr — we were part of a group, said Lucjan. We managed to do some useful things. We raised cash for people who had to leave Poland in a hurry, we circulated information. Ewa and Paweł performed their plays at home and in other people's flats. That's when I started the cave paintings — it was one of my jokes — life underground — I painted them as a signal to the others, a wave, just a stupid bit of mischief.

Then I made the Precipice Men — sculptures that I mounted on the roofs of buildings. Ewa and Paweł helped me. We worked at night. First we put one figure on the roof of the building where I lived, and then three more on theirs. I made them from clay, just mud really, reinforced inside with scrap metal. They wouldn't last and that was part of it; and I liked that it was scrap that held them together. I could make them fast, they didn't cost much, and, because of the clay, they were truly lifelike. They peered over the edge at impossible angles. I got the idea from a book of Ewa's, a picture of Palladio's *Villa Rotonda*. The figures were there for weeks before anyone noticed; nobody looks up. But when people started to spot them I'd stand on the street watching. I liked that moment of surprise. It was a game, a childish game. I would have liked to put some of them on the Palace of Culture but Władka talked me out of it. She said the most disparaging thing anyone has ever said about the silly things I make: the idea isn't worth prison.

Lucjan sat up in bed. He paused.

—Then one evening, an old man waited on the roof of Ewa and Paweł's building in the Muranów. He stepped off the edge. A young man, a student, happened to be looking up and saw one of the figures come to life. The suicide left his suit jacket neatly folded, with a letter in the pocket asking only that the jacket be given to charity.

Jean sat up beside him.

— I can hardly believe what you've just said.

Lucjan covered his face with his hands.

— As soon as I heard someone had jumped, I thought of my

stepfather. I thought it was just the thing he would do to himself and to me. But of course, it wasn't my stepfather. Paweł and Ewa knew the man very slightly because he lived in their building. The man's wife had been sick for a long time, and she'd died in their flat. They'd never been apart – not once in fifty years, not even during the war. Paweł believed that I had given him a way to die, in the place where his wife had died.

Death makes a place sacred. You can never remove that sacredness. That apartment tower was built over the ghetto, where some of the worst fighting had been. All the dead trapped in the rubble under those apartments, perhaps my own mother somewhere, all that happened after. We were already in a graveyard.

Jean wrapped her arms around him. Lucjan took her arms away.

– Not long after that, Władka and I had a bad fight, the worst. I'd had a little conversation with Lena, I felt she was old enough to learn one or two things about what we were doing, the politics of non-violent action. She'd wanted to know why I was always doing such crazy things, leaving matryoshka dolls on top of things too high to reach, hanging from streetlamps, second-storey windows, etcetera, and so I explained about 'friends in high places.' And she wanted to know why the older students wore radio parts on their lapels like jewellery – and so I explained about 'resistors,' and that the first act of subversion is a joke, because humour is always a big signal to the authorities, who never understand this: that the people are dangerously serious. And that the second most important subversive act is to demonstrate affection, because it is something no one can regulate or make illegal.

A few days after that conversation with Lena, Władka said she'd had enough. I moved to Ewa and Paweł's. Soon she was making it very hard for me to see Lena; she would arrange a meeting and then, when I came, they weren't home. She sent Lena to her parents, to her friends. For several months I was crazy, I followed Władka around in the street. The swish of Władka's sleeve against the body of her plastic raincoat – day after day I listened to this irritating sound; it grew in my head to such volume that it outmeasured the calling of the crows, the grinding of the endless trucks dumping their rubble, the planes overhead. Every other sound fell dumb to the over-powering swishing of her plastic sleeve. I watched men and women at the building sites as if their actions and gestures were taking place behind glass – all I heard was that enraging, incessant brush of her raincoat as she walked ahead of me. There is one thing I can say for Władka: she bore this madness too. Following her around like that, I knew I would never want another child. I will never forget that sound and that feeling of being imprisoned out in the open air. We can rebuild cities, but the ruins between husband and wife . . .

Even before this, with Władka it always came apart the same way. I'd ask a question, a simple question – 'what would you do in the same circumstance?' – but really I was probing like a monkey with a stick down a hole, looking for ants. They dribbled off the stick, dripping globs of moral ambiguity – that moment of hesitation, of her not taking the question seriously, or of plain, shocking, moral uncertainty. And each time it sickened me to discover the spot, soft like a bruise, the moral line she was always willing to cross, even though I understood it was out of a very sensible fear. It sickened me with triumph. There it was, proof it was foolish, crazy, to trust her, and how close I'd come to forgetting. That twinge of satisfaction – it was almost a feeling of safety, that inner smirk – while all the time she would go on stroking my hair or reading to me and I would be disgusted by her touch and it was over, right at that moment, for the hundredth time, over.

After a year of this and when they made it easy for the last Jews to leave, I went. Paweł and Ewa were always in trouble, Ewa's cousin Witold, and Piotr – we all left. Later I learned that Władka had been working on making 'improvements' for herself and Lena, with a certain Soviet bureaucrat, and that these trysts had been going on for quite a while, even before my little talk with Lena. She might have turned in any of us – me, Paweł, and the others – but she didn't. She wanted me to be grateful – she cost me my daughter but at least didn't cost me the lives of my friends. That's just the sort of bargain Władka liked. Enemies know each other best, she liked to say whenever we argued, because pity never clouds their judgment. It was her way of telling me I was an inconvenience and nothing more, 'not even worth prison.'

Ewa had a brother, her twin. They deliberately stressed the resemblance, Ewa used to dress like him. It sometimes made me sad, like in those ballads where the girl cuts her hair short and dresses like a boy in order to go off to sea to be with her brother or her lover; there was a desperation in it, in the disguise. And when the police picked him up and he wasn't heard from again, Ewa never knew, she'll never know, if they'd really been looking for her. The truth is, either of them would have sufficed. But Ewa had always taken more risks and she feels, even now, it should have been her.

Once, I spent a whole month's money to phone Lena in Warsaw. While we were talking, Władka came home and told her to hang up. I could hear Władka yelling. Lena said she'd quieten her down. 'Just a minute,' said Lena. 'I'll be right back.' I called to her to come back to the phone. Then I waited. For twenty minutes all I heard was the dog howling and his chain sliding across the floor. A whole month's money – just to listen to a dog barking across the ocean. That was years ago, that conversation with Mr. Bow-wow. It was the last time I phoned her.

– You've never spoken to your daughter again?

– No.

Jean reached out, but Lucjan took her hand and placed it in her lap.

She turned away. The snow fell, soundless and slow, in the window high above the bed.

Everything we are can be contained in a voice, passing forever into silence. And if there is no one to listen, the parts of us that are only born of such listening never enter this world, not even in a dream. Moonlight cast its white breath on the Nile. Outside the snow continued to fall.

As Jean spoke, Lucjan could see the gauze of starlight on the river the night the boy drowned in her dream, the moment Jean believed her daughter floated from her, without a trace but for this dream of drowning. In her voice, Lucjan saw the hillside where Jean first told her husband he would be a father, and the bare hospital room in Cairo. Her fear of not carrying, her fear of carrying, another child. Her body abandoning Avery's touch.

— Janina, said Lucjan, fearlessness is a kind of despair, do not wish it, it is the opposite of courage . . .

For a long time they lay together quietly. Every so often the glass bowl on top of the fridge began to vibrate and then stopped. It was warm under the blankets, Lucjan along the length of her.

The absence that had been so deep, since childhood — at last Jean felt it for what it was, for what it had always been — a presence.

Death is the last reach of love, and all this time she had not recognized what had been her mother's task in her, nor her child's; for love always has a task.

From the peace of sleep, Jean opened her eyes. Beside the bed, her clothes, Lucjan's thick cabled grey sweater, the teapot, a drawing of her. She could see, barely in the dimness of dawn, the curve of her waist, the sleeping curve of her across the heavy paper. She remembered what Lucjan had said, one of their first nights together: There is no actual edge to flesh. The line is a way of holding something in our sight. But in truth we draw what isn't there.

She turned to find Lucjan, his eyes open, beside her. He had been waiting for her to wake. He drew his hand through her hair, drew her hair tight against her scalp, a gesture an observer might have mistaken for pure desire. Then, lowering his head to her belly, he slipped his arms beneath her, held her so tightly her breath went shallow. He did not let go, but held her this way, as if he would break her in half, the grip of a most painful rescue.

— Please, Janina, he said, whispering against her. Please get dressed and go home.

His words turned her cold. But he did not let go.

He did not let go, and gradually she felt her longing was not separate from his. The slow, impossible, surrender to what was true. He did not let go, and in this union, his confession of aloneness was as close to love as all that had yet passed between them; as close as love is to the fear of love.

With utmost gentleness, slowly Lucjan enclosed Jean in her underclothes, her thick tights, her sweater-dress, her coat and boots. With each item of clothing, a deepening loss soaked into her.

They stood by the front door, the house in darkness, except for the small light above the stove. Every detail now achingly familiar, a world that was also hers.

He took her arm and quietly they walked north, past the landmarks they had claimed together, through the city, toward Clarendon Avenue. The snow gave light to the ground. When they reached Jean's apartment building, Lucjan said, I only meant to walk you home, but now that we're here, Janina, I would like to stay.

They rode the small lift together and, for the first time, Lucjan lay with Jean in her own bed.

———

Just before midnight, the following night Jean stood at the front door of her flat on Clarendon. She had been almost immobile with thought, most of the day.

The past does not change, nor our need for it. What must change is the way of telling.

She did not want to disturb Lucjan, but perhaps he was awake too. She would walk there and see. This walking, she realized, was one of his gifts; this city inside the city, any hour of day or night, this walking. The snow from the previous night had melted away and the streets shone wet in the darkness.

There were no lights on in Lucjan's house except for the light in the upper window, his bedroom.

On its own it meant nothing, but Jean, standing at the gate of his house, recognized instantly the single fact that made the truth visible. She understood everything – a recombination of all she'd known – the way history is suddenly illuminated by a single "h."

She saw – leaning against Lucjan's fence, with its plastic flowers wound around the handlebars – Ewa's bicycle.

Jean saw what bound Lucjan to her, and what bound him – with the friendship and loyalty of decades – to those closest to him.

The word love, he had said, is it not always breaking down into other things? Into bitterness, yearning, jealousy – all the parts of the whole. Maybe there's a better word, something too simple to become anything else.

But what word could be so incorruptible? she had asked. What word so infallible?

And Lucjan, to whom words were a moral question, had said: tenderness.

The next morning Jean phoned Lucjan and told him she'd seen Ewa's bicycle at his gate. She heard the anguish in his silence. Then he said:

– Please, Janina, I want you to understand.

And, almost as if his words were from her own mouth, as if all along she had known he would come to speak them, he said:

– Perhaps Ewa can help us.

She walked to Ewa and Paweł's. It was two in the afternoon. The front door was open. Jean looked through the screen door, through the house to the back porch, where she saw Ewa bending over one of her projects. Jean called to her and Ewa looked up.

– Jean, come in . . . Come out . . .

Jean walked through the narrow house, past the flowered

bicycle in the hallway and a pile of scarves and mittens on the floor. Now the children's wall was a green field with horses. She stepped over a stack of newspapers by the back door.

Ewa was making papier-mâché boulders with newspaper and chicken wire. She wiped her hands on her smock and pulled a chair close beside her. Ewa gestured to the boulder-strewn porch.

– The coast of Denmark, she explained. You're welcome to roll up your sleeves. Just dip the strips of paper into the glue and cover the form. She pointed to a pile of wire shapes. Then she looked into Jean's face.

– Or maybe, she said quietly, it's time for a cup of tea.

Ewa put the kettle on the stove and they sat at the kitchen table.

– You love him, said Ewa.

– Yes, said Jean. Not as my husband, but – for who he is. Ewa nodded.

– I knew Lucjan before I met Paweł. When I met Paweł, well, it was hard. But even Lucjan saw that Paweł was the man for me.

She looked at Jean.

– How can I explain it to you? she said quietly. We're – *uwikłani* – entangled; – Paweł, Lucjan, and me. So many times we've saved each other over the years; perhaps it's as simple as that. When Lucjan met you, Paweł and I thought, If it could be anyone, it would be you. Lucjan's brought home women over the years, but none like you. He talks to you. It's your compassion, it's everywhere in you – in your beautiful face, in the way you carry yourself. It's your sadness. And perhaps the fact that you love your husband has a little to do with it.

Sometimes Paweł goes to sit with him, but it's me he needs. It's my hands he needs. I stay with him until he falls asleep . . . Do I have to have a name for it? It's not a love affair, not a romance we're having, not something psychological, not an arrangement – it's more like . . . a disaster at sea.

–You're a family, said Jean.

The two women sat with their hands around the fragile, old-fashioned teacups.

– I love Paweł, said Ewa. What would I be without him? And Lucjan belongs with us. How can I explain what bread means to us, what making things means? Those years can't be measured like other years.

Ewa paused.

– We've lived many lifetimes together.

Jean saw past Ewa's costumes, the hairstyles, the feathers and fake fur, to the most adult face.

– Of all of us, Lucjan feels everything the worst. Sometimes he can't bear his loneliness; soul-loneliness. I think you understand, said Ewa. She spoke with such contrition, Jean could hardly hear her: We teach each other how to live.

III

Petrichor

J ean took the train to Montreal, the route of the *Moccasin* of her childhood. It felt right to make the journey by train. Then she changed lines and rode another stop farther, to the town of St. Jerome, and walked the short distance to the cemetery her mother had chosen so many years before.

It was a cold April day. A high wind beat down the long grass between the church and the graveyard. Jean stood in front of the three stones, for the first time looking upon the marker for her daughter: the few words, the single date.

She put down her satchel and kneeled in the mud. How could she have left off talking at the precise moment her daughter had needed most to hear her voice? She began to chastise herself, but then let this misgiving fall away; for it was a true peace to feel the knees of her tights growing sodden with the damp earth. She had so often tried to imagine who had made the first garden; the first person to plant flowers for the pleasure of them, the first time flowers were deliberately set aside – with a wall or a ditch, or a fence – from the wilderness. But now she felt, with an almost primordial knowledge, that the first garden must have been a grave.

———

In the late morning, when Avery reached the cemetery at St. Jerome, he saw Jean's flowers. She had come, their daughter's first birthday, his instinct had been right. But he had missed her. He had driven half the night and come too late. He stood there for some time, unbelieving.

He descended the small hill to the vault, in a corner of the graveyard, just as Jean had described it, so long before. Along the rough stone building was a wooden bench. He sat, leaning back, his head against the wall. He looked out to the adjacent field, empty, without even the single black horse from Jean's childhood. He imagined her as a young girl with her father, almost as if it were his own memory, reading together by the thick oak door.

Jean's childhood, her web of memory and unconscious memory, had once been her gift only to him. Now it had been given to another. This was the loss that overwhelmed him the most. Our memories contain more than we remember: those moments too ordinary to keep, from which, all of our lives, we drink. Of all the privileges of love, this seemed to him to be the most affecting: to witness, in another, memories so deep they remain ineffable, glimpsed only by an intuition, by an illogical preference or an innocent desire, by a sorrow that arises out of seeming nothingness, an inexplicable longing.

It is not the last chance that we must somehow seize, but the chance that is lost. He had not realized how fervently he'd been waiting for this date, this April 10. Now his head ached from the early drive, from six hours of straining, mistaken hope.

He closed his eyes and soon slept, his head at an awkward angle against the stone wall of the vault. When he woke, he returned to Elisabeth's grave and left a handful of stones. Jean had cried so many tears, but he had wept only once, in his mother's kitchen, for all of them. Now he sat in the car at the gates of the cemetery and wept again; for himself.

He remembered taking Jean to the churchyard at St. Pancras, to show her Thomas Hardy's tree. The small London parish cemetery had been dug up, bones and plinths scattered, to make way for the railroad. The excavation of the graves had been overseen by Hardy as a young architect. Not knowing what else to do, and burdened by the responsibility, he had gathered the strewn gravemarkers and placed them in a tight circle, leaning them together like stone pages of a book, encircling the wide trunk of an ash tree.

The wind had been damp and chill. His arm around her, he had felt Jean's cold skin beneath the waistband of her skirt. His fingers still remembered that inch of cold. Time and weather had effaced every marking on the tombstones. Not a name or a date remained. They had been able to read only two words distinctly, on a single stone: In memory. The tree was bare, but it sheltered the dead.

It was mid-afternoon when Avery drove back through the cemetery gates and turned toward the small town of St. Jerome. The sky was blackening with coming snow. When he was almost all the way to the town, he saw her along the road, walking back toward the cemetery, a slight, determined figure, head lowered to the wind. He drove on, in confusion, a few minutes more.

———————

They travelled past Montreal and into the landscape they both knew so intimately. They did not stop, but drove through. Neither foresaw the effect of travelling again through land that had been so changed, and had so changed them. How many times in earliest days had they returned to the drowned landscape of the seaway, had they set out without a destination, only the desire to be together as the day revealed itself. They saw the phantom shoreline as it had been, even as they passed through the new towns.

Jean thought of Ashkeit, and the abandoned town of Gemai East that had been their second sight of that emptiness. There, on a bright limewashed wall, a house owner, in fluid Nubian script, had painted his poem of farewell.

The smells of homeland are those of gardens.
I left it with tears pouring . . .
I left my heart, and I have no more than one.
I forsook it not by my own will . . .

And some weeks later, when they had travelled to the new settlement at Khashm el Girba, they saw that what sparse decoration had been added, to some of the houses, did not depict the new world around them, nor geometric shapes and patterns, but the forlorn likeness of what had been left behind, the plants and palm groves of the banks of the Nile, the horizon of mesas and hills.

In all the bleak flatness surrounding Khashm el Girba, there was only one hill. It was common, a young man in the village had told them, for the settlers to walk to that solitary height, a distance of more than forty kilometres.

And what do you do, Avery had asked, when you reach the hill?

We climb, said the young man. But we can never see as far as our homeland.

Avery had placed his hand then on Jean's belly.

Now, in the car, the evening sky motionless above the fields, Jean remembered what Avery had said after their child had died. The wrong time, other words, meant to heal, futile. She remembered the thanksgiving with which his hand had touched their child that day, in the new settlement. Their daughter was still alive, in that place of banishment, in Khashm el Girba; in that place of helpless beginnings.

If there is true forgiveness possible in this world, thought Jean, it is not conferred out of mercy; nor is it conferred by one person to another, but to both by a third — a compassion between them. This compassion is the forgiveness.

We must not forget what it means to be in love with another human being, Lucjan had said. For this, once lost, can no longer even be imagined.

In the car, something settled between them. But it was not a peace. They both sensed it, the raw chance. If they spoke imprecisely, it would vanish.

Avery felt again that the dark weight of her next to him was a kind of earth. He felt the familiarity of her concentration, and now, the intensity of new experience in her, at which he could only, painfully, guess. He had missed this so completely: just being able to sit beside her, listening to her think.

It was dark now, east of Kingston. They had spoken very little, all the hours since Montreal.

The car heater was on, but Jean's feet were cold and wet in her boots. The mud of the cemetery had hardened into the knees of her tights.

— Avery, said Jean. Moving the temple was not a lie.

For some time, he did not reply.

— Moving the temple was not the lie, he said at last, but moving the river was.

— How long have you known this? asked Jean.

Again, silence.

— About a kilometre.

—You tried to tell me this before, said Avery. That I must think harder about my hand in things. For wanting to do good. Just by living, you said, we change the world, and no one lives without causing pain.

Sometimes, she thought, there is no line between one kind of love and another. Sometimes it takes more than two people to make a child. Sometimes the city is Leningrad, sometimes St. Petersburg; sometimes both at once; never now one without the other. We cannot separate the mistakes from our life; they are one and the same.

— I've known you for so long, said Avery, and still you surprise me. I remember feeling I knew the essence of you almost from the very first moment, and I think I did. But I wasn't listening to you, Jean, even though you were whispering right in my ear.

—When I saw the flowers, said Avery, I knew you'd been there.

— The flowers won't last, said Jean. It's too cold. But I planted something else. Seeds from the plants I collected on the riverbank, the day we met.

For a moment Avery thought he would have to pull over to the side of the highway. But he drove on.

— Very early this morning, said Avery, I stopped along the St. Lawrence, just past Morrisburg. I walked down to the river. In the sand, glinting in the moonlight, there was a baby's bottle. It had only been dropped and forgotten, yet the sense of violence was overwhelming. I knew there was nothing but innocence there, yet still I felt it. It was a scene my mother might have painted.

We want to leave something behind, thought Jean, a message on the kitchen table saying we'll be back soon. A suit jacket on a roof.

What does a child leave behind? Marina had asked, long ago. We cling to the children's paintings from Thieresenstadt, to a Dutch girl's diary, because we need them to speak for every war child's loss.

Some days are possible, Jean thought, only because of love.

In the long silence surrounding them, in the low noise of the car heater, Avery touched her cheek. Jean bent her head into his hand.

He had never truly believed he would feel this again, the response of her body to his touch. He dared not stop the car nor speak a word.

White patches of snow floated, icebergs, clouds, in the black fields. But nothing shone white in the blackness of the river, as it flowed past them, driving past.

———

Avery and Jean stood in the lobby on Clarendon Avenue. It was almost 2 a.m. In the Great Temple at Abu Simbel there had been stars on the painted ceiling and now, five thousand years and half a globe apart, Avery realized how ancient this desire. To replicate the sky. To hold beyond reach.

– At the cemetery, said Jean, nearby to Elisabeth's grave was the grave of another child. There someone had left a magnificent garden of plastic flowers. Ferns grew lush out of a thick square of florists' foam, and in the foliage stood two painted china dogs. Each plastic flower had been carefully chosen; roses, hyacinths, tulips, lily of the valley. There was love in each moulded crevice of leaves and petals.

I remember when I was young looking at plastic flowers in a shop. I heard someone say, 'They're not real' and I couldn't understand what they meant – I was holding one in my hand, of course they were real.

The child's garden rested on its thick green foam above the cold spring ground. It was as real as anything. A child would have thought that garden beautiful.

Everything that has been made from love is alive.

Avery spread a blanket on Jean's bedroom floor. He sat with his back to her. The desert was almost completely gone from his skin.

Beside Jean was a cup of water and Avery's paintbox. She drew the brush across his pale, thin back.

Regret is not the end of the story; it is the middle of the story.

When Jean was done, she knew how careful she had to be. Not to erase, but to wash away.

ACKNOWLEDGMENTS

"As pines keep the shape of the wind . . . so words guard the shape of a man." – George Seferis

Many histories of Egypt, Sudan, Abu Simbel, Poland, and the St. Lawrence Seaway were consulted during the writing of this novel, but I wish to acknowledge two sources above all: *The Salvage of the Abu Simbel Temples: Concluding Report* (Arab Republic of Egypt and Ministry of Culture, Vattenbyggnadsbyran [VBB] Sweden) and Hassan Dafalla's *The Nubian Exodus*. It is my hope especially that Hassan Dafalla's memory is honoured by the account I have made here. I am grateful to the Lost Villages Museum near Cornwall, Ontario; to Marian Wenzel's *House Decoration in Nubia* for the poem written on the wall; to David Crowley's *Warsaw*; and to the *Guardian Weekly*, where I came across the term "petrichor."

Especial, long-standing thanks to John Berger, Joe McBride, Janis Freedman Bellow, Sam Solecki, and Gareth Evans.

Many thanks to Ellen Seligman, as always as deeply astute and generous an editor as one could wish. To Marilyn Biderman for her acuity and kindness. To Liz Calder, Sonny

Mehta, Robbert Ammerlaan, Roberta Mazzanti, Arnulf Conradi, and Elisabeth Ruge. To Helen Garnons-Williams, Diana Coglianese, Deborah Garrison, Anita Chong, and Heather Sangster.

Thanks to Dr. Elaine Gordon and Dr. S.J. Batarseh for confirming details regarding treatment of a still-birth in late pregnancy, in the time and place in which this event is set in the novel. And to Dr. Lorraine Chrisomalis Valasiadis for her advice.

Thanks to Margaret and Chris Cochran for the extraordinary tour of Wellington, New Zealand. Thanks to Andrew Wylie, Simon McBurney, Stephen and Mary Camarata, Mark Strand, Wallace Shawn and Deborah Eisenberg, Dan Gretton, Jack Diamond, David Sereda, Eve Egoyan. Thanks to Rebecca and Evan. Thanks to Zbysiu, Marzena, Dennis, Jeff, Luigi and Nan, the entire Freedman family, Arlen and Jan, Jane and Andrew. Special thanks to Sheila and Robin for invaluable gifts of time.

The beginning scenes of the book, set on the houseboat, were first read publicly at various venues in Canada and the United States in 1997. My thanks to these book-sellers and festivals. And special thanks to the Elliott Bay Book Shop, A Different Drummer Books, and The Flying Dragon Bookshop.

This book remembers Rose Kornblum, Rubye Halpern, Ida Rosen, Robert Mirvish, Robert Muma, Professor Michael Dixon, and Connie Rooke. This Warsaw honours Isaiah Michaels. This seaway, the dear lost. And these pages are an embrace for the daughters: dearest Rebecca; Naomi Rose; Gemma; Mary; Jaymes; Viva. May you fare forward with strength and love.

JOHN BERGER

TO THE WEDDING

From the Booker Prize-winning author of *G*

With an introduction by Nadeem Aslam

'No one knows more about the necessity of love than John Berger: what love makes us capable of, and incapable of. This is a book of the most precise humanity. No one who reads it will forget what it makes us understand: every action has its twin, conscionable or unconscionable; every truth, its shadow in the world; everything lost, alive in love'
ANNE MICHAELS

A mother and father, estranged for years, are travelling across Europe to their daughter's wedding. Vibrant, beautiful Ninon has fallen in love with the young Italian Gino. She is twenty-three years old – and she is dying of AIDS.

As their wedding approaches, the story of Ninon and Gino unfolds. On their wedding day, Ninon will take off her shoes and dance with Gino: they will dance as if they will never tire; as if their happiness is eternal; as if death will never touch them. *To the Wedding* is a novel of devastating heartache, soaring hope and above all, love that triumphs over death.

*

'A great, sad, and tender lyric, a novel that is a vortex of community and compassion that somehow overcomes fate and death. Wherever I live in the world, I know I will have this book with me'
MICHAEL ONDAATJE

'A wonderful book, one which yields immediate pleasure and promises to stay long in the mind'
THE TIMES

'The finale, the wedding itself, is a masterpiece ... this is a novel that will haunt you'
SUNDAY TELEGRAPH

*

ISBN 978 0 7475 9939 5 · PAPERBACK · £7.99

B L O O M S B U R Y